THE QUARRY

A NOVEL

by

Valerie Hansard

Grosvenor House
Publishing Limited

This book is published by
Grosvenor House Publishing Ltd
Link House
140 The Broadway, Tolworth, Surrey, KT6 7HT.
www.grosvenorhousepublishing.co.uk

A CIP record for this book
is available from the British Library

ISBN 978-1-78623-398-1

Main Characters

English

Jo Perry:
Alan Perry: Jo's husband
Gerry Nolan
Kate O'Leary
Victor Fleming

French

Didier Pérnot:	Mayor of Laronne
Lucien Gautier:	Baker
Colette Gautier:	His wife
Roland Paillard:	Architect
Madame Paillard:	His mother
Jules Gilot:	Postman
Chantal Gilot:	His wife
Georges Lefèvre:	Plumber
Josette Lefèvre:	His wife
Marcel Legrand:	The Perry's neighbour
Jeanine Legrand:	His wife
Emile Marceau:	Schoolteacher
Anne-Marie Marceau:	His wife
Louis Durant:	Undertaker
Grégoire Bazalet:	Notaire
Bernard Roger:	Cattle farmer
Denise Roger	His wife
Luc Roger:	Their son, aged 11
Jean Bertrand:	An unpleasant youth, aged 22
Jean-Pierre Floret	85-year-old neighbour

Chapter One

Jo Perry first saw the young man slightly ahead of her on the steep staircase leading from the car deck to the upper decks on the cross Channel ferry. Although it was only the middle of May, the ferry was unusually crowded. Jo struggled to keep her balance, clutching the rail as passengers crammed the staircase, cars disgorging more people than the small boat could comfortably accommodate. She saw him again in the queue for the self-service restaurant on the top deck. He was tall and lean, his broad shoulders narrowing to slim hips, his brown wavy hair worn a little long. Jo didn't generally take much notice of people from behind. It was features such as eyes and hands, seen from the front, that attracted her to people - or not, as the case might be.

She took a tray and joined the disorderly throng of hungry passengers, many pushing in to inspect the various dishes on offer. The hot dishes, standing in their large sunken metal containers turned her stomach, the tepid half-congealed food slipping down the shiny metal sides as if in protest, but she thought of the long drive ahead and helped herself to a sausage and a few mushrooms. The canteen routine always reminded her of boarding school: the endless queues for a tray, a plate and cutlery; shuffling along with her chattering, giggling peers; watching as their plates were piled high with indifferent, tasteless food which they were all too hungry to refuse. The memories flooded back, triggered, no doubt, by the smell of bacon, egg and sausage and the slightly rancid cooking oil. Boarding school had made her more fastidious than catholic; she had become more conformist than innovative.

She selected grapefruit juice from the choice of four fruit juices on offer. Alan had preferred grapefruit juice, which made her decision a little easier. Having completed her choice with a crispy roll and coffee, she paid at the cash desk, and precariously balancing her unevenly loaded tray against her bulky hand luggage, she wound her way through the ever thickening groups of diners all looking for somewhere to sit before their food got even colder.

Seeing a vacant table in the far corner, she pushed her way through the milling crowd and set her tray down at exactly the same moment as the tall slim young man she had just noticed in the queue and on the stairs a few moments earlier.

'Oh, I hope you don't mind...'

The young man had already sat down and was busily rearranging his tray. He looked up, smiled and indicated the vacant seat.

'Yes, please do. Go ahead.'

His voice was soft and attractive. Possibly Irish.

He turned his attention back to his food, stretching across the table for the salt and pepper, which he sprinkled liberally over the whole plate. Still not satisfied, he reached out for the mustard. Removing both the lid and the serving spoon from the jar, he dug his knife in deep, smearing a large dollop of the nauseous-looking yellow paste over a curved and corpulent sausage. Glancing quickly around the table, as if to make sure he hadn't missed out on anything else on offer, he picked up his knife and fork with the determination of a man going into battle.

Jo sat down and began to eat. Under half-closed eyelids she glanced at her companion as he sat, slightly hunched up, head down, busily concentrating on his food, tucking in ravenously as though he had eaten nothing for days. She was unable see his eyes as they were focused on his plate, but she did notice his hands; square and strong, larger than one would have expected for a man of his slim build. He held his knife and fork more as though they were weapons rather than dining utensils: gripping each object with clenched fists, his knuckles showing white as he slowly sank the point of his knife deep into the succulent sausage.

It was the first time Jo had undertaken the long drive on her own. Until now she had always had Alan to do the organising and bear the brunt of the driving. But now Alan was dead and Jo had not yet come to terms with her loss. For several days afterwards she had felt too numb to cry. She had gone about her daily domestic tasks as though he were still there. She laid his place at the table, having cooked enough food for two, which she forced herself to consume for lunch the following day. She washed and mended his clothes, returning them to their correct places in the cupboard. She even had a pair of his shoes re-heeled and took his winter coat to the dry-cleaners. At meal times she imagined he was there, sitting opposite her, gravely elegant as he picked fastidiously at his plate, blue eyes smiling behind the thick, horn rimmed spectacles, his greying hair thick and luxuriant like a halo. She had his body flown to back

England for the funeral. She wasn't sure it was what he would have wanted. He had loved France passionately. He always talked about it, whether they were actually there or just planning another visit. He loved the people, the food, the scenery, the atmosphere and he spoke virtually faultless French. He probably would have wanted to be buried there too, but they had never discussed it. It hadn't seemed necessary. Alan was, after all, only forty-three, still in the prime of life and perfect health. It was really for her that Jo had arranged the funeral in England. Alan could have been buried in France, of course. It would have been a lot simpler and saved a great deal of money. She had no idea of the enormous expense of transporting a body just a few hundred miles by aeroplane. When she discovered the cost she almost went back on her decision. But then she saw in her mind's eye the bleak cemetery in the tiny village of Laronne; well kept, but full of unyielding, discoloured plastic flowers and sad inscriptions in French, most of which she didn't understand. The idea of visiting Alan's grave in a foreign land did not appeal to Jo in the least. She was no lover of France, or any foreign country for that matter. To Jo abroad was for holidays; England was for living in. She had only gone to live in France to be with Alan.

Then there was the family to think of. Alan's family. Even after almost seven years of marriage Jo still couldn't consider Alan's family as hers. They were all too different. Even so, Jo felt sure they would have preferred the funeral to be in England. And Alan's mother, at seventy-nine, was no longer in sufficiently robust health to withstand the journey to France, on top of the sudden shock of losing her only surviving son.

Now the funeral, harrowing occasion that it had been, was over at last. The two weeks in England had been a great strain. Of course she had wanted to stay there. She would have preferred never to return to France again. To live in Laronne on her own without Alan was unthinkable, but at present there was no alternative. The house was there and so were the paying guests. She had nowhere else to go and no way of financing a home in England unless she could sell the house in Laronne. She realised the next few months would be fraught with heartache and practical problems. Not only would she mourn Alan's loss, and feel it even more keenly on her own in Alan's home than she had ever felt it in London staying in her parents' house surrounded by family and friends. But she also had a myriad of practical matters to attend to. Matters that might cause unforeseen problems, taking place as they would in a foreign country where she knew few people and had a very poor command of the language.

Glancing in her rear mirror, she saw a battered Mini, towing a caravan, coming round a steep bend, three cars behind. She had an odd feeling it was following her and her stomach tightened a little. Ridiculous, she thought. Why shouldn't a caravan also be travelling on the motorway? It was, after all, the autoroute to the South of France. She felt her eyelids becoming heavy. Her head ached and began to nod. This won't do, she thought. I've just passed Chalon-sur-Marne. At least another three hours to go. I'll have to stop at the next *Aire* or I'll fall asleep at the wheel. A large sign flashed over the motorway:

Dormir ou Conduire.

Quite right, she thought. Sleep or drive. In about three or four minutes she passed a motorway sign announcing: *Aire de l'Espèrence:* Area of Hope, with an attractive brown and white notice of a pine tree and two people sitting at a picnic bench. It was the simplest kind of stopping place with no knife, fork or plate sign announcing food. There was no petrol pump either, but at least it was an official parking place off the motorway where she could pull off and either have a kip in the car or get out and stretch her legs.

She looked again in her rear mirror. Yes, the Mini van was still there, but no doubt if she were to turn off, it would drive straight on down the motorway, towing its caravan, in search of peace and tranquillity at a campsite in a pine forest, bordered by the sun drenched beaches of the Côte d'Azure. As the slip road approached she signalled right and slowed down. The three cars behind her sped along the motorway but the Mini van, right-hand indicator flashing, followed her up the slip road to the parking area. The driver hesitated for a moment before deciding whether to drive to the area designated for caravans and commercial vehicles or the one which said 'cars only.' He decided on the latter, made a sharp left turn and drew up at an awkward angle beside Jo's white Peugeot. Jo saw the caravan at close quarters for the first time. It was shabby and dented in places. Once possibly a sparkling white it had now dulled to a streaky grey. The curtains, drawn across the windows, were of different fabrics. One of the curtains hung askew, some of its hooks missing. The caravan was being towed by a small blue Mini van without side windows. The blue was two-tone, which could have been quite smart had it been done professionally, but the 'Do-It-Yourselfer' had run out of paint before finishing the second side, so the rear off-side and the back had been painted in a darker shade of blue, which clashed slightly with the predominant colour. It was a British car with the registration number A 410 IOU.

As the driver got out of the Mini van, Jo's heart missed a beat. It was the tall young man whom she had noticed on the boat, whose table she had briefly shared at breakfast. He came across to her car, smiling. The *Aire* was quite empty. There wasn't a soul about.

Chapter Two

'You mean, actually live here? All year round?'

'Well - yes.'

Jo held her *croissant* in mid-air, too shocked to take a bite.

'What about your job?'

'I'm tired of my job. I've been teaching for the last twenty-four years and I'm ready for a change.'

'The school won't like it. You've been head of modern languages for more than fifteen years.'

Alan laughed. 'They'll soon get used to it and find a younger replacement who's probably a great deal better than I am.'

'Oh, Alan! Don't be ridiculous. Of course there isn't anyone better than you are.'

'At least as good then.'

'What'll you do instead?'

'Write. Paint. Perhaps try some pottery. We'd take in paying guests and maybe open a restaurant...'

'You can't cook,' protested Jo.

'But you can.'

'Not the sort of cooking that would bring diners to a restaurant in France.'

'It wouldn't take you long to learn. You could always go on a course.'

'Why don't you go on a course? It's your idea.'

'Perhaps we could both go on a course.'

'Not much use opening a restaurant out here even if we could cook. Nobody would find it in this remote spot.'

'We'd advertise. *Le Mirabellier* isn't in a town but it does very well because it advertises everywhere.'

'But it's on a main road. Our road doesn't even have a number!'

'I'm sure the Mayor would give it a number if we asked him. He'd love it if we opened a restaurant. So would everyone in Laronne.'

'Alan, I wish you'd be more practical.'

'I am being practical!'

Jo was silent. She couldn't tell whether Alan was serious or not. He often made flippant remarks. She thought when she first met him that he did it deliberately to wind her up, but he always assured her that he didn't mean to. She sipped her coffee. It was hot, strong and very French. She didn't know whether she'd like it every day of the year. The bread too. They'd stopped buying the *baguette*, the staple diet of all the tourists. It didn't remain fresh even till lunchtime. The *batard*, being a broader loaf, kept better. The *pain de campagne* kept best of all, but often the village bakery was out of it by the time they got there later in the morning. After all, they were on holiday. They had also tried the *pain complet* a few times, but it was hard and dry and most unappealing. Even Alan referred to it as 'the complete pain.'

'I thought we bought this place as a holiday home.'

Jo took the delayed bite of *croissant*. Very nice, but she would heat them up next time, whatever Alan said about cold *croissants* being more French.

'We did. That doesn't stop us living in it permanently.'

'There's nothing to stop us.'

'Good. So it's settled then.'

'What do you mean, settled?'

'You've just said there's nothing to stop us.'

'I meant there's nothing actually to stop us physically. That doesn't mean it's a practical possibility.'

'What's impractical about it?'

'Just about everything. We can't just come and live here for ever just like that.'

'Why not?'

'What about money? What'll we live on?'

'I'll have my teacher's pension.'

'Not your full pension if you're going to retire early.'

'No. I'd have to go into it. But I've still got some of my godmother's inheritance left. And of course we'd sell the house in Clapham.'

'What! Sell Lavender Garden!' Jo was appalled.

'Why not? We won't need it if we're going to live here. We can't be in two places at once.'

'And in addition to the question of money there are many other things.'

'Like what?'

'The French language; the French people; the countryside.'

'You'd soon get used to it.'

'Would I?'

'Yes. You'd be so busy...'

'Making ends meet.'

Jo was silent again. Sometimes Alan was ridiculous. She couldn't really believe he was actually serious about coming to live in Laronne. There was nothing there except fields full of cows and some vineyards down the road. There was nothing to do except look at the cows - and the vineyards down the road. There were no shops, no restaurants, not even a proper *café* in the village, only a crude bar called *Le Bar des Sports*, where the locals, mainly retired old men and spotty, unemployed youths spent most of the day killing time. And there were hardly any people. There were barely five hundred inhabitants in the *Commune*, which comprised Laronne and several tiny outlying hamlets. They seemed friendly enough, but they were peasants and she had nothing in common with any of them. They were country people, totally unsophisticated, with no knowledge of anything outside their small rural community. Most of them only vaguely knew where London was, had never been to Paris and rarely visited the local market town, a mere twenty kilometres away; the general opinion being that it was too far. Jo shuddered as she saw them in her mind's eye: the little old ladies struggling along the road on their sticks. There were a few younger men, but most were old; tilling the fields in their grubby faded, blue overalls; loading the cattle into trucks to be sent off to the slaughter-house.

Last February they had paid a brief visit to Laronne to sort out some practical problems. The house had been cold and damp, the trees were bare, the skies a leaden grey. The fields were waterlogged, emptied of cattle, which were now all in stables, not for their own protection, but to save the land from the ravages of their hooves in the cold, wet weather when the grass no longer grew. They had gone for a long walk, well wrapped up. Alan relished the fresh air free from petrol fumes, whereas Jo hated the silence and the emptiness. They had put their heads round the open door of one of the cattle sheds, warm and dark, the floor covered in dung, the whole place extremely smelly. While Alan had chatted at length to the farmer about the intricacies of cattle rearing, Jo had stood aloof, not understanding a word and loathing every minute of it. With each succeeding visit to Laronne, Jo realised how much she was beginning to dislike the country. It would be impossible to live there permanently. Nor could she understand peoples' desire to live abroad. To her it seemed like going into exile.

They were having breakfast on the terrace as they nearly always did. The house faced south and got all the sun that was going, which in the summer was generally a great deal. By eleven o'clock in July and August they were forced to move into the shade, sometimes until well after three. Now it was just after ten am and already they could feel the heat of the sun beating onto the tiled terrace they had laid with such pains last summer, utterly exhausted by the evening. The tiles reflected the sun, so by midday the heat on the terrace was unbearable.

Jo stood up and started to clear away breakfast. For a moment Alan sat and watched her, absorbed in her task, piling up the plates, then the two saucers followed by the cups, tidily onto the tray. Always neat and methodical, Jo left the glasses and the coffee pot until last, screwing up the paper table napkins prior to putting them in the bin.

Goodness, I am lucky to have found her, thought Alan, noting appreciatively her slim, tanned arms and legs, her shapely body; firm breasts just discernable under the cool sleeveless top; well-cut, white shorts sitting elegantly on her trim waist. Her fluffy corn-coloured hair had fallen forward over her face as she reached gracefully across the table to retrieve a teaspoon, brown tapered fingers curling around the spoon, placing it on the tray with the rest of the breakfast debris. Jo felt his eyes on her and looked up and smiled, her deep violet blue eyes full of warmth and laughter.

'Would you be a love and help me in with this lot?'

'Of course, my darling.'

Alan got up hastily, picked up the tray and carried it in to the kitchen. The large oak beamed room was cool and dark after the bright sunlight on the terrace.

'Can I help you wash up?'

'No, that's fine, thanks. I'll have it done in a jiffy.'

Jo was already donning hideous, lurid pink plastic gloves and running water into the sink.

'Go and put out the chairs, darling. Fair division of labour. I'll be almost finished here by the time you've got them out.'

'OK. Will do. Sun or shade?'

Jo glanced at her watch. Ten-fifteen. A good three quarters of an hour before she would start to burn. She smiled up at him again.

'I'll try the sun for a bit. After all, I've already got a slight basic tan.'

'A beautiful tan if you ask me.'

Alan stroked her arm and kissed it. Jo laughed.

'It's the suntan lotions they make nowadays. If you take care and use them correctly you can't really burn.'

'Famous last words.'

Alan kissed the other smooth brown arm, feeling desire for her and wondering whether he could just carry her off to bed. On the other hand, they had already made love this morning. Jo would probably say he was being greedy and plead that she wanted to get on with the day's activities. Alan moved one of the reclining chairs into the sun, brought out a mattress and laid it on the chair, covering them with a towel. He crossed the courtyard to fetch another chair for himself, putting it in front of one of the outbuildings. The French called it a *dépendance*. Alan had named it *La Petite Pièce*, meaning the small room. He collected a second mattress and a towel with which to cover his reclining chair, still in the relative cool shade of the outbuilding. He took off his shorts and shirt, revealing swimming trunks underneath. His torso was lean and muscular without a spare ounce of fat, undoubtedly due to years of coaching schoolboy cricket and football. His youthful figure belied his forty-three years. He went back into the house to fetch a book. Jo was just putting away the clean crockery. Alan gave her another kiss.

'You are marvellous. Leave the rest there and have your sunbathe before it gets too hot.'

'Yes. Good idea. What's the book?'

'The poems of *Mallarmé*.'

'You never stop working, do you?'

'I enjoy it. A few of the poems are set for A Level. I'm reading all the others because they're so beautiful. Most romantic. All about love and longing.'

'Sorry I wouldn't understand them.'

'Yes, a pity. But never mind. You have many more important talents.'

'Like cooking, in order to open a restaurant in Laronne.'

'Yes.'

They both laughed.

Alan settled down in his chair in the shade of *La Petite Pièce* and started to read one of the poems. In the silence and stillness of the countryside he found it hard to concentrate. The air was torpid, heavy and still. A slight breeze rustled the full leaves of the magnificent plane tree already casting its dappled shadow across the far corner of the courtyard.

La Belle France! France in the summer! Even better. He had always loved the countryside, the small towns and villages, the charming, simple people, the language, the food. He felt he could live here forever and never return to London, except perhaps for weddings and funerals. Would he miss it? Theatres? Bustle? English newspapers and TV? He really didn't think so. His problem would be persuading Jo to come and live here with him. He thought back to the time, two years ago, when they had already been happily married for nearly five years. They were well settled into their comfortable middle-class existence in an attractive Victorian house in Clapham. He was head of modern languages in a large South London comprehensive school. Jo was the secretary in a primary school. At the time Alan thought he had the rest of his life mapped out. They would raise a family: his second family. He would continue in his teaching job until he was sixty-five. There had been no question of his doing otherwise. He enjoyed it. He was trained for it and he was good at it. In fact he couldn't do anything else.

But the second family failed to appear and Alan began to grow restless. Then over two years ago, in the spring of 1988, Alan received a handsome legacy from his godmother of just over one hundred thousand pounds. They decided to celebrate in the summer holidays by making a three-week tour of France by car, booking into hotels as they went. One day on a visit to Beaune, they happened to look in the window of an estate agent, and there it was: the most beautiful farmhouse either of them had ever seen. It was remote, it was a wreck, but it was irresistible and they could afford it. So they bought the rambling property on the outskirts of the village of Laronne, right in the middle of Burgundy, the smoothest house purchase that Alan could ever remember. They were both consumed with enthusiasm. During the next two years they spent all of the Easter and summer holidays, and sometimes the half-term holidays as well, renovating their vast property. It was impossible to do all the work themselves. The main house, a long, low, two-storey building, about three hundred years old, needed re-roofing, as did the vast barn and the motley collection of outbuildings. The vendors, a retired couple who had found the place too large for their needs, had recommended an architect, Roland Paillard, who lived locally and had an excellent reputation. The plumbing was done by Georges Lefèvre, who lived in Laronne, and the superb carpentry by Didier Pérnot, Mayor of the *Commune*. As the work progressed, Alan and Jo became friends with their workforce, whom they found to be warm, generous people, always ready to invite them to their homes for *un apéritif* after a hard day's work. Alan began to feel they were becoming part of the neighbourhood scene. He felt a sense of belonging. Then gradually the school terms became longer than they used to; teaching grew irksome. The children appeared worse behaved than before and his colleagues were becoming more irritating. London was too large, too noisy and over-crowded. The air was full of petrol fumes, buses never arrived and it always seemed to be raining.

Whereas Laronne was small and silent, with very few inhabitants. There were no petrol fumes; no buses and the sun always seemed to shine. So why return to London? Why continue in a job that had now become a chore? Why not take the plunge and leave it all? Why not come and live in quiet peaceful rural Laronne?

But what about his family? Would he miss them? He had never been really close to his mother. Now well into her seventies, she was feeble and confused with the onset of Alzheimer's Disease. She might resent it if he went to live abroad. As her only surviving child he felt he owed her something. On the other hand, if he were to wait a year or two the Alzheimer's might be sufficiently advanced for him to settle her into a care home and he would be free to go wherever he wished.

Would he miss his children? Sebastian, tall, gangling and spotty at twenty, reading PPE at St John's College Oxford, his old college. He, Alan, had got a County Award, though it hadn't amounted to much: it had hardly paid for his dinners in Hall for one term. Just as well they had been scrapped. Then there was his daughter, Petra, who had just turned eighteen.

At school Alan had always been considered a high-flyer. He was expected to become a don and write lots of erudite books on medieval French. But he hadn't. He had got his predicted first, stayed on to do a doctorate and then got fed up with the whole thing: the confines of the College, the petty regulations, the pomposity of the dons. So he had left in the middle of term, bored and frustrated and gone to India. And that was where he had met Melissa.

He put his book down on the fine gravel beside his chair, the page carefully marked. Now he had started on a trail of reminiscence he found it impossible to read. He remembered the meeting so clearly. He was trying to take in the magnificence of the Taj Mahal, dazzling white, a sparkling jewel in a sky almost white too in the fierce heat of the sun. There were hundreds of tourists milling around. Most were clad in shorts, a few in trousers, many of the western women in cotton dresses with necklines scalloped low, their skin scorched and blistered in the heat. And there was Melissa, cool, elegant and pale-skinned in a sari. After dinner together that evening in the square, they had gone to bed. He had fallen madly, hopelessly in love with Melissa, the visionary, the lover of Buddhism and The Orient. He had chased her all over India in vain and only managed to win her when she finally returned to England two years later. By then Alan had completed his year's teacher training course and was in the middle of his first year teaching.

They were married in the summer. It was a large and opulent affair. Melissa's accountant father had more than a penny to spare and was delighted to lavish some of it on his only daughter. There were four hundred guests, a marquee in their spacious Surrey garden, a band until two am and non-stop champagne. An exquisite oyster-white wedding dress had been ordered, supervised by Melissa's mother, who was utterly distraught when her daughter arrived at the altar in a scarlet sari, complete with the customary Oriental mark on her forehead. She was heard to remonstrate with her husband during the reception that surely he could have persuaded Melissa to change into her white wedding dress. He assured her he most certainly would have done had it been at all possible, but their daughter had been quite adamant in her choice of wedding garment.

The first few years of their marriage had been happy. They spent a great deal of time in bed, resulting in two children in less than three years. Then the quarrelling began. Melissa felt lonely and trapped with two small children to take care of. Alan's responsibilities at school increased and there seemed less and less time for lovemaking. As many people had predicted, they drifted apart and after only seven years of marriage, a mere three of which were truly happy, Melissa went off to India with her guru, leaving Alan in sole charge of their two young children, aged four and six.

Alan opened his eyes with a start, unaware he had begun to doze off. And it wasn't yet eleven o'clock! They had only been up two hours and he was already falling asleep! This is the life, he thought. This is the way to keep young and live long. Just spend most of the day lying in a chair out of doors, dozing. There was a scraping sound on the terrace as Jo moved her chair a little to face the sun more directly. Alan sat up and waved. Jo got up and walked over to him, wondering if he needed his sunglasses or wanted a cold drink. The day promised to be a scorcher. The sky was a cloudless, azure blue, without a breath of wind. Jo had already slipped off her shorts and sleeveless top, and striding across the courtyard in her turquoise bikini showing off her tan, she looked almost like a model on a catwalk. Alan felt desire rise in him again as she stood beside him, slim, poised and fragrant. He stroked her back, running his finger down her spine, slipping his hand inside her bikini pants to caress her slim buttocks. Jo gave a little frisson of pleasure. Then she laughed and pushed him away gently.

'Greedy. You've already had your oats to-day.'

Alan withdrew his hand. A second helping was too much to hope for so soon.

'I thought you came over for more.'

'Out here?'

'We've never tried it.'

'Say someone calls round?' Jo sounded doubtful.

The gate at the front of the house squeaked and footsteps crunched along the gravel.

'I told you!' said Jo triumphantly.

'I was planning to oil that gate,' replied Alan, 'but I think it might be wiser to leave it as it is.'

Jo laughed. 'I agree,' she said, as their nearest neighbour, elderly Marcel Legrand, the retired farmer who lived at the end of the lane, walked round the corner of the house. He closed the gate carefully, bending to inspect the lock as it squeaked again in protest. He walked slowly into the courtyard, shuffling, and a little bent. He was of medium height, thickset, certainly not thin, but not really fat. His observant light blue eyes twinkled in a ruddy, weather-beaten face, creased and care-worn after seventy-five years of harsh living. He wore faded blue trousers and a jacket which no longer quite matched. A flat cap covered his wisps of straggling grey hair. He looked inquisitively round the courtyard, his observant eyes darting round, missing nothing, noting all the changes which had taken place since his last visit. He moved across to where Jo and Alan had hastily resumed their places on the sun beds, quickening his pace slightly, his ambling gait resembling a tortoise in a hurry, his right arm already extended for the ritual handshake.

'*Bonjour, mes amis. J'espère que je vous ne dérange pas ? Il fait beau, n'est-ce-pas ? Pas trop chaud, hein?* Will you come round for a drink this evening?'

'We'd love to,' replied Alan, always pleased to have a French speaking evening in prospect.

'*Vers six heures et demi?*'

'Half-past six? *Excellent.*'

'*Bon! Parfait! Entendu. Alors, à ce soir.*'

'*Au revoir, Marcel. A ce soir*'

There was more hand shaking and Marcel shuffled back across the courtyard, beady blue eyes flashing round to make sure he hadn't missed anything the first time.

When he had left, Jo laughed. 'Funny old bugger.'

'Yes. But kind. Very well meaning.'

'Insatiably curious.'

'But he's got nothing else to do.'

'Nor will we if we come and live here.'

Jo considered the prospect: she and Alan at home all day on their own together. It mightn't be too bad. The weather was certainly better than in London. She would be free to do as she liked all day. Maybe she would take up painting too. She had enjoyed art at school. Her job as a primary school secretary was becoming repetitive, even boring. They say a change is as good as a rest. Perhaps living France wouldn't be so bad. It would certainly be different. Perhaps she was coming round to it after all? Jo closed her eyes, too lazy to read, and applied herself fully to the art of sunbathing. Well, they had a French session in prospect this evening, probably two hours of it. It would do her French good. Alan, much to Jo's chagrin, spoke virtually flawless French so he hardly needed the practice, but he would certainly enjoy the evening. She thought back to their first visit to Marcel and Jeanine Legrand, almost exactly a year ago. Having no idea what to expect, they had showered, changed and presented themselves *chez* Legrand at six thirty-five. Jeanine let them in, smiling, courteous, full of handshakes, chatting continually.

'*Bonjour. Entrez, je vous en prie.* Marcel will be here directly. He has a few little problems... But it can't be helped.'

Tall and rather large, Jeanine had a kindly face with a ruddy complexion, remarkably soft and unlined for her sixty-eight years. She had short-cropped thick grey hair and wore half-moon glasses, which slipped constantly down her nose. She wore a purple hand-knitted wool jumper, several sizes too small and a nondescript skirt of indeterminate length, which she had undoubtedly bought from a market stall. The Legrand's farmyard was large and immaculately tidy. The house was tiny and spotless. A pair of rubber clogs stood neatly on the freshly scrubbed doorstep. They went in through a narrow entrance passage, the floor covered in shiny, brightly patterned lino. A pair of men's slippers lay equally tidily on the floor by the radiator just inside the door. Jeanine led them in to the moderately sized kitchen, sparsely furnished and very neat. Along the far wall stood a cooker, fridge and a washing machine. There were cupboards and a kitchen sink under the window on the right. In the centre stood a table covered in a plastic cloth of a garish, tasteless design, flanked by four wooden chairs. Although it was still broad daylight, a neon strip-light, running almost the whole length of the ceiling, bathed the room in a harsh white light. The room was convenient, extremely functional, but there was nothing aesthetic about it at all. Jeanine invited them to sit down at the table.

'*Asseyez-vous, je vous en prie.* It was a nice day today, yes? Not too hot. I hate the heat. Maybe it's because I'm too fat.'

She chatted on, her soft burr with gently rolling rs reminding Jo of the West Country accent. But it was difficult to follow unless one spoke good French. The three of them sat round the table for at least half an hour, awaiting the arrival of Marcel, apparently caught up in some little problems; events beyond his control.

'Problems make him happy,' explained Jeanine. 'They occupy his time and make him feel needed. He likes to be busy, to fill his day. But there isn't enough for him to do now since he sold the cattle. He misses his youth,' she went on sadly, full of understanding. 'Twenty years ago he didn't have enough hours in the day. But it was a difficult life, farming here in those times. We suffered badly in the war, you know. Many people were starving. They were so hungry they sold their souls to the Vichy Government just to get food. The children ran barefoot. Many had no coats. Rural France was hard in those days. The cities picked up first after the war. We seemed to have been forgotten, left behind. It wasn't until the beginning of the sixties that things slowly began to improve. In 1961 we got water. Have you noticed how many wells there are around here? Most farms have wells. They were our only source of water. I couldn't believe it the day I turned on a tap and the water came out! It was like a miracle! And the shower! I was thirty-five before I had my first shower. Nowadays it seems unimaginable. But then everything was different. In those days there was no electricity either. That came in

1962, or was it 1963? Almost thirty years ago now. It's difficult to remember.'

Alan sat listening, absorbed and fascinated. Jo, trying to concentrate and only understanding a few words, began to feel sleepy. They sat on round the empty table covered in its garish plastic cloth, the pattern glinting in the relentless white neon light. No bottle or glasses had been produced. There wasn't even a bowl of nuts on the table. Jo began to wonder if *les apéritifs* had been a myth, a figment of the imagination. Perhaps even Alan had misunderstood the invitation. She needn't have worried. Just after seven o'clock Marcel arrived, full of apologies:

'Je m'excuse... I'm so sorry... I had a number of problems...' And, glowing with importance at having problems to solve Marcel got out glasses and several different bottles. Then the serious drinking began and continued until well after nine o'clock.

Jo didn't realise she had fallen asleep until she heard footsteps crunching on the gravel. I bet it's that nosey-parker Marcel again, she thought, struggling to sit up. But it was Alan, smiling gravely, as he stood beside her, looking down.

'Good heaven's! I must have fallen asleep,' she said, feeling rather guilty at having wasted the morning.

'That's what holidays are for,' said Alan. 'But I'm afraid this one's going to come to an abrupt end.'

'Oh, why?' Suddenly Jo didn't want to leave Laronne.

'That was Sebastian on the phone. We've been burgled.'

'Burgled! Where? At Lavender Garden?'

'Where else?'

Their little Victorian terraced house had been completely vandalised. The walls had been daubed with paint, the curtains torn down, upholstery slashed and the tables and chairs covered in cigarette burns. All their clothes had been pulled out of the cupboards and drawers and flung onto the floor. Most of their paintings were missing and all Jo's jewellery had been stolen. It was the most traumatic home-coming that either of them had ever experienced and had a great deal to do with their decision to move to France permanently.

In the end, even Jo was not sorry to see the last of Lavender Garden.

Chapter Three

Alan stood up stiffly, yawned, stretched and looked at his watch. Twenty minutes past five. Being a weekday, Wednesday in fact, he had meant to go on working until six o'clock but he felt much too tired. Creative writing was much harder than he had expected. The writers' handbooks made it all sound so simple. Map out the plot; make sure it moves along at a good pace, full of action, conflict and surprise twists. Make sure the characters are likeable people with whom the ordinary reader can easily identify. Write about events you have experienced; the sort of people you know; places you have visited. He had read several handbooks and many, many contemporary novels with vastly different characters and plots, in English and in French. He felt very well prepared. And yet some things were easier in theory than in practice. Writing a first novel was obviously one of them.

He sighed, flexed his shoulder muscles and walked over to the window. He looked at the scene below and smiled with pleasure. The sun was curving down to the right across the courtyard, a spacious oval covered in pale fine yellow gravel, which the French called *tout-venant*. To the left of the house was an enormous barn, recently re-roofed and completely renovated as a store and garage. Next to the barn was another outhouse, consisting of one small room, which he and Jo affectionately called *La Petite Pièce*. They had spent the last summer holidays renovating it and now it was rented out on a weekly basis, mainly to English paying guests. Opposite the barn were more outhouses, long and low, not yet renovated and in a bad state of repair, but Alan was well aware of their potential as additional guest accommodation, with possibly two extra apartments. Plans for their refurbishment were already well advanced. At the far end of these buildings was a Burgundian Round House, which Alan had spent the winter re-roofing and repairing, transforming it into a beautiful two-room apartment, complete with luxury bathroom and fully fitted kitchen. The advertisements in *The Sunday Times* emphasised its unique Burgundian charm and so far they had had no difficulty in filling it with paying guests every week, despite the devaluation of the English pound. Alan sighed with relief each time his English agent rang with a new booking. He knew how much the French hoteliers and restaurateurs were suffering from the dearth of English visitors. It took very little to destabilise precarious finances; and theirs were certainly precarious. Having retired early, Alan's pension was inevitably reduced and despite not having yet spent all his godmother's inheritance, they needed every available booking to make ends meet. If the punters didn't arrive, they were in trouble. But at last they were beginning to break even. If their luck held, they would be all right. If only he could get a novel, or even some short stories, into print, it might swell the coffers a little.

So far he felt they had made the right decision to come and live permanently in Laronne. It was the appalling burglary of their house in Lavender Garden,

Clapham in 1988, which had finally persuaded them to move to France. Now two years later, after extensive renovations, they were beginning to settle down to an entirely new life.

Beyond the Burgundian Round House stretched the rolling, gently undulating Burgundian fields, dotted with silent, white, slow-moving cows: Charolais, the best beef in France. A walk. That's what he needed. A walk somewhere in the calm and peaceful countryside, far from the pressures of urban life. He looked down at his legs; bare, tanned and shapely. Should he put on trousers? But why? This was the country, not Hampstead Heath. Surely he was unlikely to meet a soul. He wondered if Jo would want to join him on his walk. At first she had enjoyed country walks, but now she seemed to make any excuse to avoid them. 'Too much to do in the house,' she would say. But when he arrived back home she was either stretched out in a garden chair fast asleep or engrossed in some paperback with a lurid cover. She had become increasingly silent of late, verging on the withdrawn. He was beginning to become anxious about her. He hoped the move to France hadn't been a mistake. Jo had been so enthusiastic about it in the early stages but now he wasn't so sure. She seemed restless and unsettled. She wasn't making any effort to improve her French either. He felt they should give it another year or so at least, though God forbid, another move in reverse was a truly horrendous prospect; assuming they would be able to sell their remote, rambling property in the first place.

A baby would hopefully solve everything. And it was certainly not for want of trying. Strange thought. The infant would be a French born child, brought up in

France, with a mother who spoke almost no French. It was a thought that had not occurred to him before. He crossed the landing into their bedroom to fetch a light sweater. One could never completely trust Burgundian weather, particularly at the beginning of May. He selected a beige sweater from the vast built-in wardrobe he had spent so many trying hours constructing. He had pointed out at the time that they would not need such an extensive and elaborate wardrobe for their new simple French rural existence. Not nearly so extensive as their busy sophisticated London life had required. He was quite sure they would both be able to manage on three or four pairs of jeans, a dozen or so shirts and tee shirts and a few sweaters. Anoraks and raincoats hung downstairs by the front door. Of course Jo wished to have a few skirts as well, but surely she would have no need of smart town suits or well-cut jackets; and certainly any evening wear would be totally unnecessary.

However, Jo had other ideas. In fact, she had 'topped up' her already substantial wardrobe before they moved. 'We're bound to meet some really interesting and amazing people,' she had said. Alan had thought otherwise and felt some clearing out would have been more appropriate. Now Jo's clothes were in the vast cupboard, in two sections: winter and summer, each section carefully graded according to colour. All that remained were the occasions to wear them. The amazingly interesting people seemed to be in short supply.

Alan clattered down the beautiful, uncarpeted oak staircase, built with loving care and at enormous expense by the local carpenter, Didier Pérnot, since retired, but still, as he had been for over twenty years, the Mayor of Laronne.

'Jo! I'm finishing early! Can't take any more! How about a walk? It's such a lovely evening.'

The staircase led directly into the living room, an enormous rectangle with a dark, oak-beamed ceiling. An archway separated the living room from the cosy intimate dining area, which led into the kitchen, immaculately fitted out, no expense spared, by a top firm of kitchen experts based in Chalon-sur-Saône, about thirty kilometres away. Jo and Alan had decided that as they planned to live in Laronne, presumably forever, they would convert their own living quarters to the highest possible standard. What would pass muster for the weekly punters would not be good enough for them.

'Jo, darling!'

'Yes.'

Jo came out of the kitchen wearing an apron, her corn-coloured hair slightly awry. Slim, trim and lightly sun-tanned, her youthful appearance belied her thirty-two years. Her slight frame made her seem taller than she really was, though in fact, her head only just reached Alan's shoulder.

'You look busy.'

'Yes.'

'What are you up to?'

'I'm having a bit of a spring clean in the kitchen.'

'In May! It's nearly summer!'

'I know. But I never got round to cleaning the kitchen properly. Too busy getting the apartments ready for the punters.

'Yes. The punters are a lot of work but they do bring in the much-needed lolly.'

'Oh, I know. I'm not complaining, just remarking. I think the punters are well worth it and very nice to have around too. They fill the silence in this empty place.'

They fill the silence in this empty place. Alan's eyebrows went up but he said nothing.

'Anyway,' Jo went on, in a more positive tone of voice, 'you know I rather enjoy a thorough spring clean.'

'With a few large plastic dustbin bags so you can throw most of the stuff away,' teased Alan lightly.

'Exactly. Most satisfying.' Jo smiled, her deep violet blue eyes twinkling with merriment. 'But I fear you are planning to disrupt my labours?' she mocked.

'Oh, no. How could I do such a thing?' Alan feigned seriousness. 'How far advanced are these labours?'

Jo frowned thoughtfully. 'Another couple of hours should see me through.' She looked at her watch. 'Five-thirty. That gives me over half-an-hour to have dinner ready for eight. OK?'

'Yes, of course. Sounds perfect.'

'What were you going to suggest? Another country walk?'

'Well, yes, I was. It's a really beautiful evening and I thought perhaps...'

'Alan, most of the evenings here are beautiful and the days too, thank heaven, but I do feel we've run the gamut of country walks. After all, we're living in the country; we're surrounded by the stuff. We're looking at it all the time. There's nothing else to look at. We don't have to go for walks in it as well.'

Alan laughed, a little surprised. 'Two years ago you loved country walks.'

'Two years ago I had never lived in the country.'

'Aah. Missing the city?'

'A bit.'

'Noise, traffic, pollution?'

'People, shops, bright lights, pavements.'

Alan leant against the doorpost. 'I see. Don't you like the peace, the tranquillity, the space, the silence and the beautiful white cows?'

'No,' said Jo shortly. 'I thought I would at the beginning. But I find the country doesn't improve with familiarity. It's too empty, too green and the silence is almost deafening. And as for the cows - well, I prefer them on a plate.'

Alan roared with laughter. 'You prefer cows on a plate! That's really good, that is. Does the same go for sheep and hens?'

'I'd say so.'

'And vegetables, plastic-wrapped on the supermarket shelf? Rather than freshly picked, really tasting of something, even though they're covered in mud...'

Jo laughed. 'The vegetables are OK. They certainly taste good.'

'Provided you don't have to pick them and clean them yourself.'

'Well, yes.'

'It all takes a bit of getting used to.'

'It certainly does.'

'I know.' Alan felt guilty.

He was afraid to touch her, or even look at her, in case she would cry.

'We could always...'

'No. It's fine. I'll adjust in time. Go for your walk, darling. You love your long, isolated, rural walks. I'll finish clearing out the kitchen. I'm enjoying it. It's what I'm used to. I'll put on a CD to fill the silence.'

'Good idea.'

Alan realised it wasn't the right moment for a serious discussion about the advantages and disadvantages of rural French life.

'Dinner at eight?'

'Yes. That sounds just about right.' Jo smiled. 'Take Max with you, won't you?'

'Of course. Be back by seven-thirty.'

Alan put his arms around his wife and brushed her lips with his. He felt a stirring in his groin, as he nearly always did when he was close to her. He held her more tightly and tried to part her lips gently with his tongue. She stiffened and withdrew from his embrace. She laughed lightly.

'Off you go! You need your walk.'

Alan whistled tunelessly as he wound his way up the steep, narrow path to the old quarry beyond Dracy. He had been walking for a good half-hour and hadn't stopped thinking about Jo. He had known something was wrong. He could see now that she wasn't happy living here, deep in the remotest part of Burgundy. He had thought she would eventually adapt to the French way of life. The weather was better, especially in the summer. The food was delicious and eminently drinkable wines were readily obtainable for a fraction of the price one paid in England. But there were other things, more important in life, than good food, wine and the weather. There were human relationships. He and Jo had been married for nearly seven years now and Alan felt the marriage was a good one. Of course he tended to take the initiative and Jo was more inclined than not to agree with him. But wasn't that one of the basic differences between men and women? Didn't the man generally make most of the decisions in a partnership?

But when he really thought about it, when he really asked himself the question: did you really consider Jo in deciding to move to France permanently? He felt guilty. He knew he had done just what he had wanted without sufficiently thinking how Jo would settle down and fit in with French country life. To start with, she hardly spoke any French. His French was fluent. He had suggested they speak French together for an hour each day. They had tried it during the first few weeks but he discovered it was uphill work. It was only then he had discovered how little French Jo actually knew. Secretly he was appalled. Where had she been during French lessons at school? She hadn't learnt a musical instrument, so she didn't even have the excuse of being taken out of class. She once said she had started French lessons at the age of ten. That made six years of French instruction. Amazing to have completely forgotten something one had studied for six years. She had said she was working at it - that she still had her old school grammar book. He had bought her another one for a bit of extra help, but he never saw her use it.

She was crafty, though. When they visited the neighbours for *apéritifs* (which appeared to be a favourite pastime in Laronne), Jo always seemed to understand what was said. She joined in the laughter and never appeared to be at a loss. Perhaps she was pretending to follow the conversation? Perhaps she knew more than she let on? Perhaps she was studying in secret? Perhaps she was even enjoying life in Laronne after all? Perhaps, perhaps...

Alan reached the top of the steep, narrow path. The last ten minutes had been quite a scramble, as the path was stony and very dry. It had been difficult to find footholds in the hard white ground and there were few handholds either. There were just some prickly scrubby bushes, which had only very shallow roots. Alan looked down at the path he had just come up and rather regretted it. The descent was certainly steep. One misplaced footstep could be fatal. The ground was so dry it was like a slide and there was nothing to hang on to at all. He shuddered and heaved himself carefully onto the path at the top of the hill.

He sat down on a convenient boulder and took stock of his position. He had taken a completely new route and had arrived at the opposite side of the quarry to the one at which he normally arrived. He tried to think back to where he might have taken a wrong turning, but realised immediately it was a wasted exercise. It didn't matter. He had arrived at a new location, and although the ascent had been steep and potentially dangerous, what mattered was that he had arrived without mishap in a remote and beautiful place with the most stunning view over the valley. He could make out Laronne, straggling up the gentler slope on the other side, and the vineyards of La Côte Chalonnaise stretching away to the south.

Maxwell sat down in front of him, tail wagging, tongue hanging out, panting. Alan leant over and scratched behind his ear affectionately.

'Well done, old chap. You feeling your age too?'

He stood up and tried to get his bearings. It was strange how he had arrived at the other side of the quarry Normally he walked in a more direct line. This time he seemed to have made a large semi-circular detour. Maybe he had just followed Maxwell, who had been even more engrossed than usual in chasing rabbits. He took a step nearer the quarry. There were places on the other side where it was almost level with the path, but on this side, the higher side, the ground fell away quite sharply, so he was, in effect, standing on a parapet with steep slopes on both sides. He had the choice of going either right or left. If he went left he reckoned he would arrive quite soon on already familiar terrain. Hopefully he was not too far from the derelict cottage where, from time to time, he would meet up with Didier Pérnot and his friends for gambling and drinking sessions. Alan wondered if perhaps they were in session at the moment and whether he could just call in. On the other hand, that might be considered rather presumptuous. He had never been before without a special invitation. A letter, carefully worded, with a rather sinister sign like an upside down cross at the bottom would arrive with the warning: *'Ne réponds pas. Viens si tu peux et ne dis rien à personne.'* 'Don't reply. Come if you can and say nothing to anyone!' No. He certainly couldn't just turn up.

There was also the possibility that he might be spotted by one of the members of an artistic group called *Les Projets Créatifs,* who used the old tile factory as a base for their activities. Approaching Didier's derelict cottage from this new angle would mean walking past the old tile factory in broad daylight. If Didier and his friends were having a session in their hideout, they might take a dim view of the fact that one of their circle, albeit a less regular member, had been spotted by what was considered a member of an opposing group. Alan had only one choice. He would have to turn right.

After twenty minutes walking along a rough uneven stony path, though fortunately dry, Alan reached a narrow road. It wound tortuously, following the contour of the uneven hillside, but as he had found almost throughout Burgundy, the local *Commune* kept the ditches clear and the hedges well trimmed.

Suddenly he heard the sound of a car coming towards him, taking the bend at a greater speed than was prudent. As a white van shot past him, Alan leaped into the ditch. The driver applied the brakes violently and the vehicle screeched to a halt. The window was lowered and the driver leant out. He was a well-built man in his early forties, his unruly dark curly hair mirrored by a similar mop of hair bushing through the top of his open-necked shirt.

'*Bonjour, Alain! Ça va?*'

'*Bonjour, Lucien! Merci, je vais très bien. Et toi? Qu'est-ce que tu fais ici?*'

Lucien Gauthier laughed, flashing his even white teeth. 'I could ask you the same question, *mon ami*. What are you doing here? On another of your mad walks, eh?'

'Yes. But not so mad as immensely enjoyable. I didn't realise you delivered bread so late in the day, and in such remote places.'

'I deliver wherever I'm needed; remote or not,' replied Lucien, good-naturedly. 'But you're right of course. I don't usually deliver so late but today is rather a special day. It's *Monsieur* Floret's eighty-fifth birthday, so I am bringing him my exquisite *tarte aux fraises*. There's a big family dinner for *Monsieur* Floret this evening so I mustn't be late. *Au revoir, mon ami. A bientôt.*'

And Lucien ground into gear and waved to Alan, as he shot off round the corner at a highly dangerous speed.

Alan was now beginning to get his bearings. He knew where Jean-Pierre and Germaine Floret lived: in a remote farmhouse several kilometres distant from Dracy. He certainly had come the long way round. He walked on slowly, enjoying the solitude, admiring the beautiful view and turning around now and again to watch the progress of the golden sun slowly sinking across the wide valley behind the straggling village of Laronne.

Around the next bend he saw the slight wiry figure of Jules Gilot struggling valiantly up the steep hill on his battered old bicycle. A broad grin on his lean olive-skinned face, Jules dismounted with relief when he heard Alan call: '*Bonjour, Jules*!' and waited for him to catch up. Alan expressed surprise that Jules should also be out on such a late delivery.

'*Ah ! Quelquefois il faut travailler tard, Alain.* I am the only postman for miles around and sometimes I have to make late deliveries. I'm on my way to deliver an urgent letter to *Monsieur* Paillard. He's the only architect in the area so he is an important man. It's up to me to make sure that he receives any urgent letters as soon as they arrive *au bureau de poste*. Are you on another of your long mad walks, *mon ami?* It seems to be only the English who go walking. England must be full of mad walkers, *n'est-ce-pas?*'

Alan laughed. 'Not so full as you might think. But yes, the English do tend to take more walks than the French. Maybe it's something to do with the obligation to walk the dog. The French never seem to walk their dogs.'

Jules's eyes widened. '*Mais non,* of course not. Why walk a dog?'

'Dogs need the exercise and they enjoy it.'

'But why give pleasure to a dog? Surely they exist only to give pleasure to humans. That's their purpose, after all. As for their needing exercise: in my experience they become better guard dogs without exercise, because they're more ferocious when they're chained up all day.'

Alan laughed. 'Your opinion is certainly the majority view in this part of the world.'

Jules looked very serious for a moment. 'Perhaps in England there is no need for guard dogs? Perhaps there are no burglars?'

'Yes, we have burglars and a special breed of guard dog which is usually kept hungry when it's on guard.'

'Hungry! But that's intolerable!'

'But it's fed when it's done its spell of duty...'

'And then taken for a walk?'

'Exactly.'

'I must visit England one day and see these wonders for myself. And now if you will excuse me, *mon ami*. I must cycle quickly down the hill and give *Monsieur* Paillard his urgent letter.' And with a wave, he shot off down the hill, around the corner and out of sight.

Alan walked on slowly, musing on the gentle pace of county life and the kindness and warmth of the people. Even if by English standards they neglected their dogs and often their pets in general, they more than made up for these shortcomings in their consideration for each other.

It was further than he realised to the Paillards' house, a large imposing structure on the hill above the quarry, reached by a long, steep unadopted road. On the occasions when they had dined with the Paillards, they had always approached the house from the other direction, taking the road through Dracy. He had just passed the turning to the road up to the house when a car stopped just behind him. The driver got out and waved.

'*Bonjour, Alain! C'est vraiment un plaisir de vous voir ici!* When are you coming to visit us?'

Small, dapper, with trim moustache and neat goatee beard, Roland Paillard was always immaculately turned out. He shook Alan's hand warmly. 'And how is Jo? *Maman* always enjoys her company. She is still giving piano lessons, but,' he looked at his watch, 'in twenty minutes, at seven-thirty, the lessons will be finished and there will be no more students up at the house. Perhaps you will join us for *un apéritif*? But I must post this letter first. It's rather urgent and as Jules Gilot was kind enough to make a special delivery, I feel I should post my reply equally promptly. I will meet you back at the house, *n'est-ce-pas?*'

Alan particularly enjoyed Roland's company and was sorely tempted to accept his invitation. The local residents frequently proffered invitations on the spur of the moment and he found their spontaneity quite touching.

'Roland, there is nothing I would like better than to have *un apéritif* and a nice chat with you and *Madame;* but the fact is, I have come out for a walk which has already taken a great deal longer than I had planned. Jo is expecting me back at half-past-seven and as I see it is already a quarter past, I may have to run all the way home.'

Roland laughed. 'You English and your long mad walks! I don't know what you see in all this walking. The car was invented to avoid the need for walking, *n'est-ce-pas?* Look, why not finish your walk by coming up to the house? By that time *Maman* will have finished giving her piano lessons. You could phone Jo, explain that you are with us and suggest she join us also for *un apéritif.*'

Again Alan was tempted. But he thought of Jo, engrossed in spring-cleaning in her grubby jeans, her hair awry. He knew she wouldn't want to make the effort to wash her hair, change and drive fifteen minutes just for a glass or two of *Pérnod*. For a second he considered taking up Roland's offer of using the telephone. It was a great deal later than he had realised and he knew he had no chance of getting home even by eight-thirty. But he knew that once he had arrived at the Paillards' house he would feel obliged to stay for at least half-an-hour.

'Roland, I'd love to. But Jo is doing something special for dinner and I really ought to get back.'

'*Entendu.* I won't persuade you any longer. Then come to dinner on Saturday week. I know *Maman* would love it. Seven-thirty. I'd ask you to come sooner but I have to go away on business tomorrow'

'*Merci,* Roland. We'd love to come to dinner on Saturday week. That's most kind. See you then. Seven-thirty.'

'*Entendu. Au revoir.*'

'*Au revoir.*'

They shook hands again and parted. Roland drove off up the hill towards the post office as Alan set off in the opposite direction. The light was fading a little and the dusky magical twilight accentuated the stillness and the silence. It certainly was a remote spot. Alan decided his best course would be to follow the road a little further and see if there was a suitable short-cut across one of the fields, providing there were no bulls around. He caught a glimpse of a red car further up the road and rather hoped it would pass him and offer him a lift to Laronne. He would have absolutely no hesitation in accepting a lift from a stranger in this delightful and friendly neighbourhood. But the car's engine grew fainter as it climbed slowly upwards towards La Roche.

Around the next bend the road curved sharply to the left and then levelled out. Alan hadn't seen Maxwell for several minutes and presumed he had run on ahead in search of more rabbits. Suddenly he heard Maxwell's bark, at first his normal bark of excitement, then rapidly becoming hysterical. Alan thought it sounded as if the dog was yelping in pain and he started to walk faster. Then he saw a figure at the side of the road, waving his arms and shouting. Assuming the figure was frightened of the dog and needed protection, Alan broke into a run. As he came nearer he recognised the figure of Jean Bertrand, the twenty-year-old son of Jean-Yves Bertrand, who had recently moved to Laronne with his large family. Unpleasant rumours were circulating about the family, who were extremely unpopular in the neighbourhood. Alan had already had a violent argument with Jean a few weeks ago when he caught him stoning a herd of cattle only a few feet away. Alan saw Jean bend down, pick up a stone and hurl it in the direction of the frantically barking Maxwell, still out of sight. As he approached, the youth bent to pick up another stone. Alan reached the edge of the road and immediately saw that they stood at the top of a very deep gorge with a small lake far below in the quarry. A few feet from the top of the precipice, trapped on a ledge, howling in fear and pain, crouched Maxwell. The boy coolly raised his arm and threw another stone at the terrified dog.

'How dare you throw stones at a poor dumb animal!' shouted Alan, his French forgotten in his towering rage.

The boy turned towards him, uncomprehending, a half crazed look in his eye. '*Quoi?*'

Alan repeated what he had said, in French this time.

'I don't like dogs,' replied the youth, 'especially English dogs. They deserve stoning.'

Alan was incensed. He walked up to the boy and grabbing both his arms, tried to drag him away from the cliff top. Maxwell continued to bark, but realising he was no longer being pelted with missiles; he managed to jump off the ledge and struggled to the top of the cliff. He reached the road as Alan and Jean, now arm-locked as if in a wrestling match, teetered back again to the edge of the cliff. Sensing his master was in trouble, the dog circled behind the youth and gave him a sharp nip on the backside. Screaming in pain and terror, Jean pushed Alan closer to the edge. Alan, taken completely unawares, lost his balance and fell over the edge of the precipice. Luckily, there was a bush just below the rim of the cliff. He held onto it, thrashing wildly with his legs, trying to find a foothold. But his weight was too much for the bush's shallow roots. It came out of the ground with a sudden jerk, increasing the momentum of his fall. He fell onto a boulder, encircling it with his arms, as if imploring it to rescue him. But the boulder was as impermanent as the bush. It started rolling, gathering momentum and taking Alan with it down the cliff face.

Entangled with the ever-rolling boulder, Alan slid down faster; frantically grabbing at anything he could get hold of. Then he reached a section with no vegetation at all, a part that had most recently been quarried, bare and sheer, like a slide in a children's playground. Meeting no resistance from any vegetation, the boulder continued rolling down the cliff on its own, gathering speed on the way, leaving Alan sliding down in its wake.

At first he continued to fall on his back, but as his body encountered the odd rock, he began to roll over. Faster and faster he careered down the precipice, hitting his head several times. By the time he reached the lake he had completely lost consciousness.

Jean stood at the top and watched, too mesmerised to do anything. As Alan's body rolled into its final resting place in the lake, the youth picked up another stone and threw it in beside him.

Making his way back towards the road, Jean Bertrand noticed Emile Marceau in his red car, driving back to Laronne. Emile had been searching the cliff top for an anorak left behind by one of the children in his class, whom he had taken on a school nature outing that afternoon.

Chapter Four

Gerry Nolan swung his shabby duffle bag over his shoulder and walked out of Wormwood Scrubs without a backward glance. Tall, lean and muscular, Gerry had shed over two stone in prison. The food had been tasteless and totally inadequate and of course, there had been no alcohol - officially - though it had been possible to scrounge the occasional gin or whisky. As a non-smoker Gerry had traded cigarettes for the odd drink. But he had missed his beer. After seven years inside Gerry was missing a great deal more than a pint of bitter. He missed his freedom, his comforts and, probably most of all, he missed women. Prison life is hard, but it was harder for Gerry than most. Gerry was not part of the criminal fraternity. He was not a member of the underground twilight world inhabited by serial killers, contract murderers and violent sex offenders. He was not in the criminal 'Club' and knew no one when he was first sent to Parkhurst Prison. He had found it extremely difficult to settle down to the harsh monotonous routine. It was bad enough coping with the long hours of confinement locked up in a cell; the poor food, the cold in winter, the heat in summer, the shattering noise at association time, the rationing of showers, the lack of privacy and the humiliation of slopping out.

But if he had had a mate to chat to, someone with whom he could have shared past experiences and derive some little consolation, Gerry might have found his prison experience a little easier to bear. But he hadn't made a single friend in any of the nine prisons he had been confined in. Gerry was a loner. On that bright April morning he walked through the prison gates without any plans. Somewhere at the back of his mind he realised he had to try and build a new life. Aged twenty-seven, he had no family, no job and no prospects. He was neither well educated nor skilled in any trade and he had just spent seven years in prison. His first thought was to find a pub. He vaguely knew the area and reckoned it couldn't be far to Shepherds Bush. He didn't want to go into the first pub he came to as he felt he might be too easily recognisable. He figured that a lot of newly released prisoners probably went into the nearest pub and he could imagine the landlord refusing to serve him. That would be too humiliating. He walked east along Du Cane Road and turned right under Westway. As he walked past White City Tube Station, shortly arriving at the BBC TV Centre, he knew he couldn't be far from Shepherds Bush Green. There were bound to be plenty of pubs. There were, but they were all shut. It was only nine-thirty in the morning and Gerry had reckoned without the English licensing laws. He stood despondently outside The Bush on the corner, feeling cheated. He walked on past the BBC TV Theatre. Now there was nothing in the world he wanted more than a pint of beer. Even the thought of being in bed with a woman faded temporarily from his mind. It was a beautiful balmy spring day and the traffic crawled around The Green emitting poisonous exhaust fumes.

Gerry felt his throat constrict and his eyes smart. He had forgotten about London traffic.

He walked across to the Green and sat on a bench wondering what to do next. He felt wonderfully liberated and not a little light-headed. He had the whole day to himself with no restrictions. There was no one in authority. No one to tell him what to do and where to go. Just think of it! A whole free day! Hang on a minute. More than a free day. A whole free life! Provided, of course, that he didn't commit another crime. He quite understood that as a convicted criminal he had only been released on licence. If he were to commit another crime he would be sent straight back to jail. But he didn't intend to commit another crime. Good God! He wasn't a common criminal! And there had been mitigating circumstances.

A policeman passed by, neat and dapper in his uniform. Gerry's heart missed a beat and his hands grew sweaty. Cor! A copper! he thought. Better make a move. Don't want any questions asked. But the policeman merely nodded, murmured: 'Morning,' as he continued on his beat.

Gerry sat quietly on the bench. The sun was shining down directly, warming him a little as it was now after ten am. Some sparrows flew down less than a foot away, searching for food. Gerry tried to breathe deeply to calm the thumping of his heart. No good if I react like this each time I bump into the arm of the law, he thought. He began to feel hungry. It was a long time since his prison breakfast and there hadn't been much of that. He wondered if there was a caff nearby, or whether they were subjected to the same opening restrictions as the pubs. He got up and left the Green on the opposite side to where he had come in. Walking along the pavement on the far side he came to a brightly lit place with plastic tabletops, plastic stools and benches and a chrome serving-bar at the far end. A list of available food hung on a plastic board in bold lettering. There was a large yellow M on a red background over the door. The place was deserted except for a young girl in a red and white striped apron and cap behind the bar. Gerry opened the door cautiously. The smell of stale cooking oil reminded him of prison. Two of the tables in the far corner were piled high with discarded cartons and plastic cups with straws sticking out of the top. Although some of the rubbish had spilled over onto the floor, Gerry found the mess rather comforting. It was at least a familiar sight. He placed his scruffy duffle bag on the floor by a chair in the window and walked up to the chrome serving-bar at the back. The girl in her neat cap and apron stared at him curiously.

'Morning, sir. Nice day, isn't it?'

Gerry came too with a jolt. She had called him 'sir!' He wasn't used to be called 'sir.' In fact, he couldn't remember ever being called 'sir.' That was how he had had to address the screws.

'Good morning. Yes. Lovely day.' He looked at the girl. She was about eighteen or twenty and very pretty. He felt desire stir in his loins. The girl smiled at him.

'Come in for a late breakfast, have you? Or is it more of an early lunch?'

Gerry looked at her doubtfully. He wasn't used to being asked questions. He was far more accustomed to receiving orders.

Breakfast. Late breakfast. There would be time for lunch later on.

'Bacon and egg burger? Or just a Big Mac?'

'How much...?' Gerry felt very unsure.

'Prices are all up there,' said the girl, nodding at the price list.

Gerry walked over and stared at the plastic board. But the prices meant nothing to him.

'Bacon and egg burger. Any beer?'

'Beer!' The girl laughed. 'Beer! What a question! McDonald's don't sell beer. You don't come in here often then?'

'No. Not very often.'

'It's good value for money, it is. But you've got to like the buns, of course.'

'Yes. Of course.'

'I'll have it for you in a jiffy. On nights, are you?'

'No. I well...'

'Been away, then? Abroad? I mean, working.'

Although he was flattered by her interest, Gerry found it hard to handle. She was very attractive. He wondered if he could ask her out. But where would he take her?

'Yes, yes. Been away working.' Sewing mailbags. Working in the prison kitchen. But she would never know.

A few seconds later a polystyrene carton arrived through a steel flap which opened in the wall behind the bar. The girl picked it up and put it on the counter in front of him.

'There you are. One bacon and egg burger. That'll be two pounds and eight pence, please.'

Gerry reached into his pocket and brought out a wallet containing a thick wad of notes, which had been given to him by the prison authorities before he left that morning. He separated a few of them and examined them carefully. Then he selected a fiver and handed it over to the girl.

'This do?'

'More than enough. You'll get plenty of change out of that.'

The girl went to the till and counted out his change. Gerry glanced at it and put it in his pocket.

'You've a right fistful of notes there,' said the girl admiringly. 'Just been paid, have you?'

'Yes,' said Gerry.

'Week's wages?'

Goodness! She wouldn't let go.

'No. Total of my worldly goods.'

The girl looked at him in disbelief. 'I must say you're a good laugh.'

'A good laugh?' It was Gerry's turn to look uncomprehending.

'I mean, you're good value for money.'

'Oh.' Gerry was still none the wiser.

'Want something to drink with the burger?'

'Oh. Well...a drink. Sounds like a good idea. What are you offering?'

'It's all up there on the board with the prices, and very good value too, if you ask me.'

Gerry hadn't asked her and the prices still meant nothing to him.

'I'll have coffee, please.'

It was more expensive than the tea so he reckoned it must be better. Anyway, he had had enough tea in the last seven years to last him a lifetime. The coffee arrived with as much speed as the burger. A fast operating place, thought Gerry, as he picked up the polystyrene carton in one hand, the plastic cup in the other and rejoined his duffle bag by the window. He opened the carton, picked up the burger and took a large bite. Egg-yoke oozed out onto his hand. He licked it off and felt the girl's eyes on him.

'OK?' she called across to him.

'Yes.' He finished it quickly and asked her for another one.

She laughed. 'You must be really hungry. That'll be another two pounds and eight pence, please.'

He took out his wallet and handed over another fiver. Jesus! The money was going fast and he had only been out a few hours.

'You keeping the change for the bus, then?' The girl's tone was conversational.

'The bus? No. I don't think so.' He had never thought about a bus. 'You short?'

'No. I just thought you wouldn't want to weigh your pockets down with coins.'

Gerry was uncomprehending again. It was a long time since he had had a pocket full of coins.

Another polystyrene carton arrived through the stainless-steel flap at the back. The girl handed it over. 'There you go. That should fill you up all right.'

'Thanks.' Gerry picked it up and tried to screw up his courage to ask her out with him one evening. Tonight perhaps? Maybe there was a film on that she wanted to see.

'I was wondering…' he began.

At that moment the door opened and a young man of about twenty came in. The girl's face lit up.

'Oh hello, Darren. Nice of you to come in so early but I'm not off for a while yet.'

'No matter,' said Darren. I'll have a burger and stay for a chat. He went round the end of the counter and gave the girl a big kiss. 'Nice to see you so soon again, anyway.'

The girl giggled. 'Isn't it? And I only saw you just over two hours ago.'

Gerry collected the second carton and returned to his window seat. Well, she seemed to be booked up for the foreseeable future. Pity. But there must be other fish in the sea, he thought reflectively, demolishing half his burger in one bite. London's a large city and it's still only the first day.

He finished the burger and the rest of his coffee and stood up. He looked across to the back of the restaurant planning to say 'good-bye and thank you' to the girl, but Darren had wrapped himself around her and pinned her against the back wall.

Gerry picked up his duffle bag and went out quietly into the bright April sunshine.

By late afternoon Gerry reckoned he had two choices. He could either go to one of the Local Authority Housing Associations recommended by the prison service or he could sleep rough. As soon as the pubs opened at midday he had had four pints of bitter in The Bush. Totally unaccustomed as he now was to alcohol, he found his head spinning as he left the pub. He spent the afternoon walking along Holland Park Road and through Notting Hill Gate. By four o'clock he was beginning to feel hungry again but was reluctant to spend any more money. The beer had been unpleasantly expensive. He was beginning to realise why ex-prisoners so often re-offended. It was going to be tough surviving in a world in which he had few advantages and from which he had been forcibly absent for seven years.

A good education must be a help in becoming successful, he mused. What hope had he, a poor country boy from County Wicklow, who had left school at fourteen? Why, he hadn't even been as far as Dublin by the time he was ten. And now he had a criminal record into the bargain. He wandered slowly through the wide streets and avenues of Holland Park and Notting Hill Gate, gazing up at the big handsome houses with a mixture of awe and resentment. He wondered what it would be like to live in a grand house with plenty of money and perhaps several servants as well. He wondered whether rich people had been born rich; whether it was the luck of the draw if one happened to be born into, say, the Royal Family, or the Guinness family in Dublin. Or were there many self-made men, people from disadvantaged backgrounds like himself, who managed to make a lot of money without cheating or breaking the law?

He still hadn't decided whether or not to go to the Local Authority Housing Association and get fixed up for the night. He looked at his watch. Once more it appeared that fate would decide his life's course. Mostly it was easier just to let things happen. If he made a conscious decision it was usually the wrong one. He had never trusted his own judgement. It was now ten minutes to six so the offices would be closed. He would have to sleep rough. It was worth trying for one night.

He stood by Ladbrook Grove Tube Station torn by indecision. If he was going to sleep rough he had several choices. He could go back in the direction of Holland Park Avenue and spend the night either in Holland Park,

Kensington Gardens or Hyde Park. He knew the parks closed at midnight, but there should be no problem in keeping a low profile and then bunking down on a bench. It might get quite chilly but fortunately he had hung on to his old sleeping bag, which would give him some protection. A warmer option would be to sleep in a Tube Station. But that would mean buying a ticket and he had to watch his expenses until he could line up some kind of job. So he ruled out the Tube.

There was always Cardboard City on the South Bank. He had never actually slept there but he had worked on several building sites round about in the past and he knew there was quite a fraternity. But they were probably very 'clubby'. He doubted whether they would take kindly to outsiders - especially someone who had just done time. No. Cardboard City didn't seem a very good option either and it was quite a long walk. It looked as though one of the parks would be the best bet. He found himself walking in the wrong direction, as if The Scrubs was drawing him back like a magnet. Instead of walking due south, as he should have done, he found himself walking underneath Westway and soon he came to a gipsy encampment beside the large roundabout leading onto the M40.

The encampment consisted of a dozen or more caravans and a few tents squeezed onto a narrow plot of land designated for 'travellers' by the local council. Most were genuine 'travellers': people who had the wanderlust in their blood and who would feel claustrophobic and deprived of their liberty if they were forced to live in a conventional house or flat. There were others too, the hangers on, who were too lazy to organise anything better for themselves. In fact they were a mixed bunch, people who rubbed shoulders all day long, mucking in together, trying to make the best of it all. As Gerry approached, there were several families sitting round a fire and a welcoming aroma of food wafted into the air to be lost among the surrounding petrol fumes. The traffic noise from Westway was almost intolerable and he wondered in amazement how anyone could possibly live in such a place.

Gerry cut a strange, rather aloof figure. Tall and thin with broad shoulders tapering to slim hips, he had light brown wavy hair worn rather long. His large wide-set eyes were more hazel than brown. He had a thin straight nose and sensitive lips. He smiled rarely, but when he did his face lit up with a warmth and humour that gave him an air of considerable charm. With his long stride and loping gait he looked more like an actor striding onto the stage than an ex-prisoner looking for a place to lay his head for the night.

He drew nearer to the small crowd gathered around the fire. There were people of all ages, a few very elderly and several children. A girl in her early twenties looked up from her plate of food and waved. She was slim and dark, with olive skin and long jet-black hair. She had large liquid, almost black eyes. She was beautiful. Gerry stood transfixed, completely overcome by physical desire for her. It was all he could do to stop himself from ripping off her clothes and possessing her right there in front of everyone.

'Hello.' Her voice was as soft and beautiful as her face and her shapely body.

'Hello.' Gerry was unable to move.

'Why don't you join us? You look as if you could do with something to eat.'

Gerry hesitated for a moment. He had heard about gipsies and he wasn't sure if it was wise to get mixed up with them. But as an ex-convict he didn't really have a great deal to lose. And he was desperately hungry. Pity to pass up a free nosh.

'Thanks. Don't mind if I do.'

The girl patted a space beside her on the rug and he sat down. Everyone stared but said nothing. The girl got up, went to a large iron pot hanging over the fire, picked up a chipped plate with a faded floral design and filled it full of a steamy, pungent-smelling stew. She walked back the few paces and handed the plate to Gerry.

'Thanks a lot.'

The girl handed him a knife and fork and he tucked in voraciously, amid hostile glances in a stony silence.

Gerry spent nearly a month in the gipsy encampment. The gypsies were a strange crowd. They neither accepted nor rejected him. Nor did they ask where he came from or where he was planning to go; let alone how long he intended to stay in their camp. He remained on the periphery, giving a little practical help in the evenings where he could, carefully avoiding participation in anything illegal. He stayed because of Kate. He didn't know whether he loved her. He didn't analyse his feelings. He didn't know how to. He didn't understand the word love. He imagined it had more to do with marriage rather than just with sex. He had never considered marriage himself. Marriage was for people with money and jobs, for people who could afford to buy a nice house and educate their children properly. Poorly educated people like him with no prospects didn't get married. They just bedded whichever woman was available, willing or not willing as the case might be, and moved onto the next one when they had both tired of each other. Gerry had never had a really permanent relationship with anybody, even his parents. He had never known his father, never loved his mother. After all, she had not wished his conception and certainly not his birth. But he felt a deeper emotion than mere lust for Kate, the gipsy girl. True, he only had to glance at her to feel arousal. But when they managed to slip off alone together and he held her, naked and silky in his arms, he felt her presence soothing and comforting. Sometimes he felt an overwhelming desire to weep on her breast and pour out all his longings and his weaknesses. But he didn't, as he felt that she too was emotionally frail and needed his comfort and support. And so they derived comfort and strength from each other.

They had just made love and were lying quietly side-by-side, happy and fulfilled. Gerry propped himself up on his elbow and leant over to study Kate's lovely face. He stroked her smooth, flat stomach, marvelling how a girl who led such a harsh life could possess such a silky skin. Where did these gipsy people wash? How did she keep herself so sweet smelling, so utterly desirable?

'Are you married?'

Kate laughed derisively. 'Me married? No. Most gipsies don't bother with marriage. What's the point? We live mainly outside the law. We have no permanent home. We don't like being tied down so why be trapped in a marriage?'

'Have you known other men? I'm surely not the first.'

'No, you're not the first.'

'Were there many?'

'No. Just a couple.'

'You never thought about having kids?'

'Kids? Here? Not much chance for them growing up in a place like this, is there?'

'There are kids here.'

'Yes. Poor little buggers.'

'What happened to your man?'

'The last one?'

'Yes.'

'He went off. I was pleased to see the back of him - vicious brute.'

'Was he from the camp?'

'No. He just arrived.'

'Like me?'

'Yes. But he wasn't like you at all.'

'How was he different?'

'You're kind and gentle. He was a cruel bully.'

'Do you think he'll come back?'

'I hope to God not.'

Gerry lay back, thoughtful.

'Kate, you're beautiful, gentle and lovely. A woman like you should have kids.'

'I told you. This is no place for kids.'

'But you don't have to stay here.'

Kate's eyes opened wide. 'Where else would I go?'

'You could come away with me.'

'Where to?'

'We'd work it out. If you agree to come with me then I'd get a good job.'

'A good job?'

'Yes.

'Like...?'

'A waiter in a restaurant.'

'A waiter in a restaurant!' Kate laughed. 'That would be wonderful!'

'It would, wouldn't it?' Gerry was amazed at his own inventiveness.

Kate sat up, excited. 'How would you find a job as a waiter in a restaurant?'

'I'd go to the Job Centre.'

'You'd have to have a proper address. Below Westway wouldn't be good enough.'

'I'd get an address. If you'll come with me we'll go to the Local Housing Authority together and they'll give us a nice flat. You'll see. They have to house the homeless. It's the law.'

'Gerry, there's a waiting list for flats and houses. That's why we're all here.'

'I thought you all wanted to be here,' said Gerry dryly.

'Well, some of us do. Maybe some more than others. But I know there's a waiting list. I read it in the paper.'

'In the paper?' Gerry sounded surprised. 'I've never seen you read the paper.'

'That doesn't mean I don't. You've only known me a month.'

'True.'

Gerry yawned. He pulled her down beside him and started gently to stroke her breasts.

'Let's talk about it in the morning. There's a time and place for everything.'

They woke early at six-thirty. As always, when he saw her lying there beside him, vulnerable, beautiful and utterly desirable, Gerry felt himself swell in joyous anticipation. She stirred; half opened her eyes, smiled gently and came towards him.

They were sitting at the table drinking tea. They had put away the beds, tidied up the caravan and turned it into a day room. It was a routine, which Gerry was now familiar with, but rather regretted. He didn't like to see the beds stowed away. He preferred them always to be ready and available. But despite her Spartan living conditions, Kate had a tidy nature. She liked the caravan to be a bedroom at night, a living room by day. Though twice she had paid the penalty for her tidiness when Gerry had made love to her on the floor.

Slowly the other gipsies were waking up and getting down to the activities of a new day. Kate's caravan was at the side of the site, almost tucked into a corner by itself, a fact for which Gerry was very grateful. The other residents rarely bothered them, communicating with Kate outside and seldom, if ever, acknowledging Gerry's presence at all. There was a gentle hum of early morning camp sounds in the distance: the chink of pots, a caravan door slamming, the scolding of a child, the child crying in protest. Gerry and Kate sat on in their haven, in their tiny home apart from all the hurly-burly of the main camp, sipping tea and chatting, utterly content with each other, discussing their future plans.

Kate heard it first but took no notice: the breaking of a twig just outside the window. Then another twig snapped and she looked up at the window, letting out a shrill scream of terror. She got up abruptly from the table knocking over her mug of tea. She had gone deathly white and was trembling violently, her eyes wide and staring, the pupils dilated with terror. She got under the table, cowering in fear, alternately moaning in anguish and muttering incoherently.

Gerry stood up, distressed and uncomprehending.

'Kate, my love! What is it? What's the matter? What on earth's wrong?'

Kate began sobbing uncontrollably. 'It's him! He's come back!'

'Who's come back?'

'That man! He'll kill me!'

'Which man - and why on earth should he want to kill you?'

'The man. That vicious man. The one I told you about. He wants me all to himself. He treated me like his slave. He'll kill me if he finds you here.'

'Why should he? He's not your husband, is he?' Gerry experienced a momentary pang of fear.

Kate sobbed louder. 'No, no. He's not my husband. But I was his woman - his gipsy woman. I was his property. He beat me and abused me... No one did anything to help me. Everyone was afraid of him.'

There was a violent knocking at the door.

'Oh, no! No! He'll break in! Help me, Gerry! Save me! Please!'

The knocking grew louder. A harsh voice said: 'Kate, I've come back! I want you. I'm going to fuck you raw and I'm going to bugger you till...'

Kate crawled out from underneath the table sobbing and shaking uncontrollably. She flung herself into Gerry's arms and clung to him in utter desperation.

'Gerry! Help! Please save me!'

The knocking on the door increased. The whole caravan shook. Then there was a ripping, tearing sound as the flimsy door was torn open and a wild-looking man bounded in, brandishing a knife. He had long dark unkempt hair and mad staring eyes. He wore filthy jeans and a torn leather jacket. He took two short steps into the tiny caravan and looked around, evil, menacing. He gave a yelp of fury when he saw Kate in Gerry's embrace. He grabbed her arm and tried to pull her away. She screamed and sobbed hysterically.

'Go away, you brute! I hate you! You evil monster! You pig!'

He held the knife against her throat. She trembled at the chill of the cold steel. He twisted the blade a little so she could feel the sharp edge. She stood motionless, transfixed with terror.

'You're mine. I'm taking you with me. I'm going to fuck you senseless. I'm going to start right now and give your precious boyfriend a lesson in how to fuck a woman unconscious.'

He ripped off her shirt, and cut off her bra with the knife, leaving her naked to the waist. He inserted the knife blade into the top of her jeans and slashed them. He moved the knife down her spine, drawing blood. With the point of the knife in her back he undid his bulging flies with his free hand.

Kate stood trembling, pleading piteously. 'No, no! Bert don't! Let me go! Gerry! Help me, please!'

The madman pulled off his trousers and tore off his underpants, standing before them, his organ huge, swollen and ugly. He ran the knife over Kate's shoulder blade. Blood, ruby red, trickled down her bare leg. For a few seconds Gerry stood transfixed with horror; then he sprang into action. He twisted the man in a half Nelson and managed to wrest the knife from his grasp. The man lunged out at Kate, but she evaded his grasp and rushed out of the caravan door, screaming for help, bleeding, naked except for her underpants.

The two men faced each other, eyes burning with hatred.

'Get out or I'll kill you.' Gerry almost spat.

'You've stole my woman,' snarled the other.

'No, I didn't. You left her. She wasn't yours by right in the first place.'

'She's not yours neither.'

There was a few seconds of deathly silence. Neither man moved. Then suddenly Bert jumped onto one of the bench seats and sprang on Gerry from behind. He got him on the floor and held him in a vice-like grip, trying to wrest the knife from his grasp. He got his fingers on Gerry's windpipe and pressed hard. Gerry, feeling his breath coming in short gasps, thought a blood vessel was about to burst. Summoning up all his strength, he brought his knee up with a violent jerk into Bert's groin. Bert screamed with pain and released his hold on Gerry's windpipe. Struggling to sit up, Gerry gave Bert an expert left hook across the mouth, smashing two of his front teeth. Bert, now beside himself with pain and fury, lashed out at Gerry, punching him wherever he could reach. Gerry, now in a half-sitting position and still clutching Bert's knife, in utter desperation and with super-human strength, managed to plunge the knife into Bert's stomach, twisting and slicing through the flesh and the thick wall of muscle. Bert groaned, his arms still flailing, fists clenched. He was beginning to pummel with less purpose and soon he was just clawing the air. Gerry felt the blows grow weaker and weaker until they stopped altogether. Bert gave one last, convulsive shudder. Then he went completely limp.

Gerry stood up and looked down at his adversary. Dark blood was oozing from the wound in his stomach. His mouth was also bleeding badly. He lay completely still and didn't appear to be breathing. Gerry didn't wait to discover whether or not the brute was dead. He was only out on licence. With a deep pang of regret at leaving the home he had shared so happily with Kate, Gerry left as quickly and quietly as possible and walked briskly in the direction of the M 40.

Chapter Five

Jo sat quite still in her car, her heart thumping, as the battered two-tone Mini drew up beside her, towing the streaky dented grey caravan. The Mini stopped suddenly, making the caravan lurch violently, its grubby curtains of non-matching fabric swinging from side to side, as if unaccustomed to finding themselves stationary. A young man got out of the car and left the driver's door open. He walked towards her, tall and athletic, his shoulder-length wavy brown hair glinting with golden threads in the sunlight. His wide-set hazel eyes were smiling. A smile played too on his thin sensitive lips. He was casually but neatly dressed in new blue denim jeans and wore a short-sleeved blue and white check cotton shirt that Jo had seen in Marks and Spencer. He didn't seem threatening but even so, Jo's stomach tightened as he walked across and spoke to her.

'Hello! I hope you didn't mind me following you in here. I knew you were English when we met in the canteen this morning.'

Jo remembered his voice as soon as he spoke. It was attractive with a slight Irish accent.

'You guessed I was English before I even said anything?'

He laughed. 'Of course. You couldn't be anything else.'

Jo's heart was still thumping uncomfortably loudly. The *Aire* was quite deserted. The young man seemed to sense her unease and backed away slightly.

'I noticed you got into a French car on the boat. Made me think perhaps you might know the country a bit and give me a few tips.'

'Oh, I see. What sort of tips are you looking for?'

'Just know-how about the country. Where to go and the like.'

'It depends on what you want to do.'

Jo was intrigued despite feeling the need for caution. She had never before met a young man, travelling on his own with a caravan, who seemed to have so little sense of purpose.

'Are you on holiday?'

'Yes.' He smiled broadly. 'Yes. I suppose I am on holiday.'

'Then I expect you're looking for a campsite.'

'I need somewhere to park the caravan at any rate.'

Jo looked up at the young man and smiled. There was something appealing about him that attracted her. He was clean, softly spoken and certainly not threatening. He seemed simple and straightforward, even trustworthy. He might turn out to be... She took a huge risk.

'I have a lot of land at my place. Plenty to spare for a caravan just for the night. I also have a house full of paying guests,' she added for good measure, just so he wouldn't think she was being too forward.

His eyes widened in disbelief. 'I hadn't meant... I didn't really think...'

Jo laughed... 'That I was going to invite you to park your caravan on my land for the night?'

'No. My name's Gerry. Gerry Nolan.' He extended his hand and took Jo's cautiously proffered fingers in a cool, firm grip.

'I'm Jo. Jo Perry.'

'Nice to meet you, Jo.'

'You too.'

Jo opened the door of her Peugeot. 'We come off the motorway in Beaune. I'll wait for you just after the *péage*.'

He looked blank. 'The...'

'*Péage*. The toll where you pay.'

Jo had been away from Laronne for just over two weeks. The guests had already booked their holidays, some since January, and of course all the bookings had to be honoured, despite Alan's sudden death. The neighbours, shocked by Alan's accident, had clamoured to help and Jo had more offers of cleaning and shopping services than she could possibly take advantage of. But her biggest problem was the fact that none of the residents in Laronne spoke any English. Alan had been the translator between the paying guests and the local residents. Now there was no one to translate – except her.

Followed by Gerry with his caravan in tow, Jo drove up the long driveway in considerable trepidation. A reception committee was waiting in the courtyard to welcome her, which seemed to include at least half the residents of Laronne. Her four guests of the week were present as well and as Jo stepped out of her car, Maxwell, barking and wriggling ecstatically, rushed out of the house to greet her. Totally overwhelmed, Jo burst into tears.

In the end Gerry didn't move out. They didn't discuss it. It just happened. Nobody knew where he had come from. Nobody asked. It was none of their business anyway. Everyone in Laronne was still shocked by Alan's tragic accident and their deepest sympathy went out to Jo. By now most people knew she had only come to live in France because Alan had wanted to. They knew life would be a big struggle for her living abroad on her own, not least because she barely spoke the language. They also knew she wanted above all to return to live in England, but there was no possibility of that happening unless she could sell the remote rambling farmhouse in Laronne. Attractive though the house was, and in a beautiful situation, everyone knew that properties in rural France were easy to purchase for very little money and almost impossible to sell. There were just too many of them.

In the first few weeks after her return Jo found herself attending to a myriad of practical problems. There were bills to pay, which took simply ages because she had never before written a cheque in French. When the first two were returned marked '*pas valable*,' she was forced to seek help from the local post office.

There were problems with the roof, the porch, the shower, one of the loos and over-loading on the electricity supply. Gerry tried his best. He went on the roof; he tried to repair the porch; he unblocked the loo and stopped the leak in the shower. But he had to confess that understanding electricity was beyond him. At first his repairs seemed successful, but slowly the old problems started to reappear and finally Jo was forced to call in the experts. Even in the short time she had been away some things had inevitably gone astray. Crockery and cutlery, which had been put away in the wrong place had to be unearthed and restored to its rightful shelf or cupboard. Furniture, which had been moved around, had to be replaced into the correct apartment. The courtyard was a mess, full of leaves, weeds and small pockets of rubbish. The area round the swimming pool was also in need of serious cleaning and tidying. The days were filled with an endless grind of exhausting work. Sometimes Gerry was helpful. Sometimes he wasn't. Occasionally he would slope off on one of his long walks, but mostly he would spend the afternoons sleeping off the effect of an alcoholic lunch. At times he was a trial but on the whole Jo was grateful for his company.

Her biggest problem was communicating with the neighbours, as none of them spoke any English, and her French was still almost non-existent. Her greatest nightmare was the telephone. She dreaded its ring and sometimes even pretended not to hear it. She would put off making essential calls, sometimes for days. It was months before she understood the phrase: *'Ne quittez pas!* Meaning: 'don't go away or: 'just hold on a minute.' She thought it meant: *'n'écoutez pas;'* which she wrongly interpreted as: 'I can't hear.' So she would shout down the receiver as loudly as possible, much to the frustration of the caller at the other end, who probably wondered why foreigners living in France couldn't make the effort to learn the language.

When Jo had invited Gerry to park his caravan for the night, it was in the knowledge that she would be safely ensconced in the house while he had his own private part of the courtyard. They shopped separately, ate separately and slept separately, an arrangement that continued satisfactorily for several weeks. Jo was busy with her guests; Gerry was busy enjoying his freedom, which at the moment was principally concerned with the rediscovery of alcohol.

At first he stuck to beer, but he found that French beer was not to his liking and the German, Dutch and English beers were more expensive. So he decided to try the wine. The first wine he bought was a litre of red in a plastic bottle with a thin metal top. He thought the wine tasted a bit sour, but after he had finished it he felt pleasantly squiffy, so the next day he purchased a corkscrew and another litre of red, this time in a glass bottle with a cork. The degree of intoxication was about the same but the taste was a great improvement on the previous bottle, so he started experimenting with different wines. He spent hours prowling round the shelves of the local shops, studying the labels on the wine bottles and trying out many of the bargains.

After Gerry had been living in his caravan in Jo's courtyard for about three weeks, he felt it was time to show some appreciation for her hospitality. So one evening he invited her to share one of his newly selected wines. He had bought three bottles and they finished all of them with the inevitable result: that night they became lovers. From then on neither of them saw any reason why Gerry should move on elsewhere.

Jo laid the table for lunch in the shade of the caravan feeling enormously relieved. Sunday was definitely her favourite day of the week. Saturday was change-over day. It wasn't just the prospect of last week's guests leaving late and the new ones arriving early. There was also the daunting and exhausting clearing up operation, which each change-over entailed. Sometimes this could reach nightmare proportions. Then, last but not least, there was the expectation of the new guests; who could be even worse than the ones who had just left.

Jo brought out the wine cooler and the corkscrew and placed them on the table. She tried to continue the practice she and Alan had started of only drinking wine at lunchtime on Sundays. They had discovered quite early on that with the abundance of cheap and eminently drinkable wine it was possible to get drunk at lunchtime and remain in that state throughout the rest of the day. An afternoon siesta was, of course, essential and they found that when they woke up an hour or two later feeling thirsty, they would assuage their thirst with yet another glass of dry white *Bourgogne Aligoté*. Although this seemed a fairly reasonable luxury while they were on holiday, they both decided, once they came to live in France, that their alcoholic consumption should be a little bit more restrained. So Jo tried to impose the same restraints on herself and Gerry but it proved to be an insuperable task.

Gerry liked alcohol.

By this time he was well into French wines. He continued bargain hunting in the local shops and was quickly learning the names of the cheaper range of the market. Already Jo felt Gerry had acquired more knowledge of wine after a month of living in France than she had in four years. He enjoyed sampling and comparing different wines, but he was more interested in quantity than quality. Most evenings he was drunk, but he was never unpleasant, never violent, never morose or sentimental.

He just liked to talk - about himself.

Chapter Six

Maxwell bounded across the courtyard, barking frantically. He jumped up and tried to lick Jo's face. Black, gangling and gauche, he was a mixture of many breeds: Labrador, sheepdog, terrier and probably Doberman and bulldog as well. Jo and Alan had brought him from England. They felt their new country lifestyle needed a dog, so they had rescued Maxwell from the Battersea Dogs' Home. He was then already over a year old, a nuisance and impossible to train. Alan had adored him. In fact the affection was mutual and Maxwell had followed Alan everywhere. Jo's feelings towards the dog were more ambivalent. Often she thought she only kept him in memory of Alan. Maxwell jumped up again, barking even louder. He knocked the bread out of her hand and it fell onto the gravel where he started to tear at it. Jo thumped him hard.

'Get off! You stupid dog! That's not for you!'

She picked up the remains of the loaf and looked at it in despair.

'Damn! That's lunch gone for a Burton. We'll be lucky if we get breakfast out of it with Gerry's voracious appetite.'

She tore off the end of the bread where the dog had bitten it and threw it at him.

'Here! Take that, you stupid animal! I've a good mind to have you put down. You'd better behave yourself.'

She walked round the corner behind the enormous barn to where Gerry still had his caravan. She was living there too at the moment. Of course it was only a temporary measure; perhaps just for a month or so until she could get her finances sorted out. It had been Gerry's idea; inspired by a double booking which had occurred ten days ago.

'You've got the extra guests and you need the money,' he said succinctly. 'Move into my 'van and let the whole of your house to the punters.'

At first Jo was appalled.

'What! Move out of my lovely home and let it to strangers! Let people I've never met before sleep in *my* bed, use *my* bathroom and hang their scruffy clothes in my beautiful cupboard! They'll read *my* books and play *my* CDs!'

It was a ghastly thought. At first she was adamant. Not even the prospect of the much-needed extra cash would make her change her mind. But her London agent kept phoning. He had another couple whose holiday booking had just fallen through; in addition to the couple he had double booked by mistake. Could she spare two more apartments? After all, it was a substantial property. There were all those outhouses. Could she fit a couple into one of them?   Jo laughed down the telephone: 'Donald, you've forgotten the state of the outbuildings. They're derelict sheds with no flooring, no plumbing and leaky roofs. I wouldn't put my dog in there.'

'But I thought everything had been renovated?'

'Not everything. Just the Burgundian Tower and one small room.'

'I thought you were going to...'

'We were. Alan was just starting on one of the sheds. Then he was killed, remember?'

'Jo, I'm terribly sorry. Of course I remember. But what about your part of the house? Could you rent one floor? Only temporarily, of course.'

So Jo moved downstairs for a couple of weeks and ten days later Donald and Gerry between them persuaded her to move out of her home altogether and share Gerry's caravan.

There was no life stirring in the caravan. The curtains were still drawn and all was as still and quiet as when she had left. Gerry must still be asleep, she thought. Lazy sod. I'll soon get him up and on the move. It's Saturday, changeover day, and we've got an extra couple arriving. She opened the caravan door as noisily as possible.

The extra couple posed a new problem. Although the advertisements in *The Sunday Times* always specified 'No Children,' the Brocklebanks turned up with their four-year-old son. Jo was angry. She felt cheated, but there wasn't a great deal she could do about it once they had arrived.

'We don't really have facilities for young children, Mrs Brocklebank...'

'But Gareth's ever so well behaved. He comes everywhere with us.'

Mrs Brocklebank, large and flabby with fading red hair and blotchy skin, wasn't in the least bit apologetic.

Jo sighed. 'It's rather more a question of where he's going to sleep.'

'A mattress on the floor will be fine.'

First find the mattress, thought Jo.

'I see you have a nice little caravan out there,' ventured Mrs Brocklebank brightly. 'Gareth could sleep in that. Nothing could happen to him. We'd be close by.'

'The caravan's booked,' said Jo shortly.

Mrs Brocklebank's eyes widened. 'Oh! So you let the caravan as well?'

'No. We let the house and we sleep in the caravan.'

'You let the whole house and sleep in the caravan!'

'Yes.'

'All year round?'

'No. Only at the height of the summer.'

'You must prefer the winter.'

'We do.' Jo felt close to tears.

And so it was settled. The Brocklebanks took the ground floor apartment and a spare sunbed was produced for Gareth. Jo felt utterly miserable. Widowhood had devastated her life. Now it appeared she was homeless as well.

Gareth was a tearaway. He was loud, hyperactive and totally destructive. On first sight he appeared to be quite normal. In fact, he could almost have been described as an attractive little boy. He had an engaging smile; which, by the end of the week, Jo was describing as wicked; wide blue eyes and curly tawny-coloured hair. He ate incessantly and his baby chubbiness was already turning into something more permanent than puppy fat. He ate biscuits, sweets, chocolates, crisps and chewing gum: anything that was fattening and induced dental decay. He loved things wrapped in paper. He would separate the paper in his mouth from whatever delicacy it had been covering. It was a skill he had perfected, was extremely proud of and ready to demonstrate at any given moment. Having secreted whatever goodie the paper had been covering in the corner of his mouth; he would chew the paper until it was quite sodden. Then he would spit it out at a carefully pre-selected target. He had a preference for aiming at clothing and soft furnishings, for he had quickly learnt that these surfaces were harder to clean than wooden furniture or stone floors. By the third day Jo was almost in despair. There were little bits of hard, dried-up paper everywhere, nestling behind cushions, down the sides of the sofa and the armchairs, sticking on the curtains, wedged under tables and behind chair legs. Spitting out paper wasn't Gareth's only vice. He was a powerhouse of energy. Jo felt sure his energy was due to the endless consumption of the starchy, sugary food that kept him going in top gear all day long. From early morning until nearly midnight, he tore up and down the stairs, into the first floor apartment without any invitation, round the courtyard, in and out of *La Petite Pièce* and the Burgundian Tower. His parents had no control over him whatsoever. The only small restriction was when the child occasionally ran up the steps to the swimming pool. Here the restraining arm of his father awaited him.

Mr Brocklebank spent the entire day beside the swimming pool. Small, dark and wiry, he was quite the opposite in appearance to his wife. Seen together they rather resembled a Laurel and Hardy double act. By the end of his first day by the pool, despite his rather sallow skin, Mr Brocklebank had turned a livid painful-looking shade of deep pink. Another day saw him turn into a grubby light-orangey brown. By the end of the week he was quite unrecognisable and looked as if he might have returned from a year in Saudi Arabia.

Mrs Brocklebank, who would probably have peeled almost to the bone were she foolish enough to venture out into the Burgundian June sunshine, spent the whole of each day indoors. She took no notice whatsoever of Gareth as he tore around the house, rushing in and out of the courtyard in the heat of the blistering midday sun. Myra Brocklebank was on holiday and she would brook no interference with her annual week of rest from either her husband or her son. Evan could fry himself to a frazzle; Gareth could create mayhem. It was not for her to interfere with either of their pleasures. Myra Brocklebank had found her own amusement, which consisted of finding out as much as possible about Jo's living habits. She opened every cupboard and every drawer. She took every single object off its shelf. All the crockery and kitchen utensils were removed from their rightful places and returned to a different one. She took all Jo's books off the shelves. She started reading some of them, turning down the top corner of the page in order to mark her place, as her concentration flagged and she turned her attention to something else. She got out the CD and cassette player. She would put on a cassette, discover it was not to her taste and return it, without rewinding it, to the wrong case. In one of the cupboards she found a collection of vinyl gramophone records, which had belonged to Alan. Having forgotten, or perhaps never having known, how to operate a turntable, she inadvertently scratched many of the records, which she then either returned to the wrong sleeves or left lying around in the apartment.

To Jo the week seemed never ending. Time stretched into eternity as the Brocklebank's intrusion took over their lives. She couldn't wait for their departure at the end of the week. The final day dawned at last. Jo and Gerry stood in the courtyard to wave them 'good-bye,' hoping they would leave fairly promptly. They had a heavy day of clearing up in front of them and Jo felt it was hardly worth starting on the operation until the Brocklebanks had left. Even to begin hoovering *La Petite Pièce* or The Burgundian Tower would probably be a waste of effort, what with four year old Gareth rushing in and out like a whirling dervish, more hyperactive than ever with the prospect of a long journey ahead, pinioned in the car for over six hours. He had woken the entire household at five o'clock in the morning, rushing in and out of bedrooms unannounced, much to the embarrassment of Sandra and Tony, the young couple who Jo had been obliged to put up in *La Petite Pièce* that had originally been earmarked for the Brocklebanks. Since when his parents had lost total control over him.

Normally guests left before nine am. Most were from England and liked to make the journey home in a day. This was quite feasible for people who lived in London and the South East. Those who lived further afield generally spent a night on the way in a hotel or with relatives. The Brocklebanks hailed from Yorkshire and seemed to have made no advance plans for their return journey. Perhaps they were waiting to see how Gareth withstood the constraints of a whole day in the car. Perhaps they were planning so many stops there would be no possibility of their ever getting as far as the coast in one day. Jo didn't enquired about their plans. As the clock edged towards eleven o'clock, all she wished was they would leave as soon as possible.

Jo looked at her watch again. Ten minutes past eleven. Would the Brocklebanks never leave? She looked across at Gerry in desperation, trying to catch his eye. He was helping Mr Brocklebank to load the roof rack; a daunting if not impossible task, as the Brocklebanks had more luggage than could be safely placed onto any roof rack or stowed in the boot of any average size family car.

'Just pull a bit harder, Gerry.'

'Yes, sir.' The 'sir' was automatic. Gerry pulled as hard as he could on the strong rubber crocodile strap, which snapped under the strain. He fell back onto the gravel with a hard thud, luckily unhurt. A wooden box marked 'toys' slipped off the roof rack, narrowly missing Mr Brocklebank's head but grazing his mahogany coloured shin and drawing blood before bursting open in the courtyard, scattering toys everywhere. Mr Brocklebank gave a howl of pain and leapt around the courtyard on one leg.

'Oh, bloody hell and damnation! What did you want to bring his bleedin' toy box for, Myra? Look what it's done to me leg! It's ruined me beautiful tan! An' all that time and money wasted on getting it too!'

Myra Brocklebank rushed towards her husband and dabbed his wounded leg ineffectually with her lace handkerchief.

'Now don't you fret. It's just a bit o' skin you lost. Skin grows back on again. It'll be back on before you can notice it were gone.'

'Not tanned skin, it won't be,' said Evan, still hopping about, his face contorted with pain. 'White skin it'll be. A bright piece of white skin right down the middle of me tanned leg like a stripe on a zebra crossing. It'll be a year now before that bit of me leg's brown again.'

'A day in the Halifax sunshine and the white stripe will have gone. It's not as if you was truly white to start with. You was born more of a khaki colour.'

Evan Brocklebank glared at his wife and continued to sit on the gravel, gazing at his leg. Jo, Gerry and Myra Brocklebank gathered up all the toys, some of which had rolled under the car, others scattered about the courtyard. With a happy bark, Maxwell bounded out to join in the fun, diving at any rolling object, mashing the more malleable things in his strong teeth, picking up anything that resembled a stick in the hope that someone would throw it for him, and generally being a nuisance. Finally all the toys were retrieved and stowed into the box, which had been only slightly damaged in the fall. Having found some more rubber straps in the barn, Gerry had repacked both the car and the roof rack. Jo had unearthed a tube of Germolene from the back of the medicine cupboard, which she dabbed on Mr Brocklebank's injury, bandaging the leg tightly to stop the bleeding.

It was now twenty minutes to twelve. Mr and Mrs Brocklebank were seated in the car all ready to go, Mr Brocklebank having assured everyone that his injury was not sufficiently serious to prevent him from driving. But there was no sign whatsoever of Gareth.

Mrs Brocklebank heaved her fleshy body out of the car with difficulty and walked around the courtyard anxiously calling: 'Gareth! Gareth! Come along now, love. We're all ready to go home.'

But the child was nowhere to be seen.

Mr Brocklebank got out of the car and started calling to his son: 'Come along now, Gareth! There's a good lad! We're all ready to go!'

But still no Gareth appeared.

Jo was beginning to feel quite desperate. She wanted them to leave, but certainly not without Gareth.

'We'll divide up,' she suggested, 'and each of us search a section of the house and the outbuildings. If I look upstairs, perhaps Mrs Brocklebank...'

Maxwell's frantic barking, coming from the direction of the swimming pool, drowned the end of Jo's sentence.

'That's a mad dog you got there,' said Mr Brocklebank. 'Not safe in my opinion. Shouldn't have a dog like that around with young children in the house. I wouldn't give a dog like that house room.'

Jo was incensed. 'Maxwell is perfectly safe, Mr Brocklebank. He's just noisy and high-spirited, rather like Gareth. And I'd like to point out, if I may, that we don't normally accept young children. It states quite clearly in our publicity that there are no facilities for them.'

Maxwell's barking rose to a frenzy and he tore into to the courtyard from the direction of the swimming pool, throwing himself at Jo, rubbing his head against her leg, nuzzling her hand, barking frantically.

'I think that dog's trying to tell us something,' said Gerry, becoming increasingly uneasy with the whole situation.

Maxwell bounded off again in the direction of the swimming pool, his barking now quite hysterical. Jo and Gerry ran after him, closely followed by Evan Brocklebank. Mrs Brocklebank, labouring heavily and sweating profusely, brought up the rear.

Jo was alarmed now, and rushing up the few steps to the pool, she saw a small bundle floating on the top. Without a thought, she kicked off her sandals and dived in, reaching the child at the same moment as

Gerry. Between them they brought him out to the side of the pool, where Gerry gave him mouth-to-mouth resuscitation.

It had been a very close thing. They all agreed that if it hadn't been for Maxwell, Gareth would almost certainly have drowned. Mr and Mrs Brocklebank were both incoherent with distress. Jo phoned for an ambulance, which arrived with exemplary promptness and rushed all the Brocklebanks to the nearest hospital. Gareth was admitted overnight; his parents being forced to spend the night in a hotel as Jo's new consignment of guests was due that evening.

The following morning a chastened and deeply grateful Brocklebank family called round laden with gifts to bid Jo and Gerry a final farewell. They were full of praise and gratitude too for Maxwell's extraordinary perception and persistence. Even Gareth, who had not taken the least bit of notice of Maxwell during his entire week's holiday, despite Maxwell's efforts to persuade him to play, gave the dog a desultory pat.

Jo was touched by their generosity and their genuine gratitude. It made her feel a little less resentful about the mammoth clearing up operation after their hasty departure the day before. She and Gerry had only just got the four apartments cleaned and tidied before the arrival of the new guests. However, she wasn't sorry to say a final farewell to the Brocklebanks, and she was extremely relieved they didn't suggest a return visit the following year.

The clearing up was a monumental operation, which Jo thought she would remember until her dying day. Not only was everything in the wrong place, but there were several burnt saucepans, missing items, a pile of broken crockery in the corner on the floor, and stains on the carpet. The washing up was left unfinished and three of the sheets were torn. The place stank of burnt food and urine.

Gareth, in addition to all his other shortcomings, had also turned out to be a bed-wetter.

Chapter Seven

Kate spent nearly two hours crouching in the bushes at the far end of the encampment. Eventually she crept out clad only in her underpants, shivering with cold, and pulled a blanket and a towel off a nearby clothesline. Still afraid to return to her caravan, she wrapped herself in the blanket, made a pillow out of the towel and, curling up under the bush again, she tried to get a little sleep. She was terrified that Bert would find her. He would certainly rape her and probably kill her afterwards. She wondered what had happened to Gerry. Was he still on the encampment? Was he looking for her? Or had Bert injured him, perhaps badly?

The day passed very slowly. Kate grew hungry and was tempted to return to the caravan and grab a few biscuits, but something stopped her. That 'something' was undoubtedly fear. In the end she decided she couldn't go back to the caravan until after dark, which would be after 9.00 pm, as it was still only May. Gipsies go to bed early. With little to keep them up after the evening meal has been cleared away, they all retired to their caravans by nine o'clock. Some watched television; others just molested their wives.

Kate waited until after nine-thirty, when, under cover of darkness, she crept cautiously back towards her caravan. No light or sound came from within. The door was closed and so were the curtains. She turned the door handle and groped for the matches. By the light of the flickering match she lit one of the gas lamps. The flame sprang into life, lighting up the tiny room with an eerie, subdued bluish light. Kate threw a quick glance around her little home. It was a shambles. A heap of books lay on the floor, half covered with bedding. Pots and pans had been ripped off their hooks and flung onto the floor. There was broken glass and crockery everywhere.

In the middle of the narrow space between the two bench seats lay a body. Peering closer in the dim light, Kate saw it was the body of a man. He lay on his back with one arm twisted above his head, as if in self-defence. His eyes were open, staring out of deep sockets, like two dark pools. His mouth was also open, lips curled back, as if in a mocking laugh. Two of his front teeth were missing. A thin trickle of dried blood had seeped out of the corner of his mouth and down his neck. His shirt had been ripped open and all the buttons torn off. There was a huge gash in his stomach, with dried blood and entrails oozing out over the floor, covering the carpet in a dark, sticky-looking stain. Beside him lay a vicious-looking knife, covered in blood.

It was Bert's body.

Vomit rising in her throat, fighting terror and panic, Kate swiftly packed whatever essentials she could salvage from the mayhem. The caravan reeked of death. She couldn't bear to remain in it a moment longer than necessary. She had no idea where she would go, but she realised she must leave as quickly as possible. All the other gipsies knew how much she had hated Bert. No one would believe she hadn't killed him herself. In ten minutes flat she had gathered what belongings she could and began walking quickly towards Shepherds Bush. She spent the first night in the shrubbery in Holland Park. The following day she continued walking, spending the second night in a ditch on the Sidcup Bypass. Although she had lived most of her childhood in a tent, she had never had to sleep rough. She and her parents had lived in a tent until her father had run off with a younger woman. Her parents had fought constantly, her father often in a drunken rage. Kate was used to violence, fear and ugliness. They were part of the travellers' life, as were poverty, dirt and often hunger as well. After her father had left there was no more violence. She and her mother had moved in with one of the elder statesmen of the gipsy encampment. He was old and ugly and smelt worse than anyone Kate had ever known, but he was kind and he had loved her mother. Best of all, he had owned a caravan.

For Kate and her mother, living in a caravan was an indescribable luxury. Gone were the occasions when high winds blew the tent down; when torrential rain had washed half their possessions away. In the caravan they were dry and warm, cocooned against the elements. And best of all they had a cooker and light supplied by a gas cylinder, which they kept just outside. At first Kate thought the gas cylinder was a miracle.

Kate's mother and the old man had over two years of happiness together. The old man died first. There were some who said he was already in his eighties. Kate couldn't tell. It was impossible to guess the age of most of the travellers; some survived the hard life better than others. He left everything to her mother, including the caravan. But relative comfort had come too late for Kate's mother. She was already suffering from severe tuberculosis and a year later she too, was dead at the age of only thirty-six. So, aged seventeen, Kate had a caravan of her own but no one to turn to or take care of her. The other gipsies mistrusted her. They had all disapproved of her mother's liaison with the old man and would have nothing to do with her. And when Kate's mother died they would have nothing to do with Kate either.

Kate woke feeling stiff and sore. It had rained in the night and the end of her sleeping bag had become extremely wet. She was reminded of the many occasions in her childhood when her father was still around and the tent had leaked or blown down. These catastrophes had always brought out the best in her father. If he was drunk at the time he would sober up very quickly; but if by some miracle, he did happen to be sober, he would be sure to remedy the situation as soon as the tent was put to rights. Now her father had left without trace, her mother was dead and she didn't even have a leaky tent in which to lay her head.

Kate began to regret having left the caravan so hurriedly. It was hers. It was all she had. She had known nothing but the travellers' life; met no other people than travellers. Wanderlust was the one thing that united them. Surely the gipsies wouldn't believe she had killed Bert? Surely they would understand that she did not possess a violent nature, nor would she have had sufficient strength to kill him.

But who had killed Bert? Had it been one of the gipsies themselves? Or had Gerry gone too far in trying to protect her? Because that's what could have happened. In that case it wouldn't have been murder. Of course not. If Gerry had killed Bert, it would have been in self-defence. Anyone could see Gerry wasn't a murderer. He wouldn't hurt a fly. He was kind, considerate, caring, a gentle lover. A sob rose in her throat. Where was Gerry? Why had he left so suddenly? Was it because he had killed Bert? She wanted Gerry. She wanted somebody - anybody. She had been walking for over an hour and she was already tired. She was desperately hungry but afraid to spend any more money. She had so little left. She had no plans, no idea where she was or where she was going.

Kate was walking along a busy road with dull two-storey houses all the same, built in pairs, with small front gardens filled with rubbish. On the far side of the dual carriage-way were identical houses with identical rubbish in the front gardens. She shuddered. How depressing to spend your life shut up in a box, exactly the same as everyone else's box, with exactly the same rubbish outside and the traffic thundering past. She had been brought up to think that mobility was the success to happiness. If travellers didn't like the people or the surroundings, they just moved on elsewhere.

Kate walked on for another hour or so. She had a lump at the side of her right big toe and a blister on her left heel. Her shoes were not made for excessive walking and she started to limp. The houses petered out to be replaced by fields, dotted about with desultory cows and sheep, lazily grazing. There were a few horses too, even a donkey. It's the country, thought Kate. How lovely! They had lived on an encampment in the country when she was little. She and her mother had loved it: the fresh air, the lush grass, the peace and the solitude. Life had seemed easier in the country; there were more resources readily available. It was easy to steal a chicken, a goose or a duck from a farm and vegetables were to be had for the picking. It was the children's task to siphon off milk from the large milk churns. Kate remembered eagerly watching it frothing out of the tap at the bottom, foaming into their chipped milk jugs. The children were also in charge of stealing eggs. Kate remembered creeping into the dim dingy hen houses, giggling nervously, stomachs contracting a little for fear they would be caught. They each carried a small bowl, with strict instructions never to take more eggs than would be reasonably missed. Miraculously, they were never caught. The farmer either didn't notice or he didn't care. They lived well off the land and from the hard work of other people. When they grew tired of one location, they simply moved on to the next.

Lost in her reverie of pleasant childhood memories, Kate didn't notice that a lorry had pulled up just in front of her. It was white, with wide blue stripes across the sides and FRIGCOLD written in the same shade of blue across the back. The driver jumped down from the cab and walked slowly towards her. He was in his early forties, of medium height and rather stocky build. He had curly red hair, piercing blue eyes and a beer gut. He wore jeans and a tee shirt that was a little too small.

'Hello.'

'Hello.'

'You don't look as if you're just out for a stroll.'

'I'm not.'

'Maybe you could use a lift?'

'Maybe I could.' Kate studied the man carefully. He didn't look threatening. Anything would be better than this endless aimless walking.

'Hop in, then.'

They walked back to the lorry. He helped her into the cab and strapped her in. He settled himself in the driver's seat and started up the engine.

'Where are you going?'

'I don't know.'

He braked sharply in surprise. 'Don't know?'

'No.' Kate decided she should say as little as possible.

'Then I suppose it doesn't matter where you end up?'

'I suppose it doesn't.'

'Then you might just as well go where I'm going.'

'Yes. Why not.'

He accelerated, put out his traffic indicator, and moved into the fast lane.

'Where are you going?'

'France.'

'France!' Kate was completely taken by surprise.

'Yes. Have you ever been to France?'

'No.'

'Well, here's your chance.'

'Have you been to France before?'

'I go at least once a week. Sometimes more.'

'Oh.'

They lapsed into silence for several miles. Although she was getting a free ride, Kate felt under no obligation to make conversation.

'Hungry?'

'You bet.'

'There's some biscuits in a tin behind your seat.'

'Oh.'

'Just help yourself.'

'Thanks.'

Kate put her hand behind the seat and drew out a tin of biscuits. Hob-Nobs. Delicious. One of her favourites. She devoured half a biscuit in one mouthful.

'Mm, lovely,' she said, her mouth full. 'Want one?'

The man laughed and patted his stomach. 'No. Better not. I've got far too fat. Eat too much on this job. Boredom. It's even worse in France. Long, straight, empty roads and no one on 'em. Do you drive?'

Kate was on her third biscuit. 'Drive? Me? Heavens no. I'm only a...'

She was going to say 'gipsy' but thought better of it. 'I'm only twenty-two. Lots of time left,' she finished lamely.

'I'll say there is. So you're only twenty-two. I'd've said you were more like twenty-five.'

Kate wasn't sure whether or not to feel flattered.

'You're very pretty. What's your name?'

'Kate.'

'Kate what?'

'O'Leary.' Kate felt a little bit reluctant to reveal her surname.

'That Irish?'

'Dunno. Never thought about it.'

'I'm Tony.'

'Oh, hello, Tony.'

'Hello, Kate.'

They drove another few miles in silence.

'What do you do, Kate?'

Do! She didn't do anything. Did people have to do something?

'A bit of this and that.' Suddenly she had a brainwave. Gipsies mended pots. It wouldn't sound too incredible. 'I mend things.'

'What things?'

God, he was curious.

'Garments and curtains - and things.'

'Take in mending? At your house?'

House! If only he knew the half of it!

'Yes. People take their mending to my - house.'

'Good money?'

'I can't complain.'

Tony put her hand on her thigh.

'Pretty Kate. And only twenty-two. Ever been kissed, eh?'

'Yes.' Kate felt the need for caution.

Tony stroked her thigh. 'Been fucked?'

He felt her stiffen. 'Don't worry. I wouldn't force you. I'm no rapist. I only like it if the woman is willing. Don't see the point otherwise. After all, I'm not an animal, just a man feeling a bit randy. Funny thing, being a lorry driver. You get lonely with no one to talk to and you get hellishly randy as well. Must be the motion of the vehicle. I often have a hard on for ages and there's nowhere to toss it off 'cept in the cab. But it can get a bit smelly. And then, you meet a pretty woman...' he looked at Kate out of the corner of his eye.

Kate sat quite still. 'Is that why you give lifts to young women?'

Tony laughed. 'I suppose that's summat to do with it. I don't generally pick up the blokes. Besides, you can never tell nowadays what a bloke's going to do to another bloke, can you?'

'I wouldn't know,' said Kate dryly. 'Not being a bloke.'

Tony gave her another sideways glance and took his hand off her knee.

'We needn't rush it. Just see how you feel when we get to France. We'll do the crossing and have a nice nosh-up in a lorry drivers' caff I know in Calais. It's real good food and plenty of it.'

When they arrived in Dover Kate knew it was decision time. She would have to decide whether to stay with Tony or strike off again on her own. She was starving hungry, had practically no money and was sorely in need of a square meal. Tony had money and was prepared to pay for her dinner. And if he were a rapist, he would have raped her already. She wasn't afraid of sex with different men as long as there was no violence involved. Gipsies had casual sex with many different partners without giving it much thought. Kate had lost her virginity just before her fourteenth birthday. It hadn't bothered her in the least. Sex was part of life, so why worry? But she feared and hated sadistic men. She weighed up the pros and cons carefully.

If she said 'goodbye' to Tony in Dover she would be on her own again, with no money and nowhere to go. She would probably meet up with another man who might be a great deal worse than Tony. If she stayed with Tony she would get a free nosh but would undoubtedly have to have sex with him in return. But that mightn't be too bad either.

Kate was fascinated by the ferry and the whole process of driving on and off a boat. They had a few beers in the bar and Tony was in an exuberant mood when they arrived in France. As Tony had asked, Kate lay down obediently behind the driver's seat when they were going through customs.

'It's in case they want to see your passport,' Tony explained.

'Passport?' Kate's eyes widened. 'What's that for?'

'Going abroad.' Tony didn't see that any more explanation was necessary.

They found the drivers' caff and had a slap-up meal. The food tasted quite different: rather pungent and Kate enjoyed it. They drank two bottles of wine between them and by the time they got back to the lorry Tony was extremely amorous. As he lifted her into the cab he stroked her trousers between her legs. Then Kate realised she had passed the point of no return.

He undressed her in no time, fondling her breasts, biting her nipples. But below her waist was of far more interest to him and suddenly he plunged his thumb into her vagina.

'That's my girl. Well done,' he murmured, inserting his tongue in her ear. He reached for her lips, his breath reeking of alcohol, his mouth yawning wide as if to gobble her up. His upper lip blocked her nose so she couldn't breath. With all her orifices blocked she felt she would suffocate. She tried to push him away, just so she could get her breath a little, but his fingers gripped her harder, pressing deeper into her most private and sensitive places.

'Oh, no you don't. It's my go now. You've had your free nosh. Now it's my turn for a free fuck.'

And he forced his way into her.

Chapter Eight

Victor Fleming dipped his brush into the pot of grey paint, wiping it along the edge to get rid of any excess and then drew it slowly along the back of the wooden bench. Bench number eleven. He had been painting benches now for nearly a week. Grey. Not pale grey or battleship grey. Just mid-grey. The colour of mist and fog and the London sky most of the year round. Luckily the June sky in Burgundy was rarely grey. In fact, since he had arrived almost eight months ago, the sky had been a brilliant, azure blue almost every day. Victor finished the back of the bench and stood up to admire his handiwork. Only the armrests were left now, to be painted black when the grey paint was sufficiently dry. The legs had already been painted black. After nearly a week he had a system. He couldn't recollect ever having painted a bench before, but he quickly discovered that it was best to paint the underneath first. Not only did it provide a handhold on the seat when he was forced to lie underneath on his back, but it also got the worst bit over first.

A bell sounded in the distance from the direction of the house. Hurrah! thought Victor. Lunchtime. He looked at his watch. Ten minutes to twelve. Right on the button. The French were certainly great sticklers for punctual meal hours, particularly at lunchtime. He could imagine the whole of France sitting down to lunch at twelve o'clock midday precisely. It was usually an elaborate three or four course affair with the appropriate wines, lasting for anything up to two hours. Banks, shops, garages and offices all closed. In the provinces most people went home to lunch. Others, considering themselves less fortunate, crowded into the many excellent restaurants. Many of the smaller towns even suspended parking restrictions so the good burghers could enjoy *le déjeuner*. Most laudable and so French. The only problem was that everyone was expected to be alert afterwards and feel sufficiently energetic to do at least another four hours work. Unaccustomed as he was to these expansive lunches, Victor usually felt extremely somnolent during the afternoon and found that his concentration flagged considerably.

He walked to the far end of the enormous shed where he worked and started to clean up his hands. Bloody oil paint. Impossible to get off. His hands had had a greyish tinge for days now. Oh, well, this week was nearly over. Next week he would be gardening, not a task he particularly enjoyed, but at least it would make a change. He pulled off his overalls, crossed to the door of the shed and went out into the bright sunshine.

It was blisteringly hot in the courtyard. It wasn't an attractive picturesque courtyard, just a working yard. It had served as a central dumping ground for the lorries and the light railway that used to bring lime and gravel from the quarry above Dracy to the tile factory just across the lane. But by the end of World War II the quarry had been worked out and the factory had closed over thirty years ago, causing unemployment and serious social unrest throughout the area. At first the labourers had found other employment in a large armaments factory in a nearby industrial town, but eventually that had closed too, and the workforce, again unemployed, had been forced to move to the larger towns and cities such as Dijon, Dole, Nevers, and even as far away as Lyon and Paris. In thirty years the population had more than halved and shops and businesses had closed in their hundreds. Towns and villages became ghost towns and rural Burgundy gradually became a social and economic desert. In order to regenerate economic prosperity and restore pride and self confidence, and above all to encourage people to remain in the area, various projects were devised, both by the central government in Paris and by the local *Communes*. Groups were set up in rural areas all over France, given large grants and often free premises as well; some derelict and badly in need of renovation, with the express purpose of involving the local population in practical projects and cultural events. The latter often consisted of staging large-scale pageants of a commemorative nature, in which the entire local population was encouraged take part.

Les Projets Créatifs was one such group. It consisted of enthusiastic young people, mostly in their late twenties and early thirties, who were prepared to work hard for very little money in order to give pleasure, encouragement and inspiration to their fellow human beings. Artistic talent was not a vital qualification for membership, nor was it necessary to have any practical knowledge of stagecraft, lighting or carpentry. The important ingredients were enthusiasm, dedication, patience and tolerance. Everyone mucked in together and jobs were shared on a rota basis. Everyone took their turn at cooking, gardening, painting and general repairs.

Victor went up the three shallow stone steps, past the massive oak front door, always left open during the day, through the inner glass door and into the large cool hall. The floor was flag-stoned, the lofty ceiling oak-beamed. A magnificent staircase rose in the centre, dividing in two halfway up, leading to the separate wings of the house. Victor turned right, past the bottom of the staircase and followed the sound of a Babel of voices, growing louder as he approached the dining room where the members of *Les Projets Créatifs* were gathering for lunch.

'*Bonjour, Victoire! Ça va ?*'

'How's the painting going?'

'Almost finished.'

'*Très bien.*'

Victor went round the table, greeting the people he had not already met during the morning. A formal handshake with the young men. A ritual peck on the cheek for the girls.

'*Bonjour, Henri! Bonjour Jean-Marc!*'

'*Bonjour, Victoire!*'

'*Bonjour, Sophie! Bonjour, Chantal!*'

Always two kisses. Sometimes even three. It was hard to guess the required number. Victor was never quite sure. He didn't know either whether an extra kiss implied extra status. Did it mean he was regarded in higher esteem if he received three kisses rather than two? He had seen Frenchmen in the street or in *cafés* greet their lady friends and even men friends too, with four or even five kisses. The kissing always made him feel a little dizzy. He was relieved that the male members of *Les Projets Créatifs* refrained from kissing each other. Victor sat down at the long trestle table between Sophie and Anne-Marie. No one had a set place so Victor tried to sit next to a different member of the group each time. Although the first course of cold chicken liver *pâté* had already been laid at each place, no one started eating until the whole company had assembled. Then there was a moment's silence while someone, usually one of the men, said grace. Wine was poured, knives and forks started to clatter and the small group began to concentrate on their food in earnest. Eating was a serious matter, best undertaken in silence, so the conversation didn't generally get going until most people had finished their main course. Plates were cleared away, more wine poured and cheese was served.

'Was it an accident?'

'Of course it was an accident...'

'You don't surely think...?'

'Why not?'

'But who would want to...?'

'In a quiet place like this!'

'The quieter the better.'

'For what?'

'For a murder, of course.'

'A murder!'

'You don't really think, Jean-Marc...?'

'I heard it was the dog that found the body.'

'Really? The dog?'

'What was the dog doing up there by the disused quarry?'

'Being taken for a walk.'

'Why take a dog for a walk?'

'It seems to be one of those mad English habits.'

'How bizarre.'

'The English are a nation of dog walkers, yes, Victoire?'

'Curious place to choose for a walk, with or without a dog.'

'Yes. One of the most dangerous places round here.'

'All that loose gravel.'

'Shale.'

'Very slippery.'

'Indeed. He obviously slipped and fell.'

'Perhaps he was pushed.'

'Perhaps.'

'Was there anyone else there?'

'No one knows yet.'

The conversation flowed fast. Victor had to concentrate really hard to follow it. He had no difficulty in conversing with one person at a time, but it was quite a different matter trying to listen to nearly a dozen people at once.

'Who's been killed?' He addressed Henri directly.

'The Englishman who lived in the rambling farmhouse on the edge of Laronne.'

'An Englishman?'

'Yes. Did you know him?'

'What was his name?'

'Alan something.'

'Perry. Alan Perry.'

'That's it. Alan Perry. Did you know him, Victoire?'

Victor shook his head. 'No. Name doesn't sound familiar.'

'Where was the body found exactly?'

'In the lake.'

'So he slid right down into the lake?'

The conversation moved on to other topics. Fresh fruit was served, glowing orange apricots, peaches, creamy on one side, deep pink on the other, all gleaming with a gentle down, like very fine fur. Victor poured himself another half glass of wine and sipped it slowly, his head spinning a little. He was beginning to feel drowsy and thought longingly of a siesta. Perhaps he could just slink off to his room for a little bit of shut-eye. He had no idea whether or not this would be frowned upon. He felt it probably would. Everyone seemed so earnest; so dedicated.

Hot, black, very strong coffee was served in tiny cups. It was like a caffeine injection, designed to keep everyone going during the long, hot, torpid afternoon. Grace was said again and the company dispersed, presumably to resume their morning activities. Victor thought of the two remaining benches and the deadening, acrid odour of the grey paint. His head felt thick and heavy, his eyelids drooped. Just ten minutes on the bed, he thought, as he left the room. No one could object to ten minutes. He slunk off to his bedroom and slept all afternoon.

'*Merci.*'

Victor smiled at the waiter as he put the cup of coffee down on the plastic topped table. The spoon fell off onto the tiled floor with a loud clang and the girl in the far corner stirred and moaned in her sleep.

'*Je vous en prie, monsieur. Ça fait quinze francs, s'il vous plaît.*'

Victor put a twenty-franc note on the table and waited while the waiter fumbled in his pocket for the change. He looked curiously at the girl in the far corner, still asleep, sprawled across the table, her head cradled in her arms.

'Been here long, has she?' he asked the waiter.

'All day, *monsieur.*'

'All day!'

'Yes. She was already outside this morning when I arrived to open up the *café*. She was sitting on the edge of the pavement, her head on her knees, half asleep. I opened the door and she came in. She said nothing. Not even *bonjour*.'

'Maybe she's deaf.' Victor was genuinely trying to be helpful.

'Maybe. I don't know.' The waiter shrugged his shoulders.

'Has she had anything to eat or drink?'

'Nothing at all. She's been asleep over there all day.'

'Perhaps she has no money?'

The waiter shrugged.

'Peut-être, monsieur. Je n'en sais rien.'

The waiter returned briskly to the bar, his metal heels click-clacking on the tiled floor. The girl stirred again. Victor sat and watched her. A pretty girl. Strange to spend the day fast asleep in a *café* all on your own. He picked up his paper and went back to the article he had been reading. Thank goodness he could get *The Sunday Times* in this God-forsaken spot. It had been difficult, though. The newsagent in Dracy had never heard of it. Nor, it appeared, had he ever ordered a foreign newspaper for anyone else before. He couldn't promise it before Wednesday. Today was Thursday and it had just arrived.

Victor became engrossed in an article about a new play at the Royal Court. The theatre. The real theatre. Not pageants for peasants, which for the last five years he had been helping different groups throughout France to create and perform. Perhaps after all, it was time he returned to England and found another a job in the theatre, preferably in London. He had been in Dracy with *Les Projets Créatifs* for over four months now. It was surely time to move on. On the other hand, it mightn't be very politic to desert the group before their next production, which was planned for 15 August: a large pageant to commemorate the one thousandth anniversary of the village of Laronne. The French certainly had some strange notions. Though of course he wasn't indispensable. They were sure to find an equally suitable replacement.

One of the magazine sections slipped off his knee and fell on the floor with a dull thud. He bent to pick it up. As he straightened up, a movement in the far corner caught his eye. He sat back in his chair and saw that the previously sleeping girl was now wide-awake and sitting bolt upright. She was slight, probably not very tall, with large, wide-set black eyes, long black hair and an olive complexion. She wore a crumpled white short-sleeved shirt, jeans and trainers. A rather scruffy anorak of a non-descript colour lay askew on the back of her chair and there was a small canvas bag on the floor beside her. She didn't look like one of the local residents, nor did she look like a tourist. Victor frowned in puzzlement. She could almost be - well - a gipsy or some kind of new age traveller.

'Hello!'

Her voice was soft, gentle and surprisingly attractive.

'Hello!' replied Victor in some surprise. He certainly hadn't expected the girl to be English.

'Oh! You're English,' she said in some relief.

'Yes.'

'I didn't expect to find any English people here.'

'No. I don't think there are that many. In fact, probably none at all.' Except the Englishman who lost his life a month ago, thought Victor, but he didn't mention it.

'Are you on holiday in the area?'

Good God! What a ridiculous question, thought Victor. But he couldn't think of anything better to say.

'Not a holiday exactly.' Kate was determined to give away as little as possible. For the moment, anyway. 'I'm just looking around France,' she added lamely.

'Know the country well?'

'Not at all. I've never been here before.'

'Speak the language? I mean just a little?'

'Not a word.'

Kate thought of her fractured, almost non-existent schooling.

'Would you like coffee or a glass of wine?'

'Oh, yes please.' Kate sounded very grateful.

'Perhaps something to eat with it?'

'Oh, thank you.' Kate was quite overwhelmed.

Victor went over to the bar and ordered two sandwiches and a carafe of dry white wine. To hell with dinner. He would cross that bridge when he came to it. Kate tucked ravenously into the substantial sandwich. She devoured it in seconds. Victor ordered another one, which she nibbled more slowly.

'Nice crispy bread,' she said, wiping a dollop of mayonnaise off her chin with her hand. 'Is all French bread like this? It's the only sort I've eaten so far.'

'No. There are many different kinds but this one seems to be the most popular. It's called a *baguette*.'

'*Baguette*,' said Kate slowly, licking her lips.

'How long have you been in France?'

'A few days.'

'How did you get here?'

'Most of the way in a lorry.'

'Friend's lorry?'

'Not exactly.'

Victor could see she was sensitive. She had probably been hurt. He didn't want to upset her further by asking too many questions. He wondered if she was running away from something or someone, but of course he couldn't ask her.

'How long are you planning to stay in France?'

'I've no idea. I hadn't planned to come here in the first place.'

Victor's eyebrows shot up.

'It was just chance, was it?'

Kate sighed. 'It was because of the lorry driver. He was coming to France and I happened to be in his lorry...'

'So you had to come along too.'

'Yes.'

There was a pause while Victor tried to think out the next move. He was sure she had no money and nowhere to sleep, but he was a little apprehensive about asking her to spend the night at *Les Projets*. He wasn't worried about what the other members of the group would think. They were used to visitors and there was an abundance of spare bedrooms. Kate would be made welcome, given a day or so to settle in, and then be expected to join in all the activities, doing her share of the chores. It was Kate's own reaction that bothered him.

'Do you live in France?'

Her question broke into his thoughts.

'Yes, I do at the moment.'

'How long have you lived here?

'About five years.'

'Always here in this place?'

'No. Not always. I've lived in various parts of France including Paris for over two years.'

'Is Paris nice?'

'Beautiful.'

Kate couldn't imagine any town or city being beautiful. She had only been to London, Birmingham and Sheffield and had thought they were all ugly. Somewhere like Westway had nothing to recommend it, with or without gipsies. She had always preferred the country. She liked the green open space and the fresh smell.

'I suppose you speak French?'

'Yes. Fairly well,' said Victor modestly.

'How did you learn it?'

'Well, I did it at school to A Level and then learnt more just by living here.'

'I see.'

School again. It was all right for some.

'Did you do French at school?'

'No. I didn't do much of anything at school.'

Victor looked at his watch. Half-past seven. He needed to be back at *Les Projets* for dinner by about ten-to-eight. He took the plunge.

'I wondered, that is… would you like to come back to dinner?'

Kate's eyes widened. 'Dinner? At your house?'

'Yes.'

'Are you married?'

Victor laughed. 'Married! No.'

'So you live by yourself?' Kate sounded nervous.

'No. I live in a large house with eleven other people.'

'Eleven other people?'

'Yes.'

'Like in a camp?'

'Sort of. Not quite a camp. More of a commune.'

'Commune?'

'Yes. We share everything.'

'Everything? Including sex?'

Victor was taken aback by her directness.

'No. Not sex. We each have our own bedroom.'

Bedroom. Kate couldn't imagine a room only being used as a bedroom.

'I see. So there are twelve bedrooms?'

'Sixteen.'

'So it's a big house?'

'Yes.'

'What other rooms has it got?'

'Dining room, living room, kitchen, studies, workrooms, and lots and lots of outhouses which are used for painting, carpentry, storing costumes and scenery and stage lights and that sort of thing.'

'You put on plays?'

'Big pageants. They take months to devise. Everyone joins in to construct and paint sets, sew costumes, write the play, the music and act. We need people to erect stands, put up lights. There are a million ways in which people can help. No job is unimportant.'

'Could I help?'

'Of course you could.'

'I'll come to dinner, then'

'Good. I hoped you might.'

Victor went across to the bar and paid the bill.

Chapter Nine

'So you've always lived in the country?' Jo refilled Gerry's glass for the umpteenth time.

'Yes. Always in the country.'

'Far from Dublin?'

'About twenty five miles.'

'Oh, quite near.'

'In Irish terms that's really quite far.' Gerry took another long draught of wine. 'Dublin's quite small. Nothing like the size of London. Only around a million or so people. So twenty five miles is a good way out.'

'But it's not far into Dublin either.'

'About an hour into the centre, depending on the traffic.'

'An ideal situation - with the best of both worlds.'

'Yes. A perfect situation.'

'The peace and quiet of the country with all the city attractions close at hand.'

'Plenty of city attractions. Dublin's a swinging place nowadays; full of bars and caffs and great shops.'

'And theatres and restaurants?'

'Plenty of theatres and restaurants. Dublin's a great city for all of those.'

Gerry picked up his glass, discovered it was empty and set it down again. Jo decided she would let him wait a little. They were almost through the second bottle.

'Tell me about your house, deep in the Irish countryside. What's it called?'

'Laragh Lodge.'

'Laragh Lodge! How romantic!'

'It is, isn't it?' Gerry was impressed by his own imagination.

'Why is it called Laragh Lodge?'

'It's near a place called Laragh. Have you ever heard of Glendalough?'

Jo shook her head. 'No. I don't know anything about Ireland.'

'It's a famous place in County Wicklow with two big lakes, a tower and beautiful scenery. All the tourists go there, especially the Americans. They think they're going to find their long lost relatives in Glendalough, if they haven't found them already in Connemara or Killarney. They're a scream, some of those Yanks.'

'Tell me more about Laragh Lodge. How big is it? How long has it been in your family?'

'Oh, it's big enough.'

'How many bedrooms?'

Gerry frowned. 'Must have at least six.'

'That's quite a lot.'

'But we don't necessarily use them all.'

'Not necessarily?'

'Well, like we wouldn't use all of them all the time. Some would be for visitors.'

'So your parents entertain a lot?'

'I wouldn't say a lot; just from time to time.'

'The odd dinner party and people for drinks?'

'That's it. Just a few dinner parties and the drinks.'

'Are the neighbours friendly? I mean, most country people are more friendly than townsfolk.'

'Oh, certainly. I'd agree with you there.'

'So you have a good social life Laragh Lodge?'

'Absolutely. The social life's terrific.'

'Is it a farm? Are there animals?'

'Oh, yes. A few animals. But you could hardly call it a farm, not by Irish standards in those days. We had a few cows and pigs and hens too, of course. Never had to buy an egg. I never saw an egg box until I went to school up in Dublin. I didn't know what it was when I saw one in the shop. We had horses too. I used to ride a lot as a kid and sometimes go out hunting. It was great gas, the hunting.'

'My goodness,' Jo sounded really impressed. 'Hunting does sound smart. Tell me about your parents and your brothers and sisters.'

She picked up the wine bottle and refilled Gerry's glass. She drained the rest into her own. Just half a glass left. She toyed with the idea of opening the third bottle. Gerry was certainly opening up with the help of alcohol. He seemed to need it to get him going. Jo didn't want him to dry up. She wanted to know more about his life in distant rural Ireland.

It was a beautiful evening, calm and still. She had set their dinner table on the far side of the barn from the caravan for a change, as it had a more interesting view. The view from the other side of the barn was a pastoral scene of endless green fields, of which she was now thoroughly tired. From their present position they overlooked the entire courtyard and could see everything on the terraces of all the apartments. After all, they were her apartments and her paying guests. Without her hard work the punters would not be enjoying their summer holiday. It was interesting to observe how the different couples spent the evening with her furniture and her crockery. She didn't mind the punters seeing how she and Gerry spent the evening. Most of them only stayed a week anyway.

Deciding the third bottle was a necessary lubricant; she went round the corner of the barn to fetch it from the caravan. In the few moments she was gone, Gerry drained his freshly filled glass. Seeing his empty glass on her return, Jo realised she had made the right decision. Smiling, she placed the new bottle on the table and handed Gerry the corkscrew.

'Tell me more about your family,' she said, resuming her seat. Gerry drew the cork out of the bottle and refilled their glasses.

'What kind of things do you want to know?'

'What your father does, what your mother's like, how many brothers and sisters you have. Tell me everything.' Jo settled herself more comfortably in her chair and put a cushion behind her head.

Brothers and sisters! Jesus!

Gerry had never had any siblings. Having been born unwanted, out of wedlock and suffering a childhood of the utmost deprivation, he found it difficult to imagine a normal, happy family life with brothers and sisters.

'I don't have any brothers and sisters any more,' he said slowly. 'I had a little sister what died as a baby and my older brother was run over when he was four.'

Jo was horrified. 'How dreadful! To lose both brother and sister. So awful for your parents, too.'

'It was, surely.'

'I am sorry.'

'That's OK. At least it was a long time ago.'

'Yes. Time heals, but one never forgets.

'No. One never forgets,' said Gerry bitterly, thinking of the cruelty and abuse he had received from his mother's common-law husband while his mother looked on and did nothing.

'No. You don't forget.'

'What does your father do?'

'Do? Oh, yes, I see what you mean. What did he do? He's retired now.'

'What did he do before he retired?'

This was requiring all his ingenuity. Now that he had started 'reinventing' himself he had to keep it up. He thought of a shop in Dublin along the Quays by the River Liffey where he used to go sometimes with his mother. It had a narrow frontage but went back a long way. It was dark inside and smelt of oil and paint. There were tools hanging up along one wall: garden rakes, hoes, shovels, forks, spades, loys for cutting turf; all neatly arranged; the metal gleaming and the wooden handles still smooth and shiny, waiting for a purchaser to come along and put them to use. The opposite wall was covered with row upon row of little drawers containing hooks, nails, screws, cleats, knobs, handles, levers and a myriad of other smaller items essential to house construction and maintenance. At the back of the shop were cans of coloured paints in different sizes, stripper, varnish, creosote. The shop seemed to stock every possible item necessary for building and decorating houses. Gerry loved the shop. When he grew up he wanted to work in, or preferably own, a shop just like this one. Sadly, the owner went out of business just about the time Gerry and his mother left Ireland. He had asked his mother what sort of a shop it was.

'It's a builder's merchant,' she had said.

'My Da was a builder's merchant,' said Gerry.

'Oh!' said Jo, surprised. 'That's interesting.'

'It was. Really interesting.' Gerry described the shop in great detail. At least this time he was on safe ground.

Gerry refilled his glass and took a sip. He was beginning to feel thick-headed. No matter. He wasn't expected to do anything except talk. And alcohol seemed to dull the painful memories. He thought back to his childhood and the small, shabby farmhouse in County Wicklow where he was brought up. It was near Laragh. That bit had been correct. But it didn't have a name. It was just called 'the run-down farmhouse on the hill.' He remembered how his mother had told him once, before she had hit the bottle in a big way, how she had turned up one evening in 1963, hungry, destitute, aged only nineteen, with her new-born baby in her arms. It was raining heavily, she had said, and they were both soaking wet. She had rung the doorbell and a middle-aged man had let them in.

'Oh, dear God,' said the man, 'and you soaking wet with a little baba.'

He had bustled about in the dark, grimy kitchen, preparing a simple meal of soup, bread and cheese. Gerry remembered his mother saying she was so hungry she had finished up all the bread there was in the house. The man, whose name was Connor, made up a bed for his mother in a large cold room upstairs next door to his own. The baby was laid to sleep on a rug on the floor. Connor was a short squat, ugly man with a squint. He had a cruel, sadistic streak, which was why he couldn't keep his women very long. Only the most desperate women stayed any length of time with him; women with no home, no money, no prospects, burdened with the responsibility of an unwanted child.

Women like Gerry's mother.

For the first five or six years the three of them got on well enough. Connor owned the small-holding and the farmhouse that went with it, left to him by his father. There were two horses, a few cows, sheep, pigs and hens. They were self-sufficient in potatoes and vegetables and they took plenty into the local market to sell. They were certainly not affluent, but they managed to scrape along well enough. But by the time Gerry was eight, living conditions had deteriorated considerably. Small-holdings as small as Connor's were not an economic proposition. In the mid-to-late 1960s supermarkets were springing up everywhere, demanding more uniform produce of a higher quality than someone like Connor knew how to produce. The country people were moving to the towns, so one by one the local markets closed. There was so little demand for locally grown potatoes and vegetables that they just rotted in the ground.

With much less money coming in, there was much less to eat. Connor grew lazy, morose, and started drinking heavily. Never a sensitive or a caring man, he became violent and sadistic. He used Gerry's mother as slave labour, forcing her to do heavy manual work for hours at a time without food or rest. He beat her and sexually assaulted her in front of her son, inflicting the maximum amount of pain and humiliation. In desperation, she packed their few belongings and ran away, taking Gerry with her. But Connor drove after them and brought them back to the house where he doubled his attacks of violent abuse, starting on the boy as well. Having beaten and raped Gerry's mother he would turn his attention to Gerry, stripping him naked, beating him with a leather strap, forcing pointed objects into his anus till he screamed for mercy. And all the while his mother looked on and did nothing.

When Gerry was ten Connor died of cirrhosis of the liver. Gerry and his mother hung on in the shabby rambling farmhouse, fast becoming more and more derelict, for another two years. But it didn't belong to them. Predictably, Connor had left no will; but eventually a distant cousin of Connor's tracked them down, threw them out and sold the property. Gerry and his mother hitchhiked to Dublin. They found accommodation in a hostel but Gerry's mother couldn't find any work. Gerry went back to school and resumed his patchy education, which he enjoyed, but of course it didn't bring in any money.

Then one evening, totally distraught and desperate, Gerry's mother spent her last few pounds on tickets for the Mail Boat to Holyhead. They hitchhiked again, this time to London, where they found lodgings behind Kings Cross Station. Things went from bad to worse. Having no skills, Gerry's mother was forced to go on the game. Very soon she hit the bottle in a big way and with Connor as her supreme example of viciousness, she became violent towards her own son, now aged thirteen. Gerry found himself a school to go to, but, as his mother drank more and more, she became incapable of going out to work, even on her back. There was less and less money coming in for food, heating, light or clothing. Aged fifteen and tall for his age, Gerry managed to find a job as a messenger boy. Having had almost no education, he had little or no choice in the job market. The better jobs folded one by one and by the time he was seventeen he was working as a labourer, building motorways. He and his mother continued their precarious emotional and financial existence for another three years.

Then one evening in 1983, shortly after Gerry had turned twenty, his mother, so drunk she could hardly stand, threatened him with a kitchen knife. Fearing for his life, Gerry tried to wrest the knife from her grasp. He grabbed both her arms and held them tightly. His mother struggled and fought back hard, trying to free her right arm. Gerry shook her violently, then letting go suddenly, he pushed her across the room. She swayed and fell heavily, hitting her temple with a resounding crack on the sharp corner of the ancient cooker. The knife hit the floor with a dull thud.

Then there was silence.

In fear and trembling Gerry knelt by his mother's side, shaking her gently in an attempt to get some response. But there was none. She lay on the floor, limp and inert. In rising panic he started to drag her towards the bedroom, thinking that if he could get her to bed she would recover by the morning. But she was too heavy and unwieldy to move. He phoned for an ambulance and on arrival at the hospital, his mother was pronounced dead.

Gerry was arrested, charged with murder, tried and found guilty.

'Tell me about your mother, Gerry.'

Jo's voice broke into Gerry's thoughts. He had gone so far back into his childhood memories that for a moment he couldn't remember where he was. For a moment he was tempted to tell Jo the truth, to tell her everything. But he realised there would be no point in doing so. If he was going to do anything at all with his life he had to bury the past and start again. And fond though he was of Jo, he was perfectly aware that she was only a temporary interlude. They were poles apart. They could never share each other's lives on any permanent basis.

'My mother was - well - my mother,' he started lamely.

'Was?' asked Jo in some surprise. 'If she was only nineteen when you were born she would only be - let's see – she would be forty-six now.'

'Yes. Forty-six. That's right. But not everyone is privileged to live to three score and ten,' said Gerry, searching for some inspiration.

'Sadly not,' said Jo, thinking of Alan.

Gerry must have read her thoughts. His flashback into his childhood memories seemed to have left him rather bereft of invention.

'She used to go for long walks round Lake Glendalough,' he said slowly. 'All by herself. The Upper Lake was a lonely place, haunted by Saint Kevin, who was said to have thrown his beloved into the lake. My mother was obsessed by the story and she used to talk about it a lot. One day she didn't come back from her walk. Her body was never found. No one knows what happened to her.'

Chapter Ten

Lucien Gautier first heard the news of Alan's death from his wife, Colette. While Lucien made the early morning delivery rounds, Colette held the fort at the bakery in the village. *La Boulangérie Gautier* was more than just a shop. It was an institution. Not only were Lucien's bread and pastries considered the best in Dracy; they were also renowned over a large area. People came from as far as twenty kilometres to purchase his delicious *baguettes, batards, croissants,* and mouth-watering tarts and pastries. But the customers flocked to *La Boulangérie Gautier* not only for their excellent produce, but also for the gossip. Colette knew everything that went on for miles around and she loved imparting her information to all and sundry. Colette was always the first to know about any birth, marriage, divorce, separation, accident, theft, arrest, death or murder. No one ever surprised her with any news. Colette Gautier knew everything before anyone else. In addition to his excellent reputation as a baker, Lucien was also known for his kindness and helpfulness. No special order was too much trouble: be it a birthday cake for a small child, or a pensioner, *une galette* for twelfth night, or *une tarte aux pommes* for Sunday lunch. Not only was he prepared to take orders at short notice but he was also more than willing to make extra deliveries to the most remote places at any time of the day, particularly if the customer in question was elderly and had no means of transport.

When Lucien chatted to Alan Perry at 6.30 pm on the evening of 4 May, he had no idea he would be one of the last people to see Alan alive. It was not until the following morning, coming into his own kitchen, floury and perspiring after five hours working at the ovens, that Colette told Lucien of Alan's death. Lucien was distraught. Although they had never been the closest of friends, Lucien thought highly of Alan. He admired Alan's courage in pulling up his English roots in middle age and coming to live in France. He had enormous respect for Alan's excellent knowledge of French and he hugely enjoyed the jokes and the banter they had always shared.

Lucien knew, of course, that Alan was out 'for another of his mad walks,' as he termed it himself, on that fateful evening. He hadn't seen the dog, which had probably gone down a rabbit hole during their brief conversation. He had met Alan out walking on previous occasions, with or without the dog. He accepted walks as part of the curious English culture, and questioned neither their validity nor their sanity. Lucien hadn't spoken to Alan for more than a few minutes. He didn't ask him which direction he had come from or which route he planned to take home. Lucien remembered looking at his watch just before he drove off, noting the time was 6.30 pm. He was in a hurry to deliver his specially ordered *patissérie* to *Monsieur* Floret for his eighty-fifth birthday and still arrive home by 7.30 for Colette's delicious dinner. Even when he heard the news from his wife that Alan had met his death a mere hour after their brief meeting, Lucien saw no reason to contact the police. As far as he was concerned, people were free to go for walks where and whenever they liked. It was certainly not a habit which appealed to him, but he was well aware that everyone was different and foreigners were certainly more different than most. As for Colette: no one knew how she had found out about Alan's death. It was expected she would be the first to know.

She always was.

Chantal Gilot heaved her huge bulk out of the only chair in the house big enough to accommodate her and went to answer the front door bell. As she had expected, the caller was Georges Lefèvre, the plumber, who had come to sort out an on-going problem with the lavatory cistern.

'*Bonjour, ma petite Chantal!*' Georges leaned over the woman's vast form and, with great difficulty, placed three kisses alternately on the ballooning cheeks.

'*Petite, mon Dieu!*' said Chantal scornfully. 'There's nothing little about me. I'm the largest woman in the whole of Burgundy.'

Georges laughed. '*N'importe.* What does it matter? You have the charm and a big enough dress to hold it all.'

Still, he thought to himself, it must be a hell of a problem dragging that enormous body around.

'*Eh bien,*' he said out loud, 'show me the way to the lavatory.'

Chantal shuffled into the hallway and opened the door of the smallest room Georges had ever seen, containing a lavatory flat against the wall with a cistern above.

'*Mon Dieu!* However do you fit in here, Chantal? I would have thought...'

'That's for Jules, *stupide*. I use the full-size *toilette* upstairs.'

'*Tant mieux,*' replied Georges, taking out his tool bag. '*Quand même,* we'll have this fixed in a jiffy. Then perhaps you'll give me a little cuddle in return, *hein?*'

'What time do you expect Jules?'

'Not before midday.'

'*Excellent! Excellent !*'

Chantal didn't like anyone to see her naked, so they left the curtains drawn until she had covered her huge form with her tent dress. Georges sat on the side of the vast double bed and pulled on his trousers. He was deeply fond of Chantal. She was always willing, which his wife, Josette, had not been for years. There was the extra thrill, too, of making love to such an enormous woman. Her flesh hung in vast folds, cascading over her body, soft and malleable. Her breasts were like huge over-ripe melons. Mounting her was like bouncing on an inflatable. Georges stood up and drew back the curtains.

'They found the body of the Englishman this morning.'

'What Englishman?'

'Perry. Alan Perry.'

'*Oh, mon Dieu!* A body! What on earth happened?'

'It appears he had an accident.'

'An accident! What sort of an accident?'

'No one seems to know yet.'

'Where was the body found?'

'In the lake on the far side of Dracy, where the old quarry is at its steepest and most dangerous.'

'Towards La Roche?'

'Somewhere up there.'

'What was he doing?'

'Walking his dog, apparently.'

'Walking a dog! How extraordinary!'

'Yes, indeed. Apparently it's a common pastime in England.'

'Tiens! And who found the body?'

'Bernard Roger.'

'What was Bernard doing in such a desolate spot?'

'Looking for some missing cattle.'

'I didn't think he had the energy to go that far.'

'No. Nor did I.'

'Who told you?'

'Colette Gautier, of course.'

'Of course. Who else.'

Chantal had every intention of telling her husband the news of Alan Perry's death, but business in the post office that afternoon was particularly brisk. She also had to cover up all evidence of her amorous session with Georges Lefèvre. It had become a fairly regular, but totally secret affair. In the end it was three days before Jules Gilot heard about Alan's accident. Shocked and saddened though he was, of course, he didn't see it was any particular concern of his. The fact that he had spoken to Alan Perry forty-five minutes before his death was pure co-incidence. He saw no reason whatsoever to go to the police. His informant was, of course, Colette Gautier.

Roland Paillard, the architect, left his large house above Dracy early in the morning on 5 May to go to Chalon. He was well known throughout Burgundy and even worked as far afield as Macon. He was away for almost a week and when he returned the news of Alan's death had died down. It was not until Friday, the day before he had invited Alan and Jo for dinner, that he mentioned the subject to *Madame* Paillard.

'*Maman,* don't forget Jo and Alan Perry are coming to dinner tomorrow.'

Madame Paillard was horrified.

'*Mais, chéri,* didn't you hear the dreadful news? Dear Alan was killed ten days ago.'

'Killed? How?'

'It seems he slipped while out walking with his dog. He fell down the steep slope by the old quarry on the way to La Roche. He landed in the lake.'

Roland was appalled. 'Who found his body?'

'Bernard Roger. About eight in the evening. It seems that poor Alan had barely been dead an hour.'

'How dreadful. But Bernard Roger? What was he doing up there?'

'Looking for lost cattle, apparently.'

'Really? What day was it?'

'The day of the accident? A Thursday, I think.'

'Thursday? *Bon.*'

Roland was relieved. He had seen Alan on Wednesday about ten minutes past seven. If Alan had met his death on Wednesday he, Roland, might have been the last person to see him alive. He would have had it on his conscience if he hadn't gone to the police. But luckily the accident had happened on Thursday, so there was no need for him to get involved in any way. Roland was most careful not to get mixed up in anything shady. You never know: it might be bad for business. But he felt extremely sad. He was fond of Alan and Jo, particularly of Alan, who was so charming and intelligent and spoke such beautiful French. He didn't think of checking up on Thursday's date. He didn't realise, either, how vague his mother was becoming. For some time now *Madame* Paillard had been unable to remember the simplest things such as the time of day or the day of the week. *Madame* Paillard was beginning to lose her memory.

Bernard Roger lived with his wife, Denise and two young children on the only fully working farm for miles around. Bernard had a small herd of white, Charolais cattle. The breed is pretty to look at and extremely good to eat. Charolais beef is at the top end of the market and no self-respecting Burgundian chef would dream of offering anything else in his restaurant. Bernard took great pride in his herd, which occupied all of his time, but he took no pride in anything else. The state of his farmyard was a local disgrace. It was filthy, and filled with junk, which had accumulated for over twenty years. There were seven broken-down, rusted tractors, two old lorries, three dumper-trucks, two combine-harvesters and nine motorcars. There were two discarded electric cookers, three refrigerators, and a tin bath. There were agricultural tools of every description, some even worth displaying in a museum. There was furniture, too: four iron bedsteads, five mattresses, a huge sofa with no seat, four armchairs, one without a seat and one without an arm. There were two kitchen tables, both of solid oak, undoubtedly worth restoring by someone who realised their value; several kitchen chairs, most without their full complement of legs; a variety of lamps and great deal of broken garden furniture. There were saucepans, jars, bottles, broken crockery, battered books, torn magazines and mouldy newspapers. There was even clothing: jackets, trousers, coats, shirts, dresses, knitwear and a plethora of footwear, all strewn just anyhow all over the farmyard. There were at least two-dozen cardboard boxes, which had once been stacked up, ready to receive all the cast-offs to be taken to the tip. But no one had ever got round to packing them up, so now they just blew around the courtyard in various stages of disintegration and decay. Farm animals wandered through the squalid mess: hens, ducks, and geese. There were three under-fed, mangy dogs, kept permanently chained up, howling all day long. There was a variable number of feral cats, seven at the present count, ambling, gambling or stalking around in the chaos, giving berth to endless litters in all sorts of unexpected places. Bernard Roger's house was in no better state than the farmyard. His wife, Denise was a slut, who preferred staying in bed to doing any housework. The family couldn't remember when she had last cleaned the house, so crammed with junk it would have been a major task to unearth a duster or a dustpan and brush. The curtains were torn and hung crookedly at the windows, which were so grimy one could neither see in nor out. The toilet facilities were also pretty grim. There was a lavatory just outside at the back, its door hanging loose. There was neither a bath nor a shower, the family taking an occasional strip-wash at the kitchen sink.

Everyone in Laronne, and even further afield, was shocked by the Roger family's living standards, but they all realised there was nothing to be done about it. The children were adequately clothed, appeared well fed and attended the local school regularly. It was even rumoured that the boy, in particular, was doing well at his studies. The Roger family kept themselves to themselves. They never joined in any local activities:

they never attended local *Fêtes* or *Soirées* in the *Salles des Fêtes* at the *Mairie*.

Bernard and Denise were never known to have attended any of the school parents' evenings. The neighbours felt particularly sorry for the Roger children. Although they looked healthy, some felt they had a hunted look, but no one ever dared to intervene. Despite his squalid life-style, Bernard Roger was careful to keep on the right side of the law. Nor did he like to become involved in any police enquiries. However, when he stumbled across Alan Perry's body, lying face down at the edge of the lake, up by the old quarry, he realised he would have to inform the authorities. After all, one can't just leave a dead man in a remote spot and say nothing. Bernard hardly knew Alan Perry, but he felt everyone deserved a decent burial and he would have the grisly image of Alan's prone body on his conscience for life if he didn't report it to somebody. So that evening he reported the incident to the police.

He told the police that he had stumbled across the body while searching for two of his cattle, missing from a herd, which grazed in a field not far from the lake. The police didn't ask him if he had seen anyone else in the area, so Bernard didn't volunteer any information. He felt he had done his bit as a public-spirited citizen in reporting the body and he didn't have the time to sit around in the police station answering endless questions. More cattle might go missing if he wasn't around to keep a constant check on them.

In fact, Bernard had seen two people in the vicinity at the time of Alan's accident. He had noticed a youth at the top of the steep quarry throwing stones at a dog, which appeared to be trapped on a ledge just below the cliff path.

He thought he recognised the youth as Jean Bertrand, an unpopular newcomer to the neighbourhood. Bernard also thought he recognised the howling dog as belonging to the English couple who had recently come to live in the rambling farmhouse on the edge of Laronne. He saw the youth throw some object in the direction of the terrified dog, but from such a long way off it was impossible to tell what it was, or whether or not it was deliberately aimed at the dog. Bernard had not seen Alan, nor did he see any of the scuffle that took place between the two men at the top of the cliff. As he walked past the actual spot where he found Alan's body three-quarters-of-an-hour later, he saw Emile Marceau up on the cliff, beyond where the youth had been standing. Emile was searching the undergrowth, as if intent on retrieving something he had lost. Bernard was sure Emile hadn't seen him; and from the positions that Jean and Emile were in when Bernard saw them both, he was fairly sure they could not have seen each other. Though of course he had no idea whether or not they had seen each other earlier. It was only when Bernard continued to walk along the lake that he heard the sound of falling rocks. But as his vision was masked by bushes and clumps of rock he thought nothing of it. Even when he retraced his steps half an hour later and stumbled across Alan's body, he did not connect the discovery of a dead man in the lake with the presence of the two other men some distance away on the cliff top.

Even if he had made any connection between these two facts, Bernard would probably not have told anyone in authority. It would have meant questioning; and questioning spelt hassle. As far as Bernard was concerned the Englishman was dead, so there was nothing one could do to reverse the tragedy.

Chapter Eleven

Emile Marceau was a shy retiring man, totally unsuited to teaching in a school. He often regretted not having chosen the post of University lecturer in some obscure provincial town, a haven of tranquillity in comparison to the hurly-burly of the schoolroom. His first teaching appointment was in the large, industrial town of Lille, near the Belgian border. The school was as large and turbulent as the town itself, but Emile stuck it out for nearly ten years, ever hopeful that a post in more peaceful country surroundings would become available, preferably in an area where he could indulge in his passion for geology. Then one day in early September he found himself almost solely in charge of the village school in Laronne. It was the biggest contrast he could ever have imagined. Relieved to be in a small school in an intimate and friendly environment, Emile settled down quickly into his new job and new routine.

Not so his wife, Anne-Marie. She was a pretty little blonde from Paris, not yet thirty, who had been married to Emile for almost three years. After the bright lights and the constant excitement of Paris, Anne-Marie had found life in the dour, northern town of Lille quite dreary enough. Now she was dreading the move to the country and tried her hardest to dissuade her husband from taking up his new post in Laronne. But Emile would let nothing, not even his wife, dissuade him and although to some extent he missed the excitement of city life and the stimulation and companionship of his fellow colleagues, he was quite sure the change had been for the best. His only help at the village school in Laronne was an elderly, semi-retired spinster, *Mademoiselle* Lafarge, who came in three mornings a week. But perhaps the biggest change of all was that there were only twenty-eight children in the entire school, with ages ranging from six to ten-and-a-half, all in the same classroom and all expecting his undivided attention for their very different needs.

With such a small number of pupils under his care, Emile soon sorted them out and became acquainted with their different talents and shortcomings. All were from the village and the surrounding hamlets so he quickly got to know their parents and the intricacies of their family backgrounds. He found most of the parents friendly and supportive. They attended parents' evenings and took part in the social and fund raising activities. They were also ready to help with extra reading in the classroom and willing to accompany small groups of children on field trips. The children were easy to handle. All country bred, they were lacking in sophistication but he found their warmth and ingenuousness very endearing. Unlike city children they were neither inquisitive nor competitive, nor were they class-conscious or snide. Fortunately, they needed to be neither vicious nor street-wise. Academically Emile found his charges to be of average ability, possessing probably the same intelligence as the urban *gamins* of Lille, but devoid of the same drive. Emile soon discovered one boy who stood out from all the rest. His name was Luc Roger, son of the farmer, Bernard Roger. Luc had both an enquiring mind and a retentive memory and Emile soon found he was devoting extra time to the boy, both in the classroom and often after school as well. The boy was now nearly eleven-years-old and in his last year at the village school. He was determined to do well and go on to the *lycée* and, hopefully, later to university.

Although bright, Luc lacked charm. He wasn't badly mannered, but he was inclined to be dour and taciturn. However, in the interests of fostering academic excellence as far as possible, Emile ignored the boy's personal shortcomings and concentrated on broadening his mind. What bothered Emile most in his relationship with this rather strange boy was the total lack of parental contact. It was exceptional in Laronne. Emile knew every other parent, calling most of them by their first names, but he had only ever seen Bernard Roger in the distance and had never set eyes on his wife, Denise.

On Wednesday 4 May, Emile took a group of school children on a nature outing. They had been studying glaciers, volcanoes and rock formations as a class topic, (his own favourite subject), so Emile decided he would pack the nine oldest, who were due to move on to their secondary school in the autumn, into the Mini-bus and take them up to the old quarry above Dracy. The children took a picnic lunch and they made a day of it, leaving the rest of the school in the care of *Mademoiselle* Lafarge and two parent volunteers.

The outing was a huge success, enjoyed both by Emile and all his young charges. It wasn't until they arrived back at the school in the late afternoon that one of the girls discovered she had left her anorak behind.

'I'm so sorry, *Monsieur*,' she apologised profusely. '*Maman* will be ever so angry. It was a new anorak, too.'

Emile's initial irritation was somewhat mollified by the little girl's contrition. 'All right. Don't worry. We'll get it back. What colour was it?'

'Red, *Monsieur*. Bright red. You can't miss it.'

'Where do you think you left it?'

'On the cliff, where we had our picnic.'

'OK. You tell *Maman* not to worry. I'll go back for it as soon as I can.'

'*Merci, Monsieur.*'

The little girl was most grateful and very relieved.

Having completely forgotten about the missing anorak, Emile worked late at the school that evening. He had fallen behind with his marking and as exams were looming, he realised he had to catch up. About ten minutes to seven he suddenly remembered the little girl's anorak. He was tempted to leave it where it was until the morning, but he realised he would need to make too early a start. So he hastily tidied away the exercise books, most of the marking thankfully completed, leapt into his car and drove as speedily as possible along the narrow winding road, which climbed steeply to the cliff top above the lake where they had picnicked earlier on. He parked his car carefully in a lay-by on the narrow road and walked slowly along the cliff top where he hoped to find his pupil's anorak. It was a beautiful evening, clear and still, and although the light was fading a little, it was still possible to see a long way. For a few moments Emile just stood on the cliff top admiring the stunning view and drinking in the beauty of the countryside.

Far down below he saw a male figure walking along by the side of the lake. He was too far away for Emile to recognise him with any certainty, but the ambling gait reminded him of someone he had often seen in the distance near Laronne. The man walked with careless abandon, carrying a long stick, which he poked into holes and jabbed at rocks. He was walking towards La Roche, in the opposite direction from which Emile had come. Thinking nothing of it, Emile continued to walk along the cliff top for a few minutes, in the same direction as the figure below. Finding no anorak, he came to the conclusion he had come too far and retraced his steps in the direction of Dracy. It never occurred to him that he wouldn't find it. He couldn't imagine anyone else would visit such an isolated spot, which he thought was only worth visiting for educational purposes. Walking in the opposite direction, he continued his search for the anorak. Here the ground dipped slightly and he could no longer see the lake or the figure walking down below. Suddenly he heard the frantic barking of a dog, a dog in fear or pain. Rounding a bend, he saw a figure in the distance raise his arm and throw something in the direction of the lake. Emile thought he heard the sound of a stone landing and then rolling down the steep slope. The dog resumed its frantic barking and then all was silent and still.

Finally Emile spied the anorak half hidden under a bush. It was bright red and brand-new, so there was no mistaking it. Picking it up, he walked away from the cliff top and the lakeside view, in the direction of the road. He wasn't sure exactly where he had left his car, but as it turned out, this time his judgement had been perfectly correct. He had overshot the picnic spot when he first arrived and had walked unnecessarily in the wrong direction.

It so happened, that as Alan Perry and Jean Bertrand were engaged in their scuffle at the top of the cliff, Emile

Marceau was starting up the engine of his car. So he heard nothing. He saw nothing either, because his car was parked just out of sight. At the exact moment that Alan Perry either lost his balance, or was perhaps deliberately pushed over the edge of the cliff by Jean Bertrand, Emile was cautiously turning his car round in order to begin his homeward journey. It wasn't until his car had slowly drawn level with the spot where the fatal accident had just happened, that Emile again saw the figure on top of the cliff. As with the lakeside walker, the person was much too far away to make any certain identification possible. Emile drove home carefully and thought no more about it.

When he heard the news of Alan's death later the next day, he deliberately dissociated it from anything he had seen the previous evening. After all, he had been unable to identify with certainty either of the figures he had seen, and he was positive they would have been unable to recognise him. Sorry though he was to learn that someone had met an untimely death, he felt no personal loss, for he had never met Alan Perry. No one knew Emile had been in the vicinity at that particular time, so he said nothing to anyone. When he returned the anorak to the little girl, he was careful to tell her that had gone to look for it immediately the children had gone home.

He did have his career to think of.

Chapter Twelve

Gerry was almost skint. It was inevitable. He hadn't done a day's work in the six weeks he had been in France. He badly needed a job, but the type of unskilled, casual labour, the only kind of work to which he was suited, didn't seem to be available. In the few weeks after his release from prison, it had been hard enough at first to find work in London. Employers would ask awkward questions and give him the weather eye. Ironically, it had helped his chances if he accentuated his Irishness. 'Just come across t' water on t' Mail Boat,' he would mumble, thickening his country brogue. Via seven years inside, he thought to himself. But the employer, realising he had another dumb Irish yokel on his hands, stopped asking difficult questions and stuck to the more practical ones about how much he could carry, how fast he could dig and how many hours a day he was prepared to work. Being tall, slim and lithe, Gerry gave the impression of being good value for money. He had earned a good few pounds back on the building sites in the short time he was under Westway with Kate. But working in France was a different proposition altogether.

To start with, there was the language problem. Gerry's knowledge of French only extended to the names of the better-known wines, especially those in the cheaper range. By now he was familiar with names such as *Côtes du Rhône, Muscadet de Sèvres et Maine*, and *Bourgogne Aligoté*. He also had a nodding acquaintance with such names as *Beaune, Pommard* and *Volnay*, wines from some of the world's greatest vineyards, which were within easy reach of Laronne. The longer he stayed in France, the more his alcoholic intake increased. So did his knowledge of French wines, but sadly, his grasp of the language did not. Having grown up in the country, in an area where job opportunities were almost nil and poverty and unemployment rife, Gerry could hardly be blamed for thinking these misfortunes were purely rural phenomena. It seemed to him that people only had to travel to a large town or city to find a bewildering choice of available employment, from an executive director at the top, through blue-collar workers and train drivers, to the road sweepers and navvies at the bottom of the heap. Apparently farmers no longer needed shepherds, cowherds or a helping hand with the harvest. By contrast, it seemed that city jobs for waiters, barmen, bus conductors, lavatory attendants and construction workers were crying out to be filled. Since he had been in France, Gerry had heard mention of *le vendange*. This is the annual wine harvest, when the vineyard owners all over France take on vast numbers of casual workers, mainly students and migrants from North Africa, to help with the grape picking. Gerry had heard it was exhausting, back-breaking work, but he knew he was well up to it; the money was good and best of all, even during working hours the wine flowed liberally into the workers' glasses. The exact time of *le vendange* varied a little from vineyard to vineyard, depending on how much rain and sun there had been in the few weeks beforehand, but no grape picking started much before the middle of September at the very earliest. Now it was barely July. He couldn't afford to wait that long.

There were also other factors in the equation. One of them was Jo. Gerry knew he wasn't in love with Jo. He was still struggling to understand love, trying to work out that although it was certainly connected with sex, it wasn't in fact, just sex itself. Gerry's harsh childhood and bleak prison experience hadn't helped to nurture any strong feelings of compassion, loyalty and affection. But he knew they existed and his soul yearned for them. It was just a question of how and where to find them. He had never met anyone like Jo before. The person who had most resembled her was his English teacher, whom he had known only briefly when he had attended a Comprehensive School for a while in London. She was called Mrs Myles and must have been about the age Jo was now. She too, was slim and pretty, with corn-coloured hair and violet blue eyes. When she read them poetry each week, Gerry would lie on his desk, his chin cupped in his hands and gaze at her. The longer her reading continued and the more he gazed at her, the happier he felt. She gave him a strange sense of warmth, peace and security. Sometimes, much to his embarrassment, he would have an erection, particularly if he were to stand close to her. He would weave fantasies about her; fantasies he knew could never materialise. Not only was she twice his age and married, but she was middle class and educated. Like Jo.

He had realised, even from the beginning, that there was absolutely no future in his relationship with Jo. They were poles apart and worst of all, he had constantly lied to her. To crown his catalogue of disasters he had spent the last seven years in prison for murdering his mother. He knew he hadn't deliberately intended to kill her; it had been an appalling accident, but that hadn't change the verdict. The jury had found him guilty and the judge had sentenced him to fourteen years in prison. He was released after seven years with remission for good conduct, but there was no denying it: he now had a criminal record.

There was also a distinct possibility that he might have to face a second murder charge. There was something about Bert's appearance as he lay still and silent on the floor of Kate's caravan, that reminded him ominously of his mother as she had lain on the kitchen floor of their shabby dark council flat behind Kings Cross Station. The comparison was inevitable: the eerie stillness after the violence and the rage: the inert body on the floor. In his heart of hearts Gerry knew Bert was dead, killed by the knife wound that he, himself, had inflicted. He knew that if caught he would be found guilty of murder; whatever mitigating circumstances the defence might offer. And there would only be one sentence: life imprisonment. He was out on licence after the first murder. This was his second capital offence.

And what of Kate? Kate, the slim, olive-skinned, beautiful gipsy girl with black eyes like two dark deep pools of water. What had happened to Kate, when she ran out of her caravan, almost naked and dripping with blood from the gash her vicious boyfriend had deliberately inflicted on her? Had she run off, so traumatised by terror that she had never returned? Had she sought refuge with some of the other gipsies, even though they had shunned her for five years? Or had she remained hidden somewhere on the campsite, returning later in the day to find Bert dead on the floor among the wreckage of her little home.

Since his arrival in France and the days turned into weeks, Gerry began to imagine he was in love with Kate. Subconsciously he felt a bond between them; a bond of shared deprivation. They had both come from poor backgrounds: they had both suffered in childhood. By contrast, Gerry was sure Jo had spent a happy childhood. It was more than apparent that she came from a well-educated, middle-class background. He could imagine how she had grown up in a substantial, five bed-roomed house in the stockbroker belt of Surrey. 'A half-timbered, mock-Tudor pile, standing in its own grounds,' as the estate agent's phrase goes; surrounded by well-manicured lawns, the curving drive dominated by a vast cedar tree and a row of quick-growing evergreens blotting out the neighbours at the end of the large garden. Her father would have been a stockbroker, a banker, or perhaps a solicitor. She probably had several brothers and sisters, who all went to the best boarding schools. Of course there would have been pets in their home, rabbits, guinea pigs, several dogs, perhaps even a pony.

Funny, mused Gerry, how Jo had never spoken at all about her own childhood, keen though she was to know all about his. Maybe she sensed the great difference between them, the chasm that divided them. Maybe she felt the chasm was so great there was no point in trying to build a bridge across it. That to attempt a bridge would divide them even further. Then she had plenty of problems. The tragic, premature death of her husband in circumstances still not fully explained was a trauma from which recovery would be extremely slow and painful. Gerry admired her courage. The police were slow in coming up with any positive information as to whether Alan's death was a genuine accident or whether there had been foul play. Although Jo constantly extolled her neighbours' warmth and kindness, Gerry felt one of them must be hiding something, otherwise the question would surely have been resolved by now. Jo also had a hard time running the rambling farmhouse for the benefit of her English paying guests, in whom her sole interest was financial. All this was compounded by her scant knowledge of French, her sense of loneliness and isolation and her overwhelming desire to sell her French millstone and return, as soon as possible, to live in England. In fact, mused Gerry, rationalising his thoughts far more clearly than was usual for him, the one thing the three of us appear to have in common, Kate, Jo and I, is loneliness and isolation. None of us seem to belong where we are.

Gerry counted his money again. 400 French francs. About £50. His car was worth about fifty pounds; the dilapidated caravan was hardly worth anything at all. Total sum of his worldly goods: one hundred pounds. But it was pointless to consider selling either the car or the caravan. If he were to sell the car, not only would he be without transport in an area where everyone was totally dependent on the motorcar, but he would have a greatly reduced chance of returning to England. If he sold the caravan, not only would he be homeless but he would compound Jo's problems as well.

He knew he couldn't afford to stay in France without a job, but there didn't seem any prospect of finding one. From the financial standpoint he should definitely return to England as soon as possible, but if he did he would, in all probability, be arrested for Bert's murder. As far as he knew there might be a warrant out for his arrest at this very moment. Perhaps Interpol had already been alerted? After all, he hadn't read a newspaper or seen any television since his arrival in France six weeks ago. He hadn't been to any large towns either. He had stayed around Jo's farmhouse, visiting the shops in the neighbouring villages and making the occasional foray to the *Géant Casino,* a huge supermarket, like a giant shed or aeroplane hangar, on the edge of Chalon sur-Saône. It was under-patronised and poorly patrolled. On his first outing, Gerry donned a thick coat with capacious pockets, into which he could stuff half a dozen bottles of wine at a time. Then he made some cheap and innocent purchases for which he paid, made for the exit and unloaded his booty into his car in the enormous, almost deserted car park. The first operation went so smoothly that he returned several times, careful to use a different checkout on each visit.

Jo wondered where Gerry's money was coming from. He was generous in supplying the tasty little luxuries they both enjoyed so much, and he was particularly good at keeping the wine flowing. He paid no rent, and although they were both living in his caravan, Gerry felt he owed Jo something.

'Your cash never seems to dry up,' Jo remarked admiringly one evening.

'No. My Dad keeps me well supplied. He's ever so good.'

'So he knows where you are?

'Oh, yes. We keep in touch. I write home every week.'

Jo had never seen Gerry write a letter, but she said nothing. She thought it odd, too, that a grown man of twenty-seven should write a letter home every week.

It was the sort of thing that was expected and required of all the girls at her boarding school. But since she had left school she no longer wrote a regular weekly letter to her parents. The telephone was so much easier and more direct.

It was a hot day; one of the hottest since Gerry had been in France. It was Monday, a day when Jo was still busy with her punters: answering their queries, making sure they knew the house rules regarding the showers and the swimming pool, retrieving missing towels and cooking utensils which had ended up in the wrong apartment, giving advice on where to shop and where to eat out. A weekly pattern had evolved in the lives of Jo and Gerry, thrown together as they had been, so unexpectedly. On Saturdays, change-over day, Gerry would help Jo with the cleaning, washing, tidying and sorting out, urging the departing guests to leave as speedily as possible so they could concentrate on their labours with the least interruption. Usually, around about five or six o'clock in the evening, the new consignment of eight guests would arrive to take up a week's residence in the four available apartments, bringing with them a barrage of new demands and a host of new problems. Jo and Gerry heaved a great sigh of relief at the departure of the previous guests. It didn't seem possible that the newcomers could be anything like as difficult or unpleasant, but occasionally that would indeed be the case. Last week's nightmare would be succeeded by an even greater one, such as the Brocklebanks. By ten o'clock on Saturday evening they were both completely exhausted, so Sunday, by general consensus, was a day of rest. Jo put it to the punters, in no uncertain terms, that their problems and enquiries would have to wait till Monday.

Having pulled his weight on Saturday by helping with the chores, Gerry had no qualms in spending Sunday soothing his aching limbs with a large consumption of alcohol. He would start soon after breakfast, so by lunchtime he was fairly well oiled. The right amount of alcohol usually heightened Gerry's sexual desire and Jo had learnt to expect his amorous advances during the morning. By the time they had finished lunch, Gerry was generally too incapable of doing anything but sleep. If the weather was warm Jo would potter round the caravan wearing her bikini, 'to top up my tan,' as she put in, but in reality to stimulate Gerry's sexual appetite while the going was good. The beds had been tidied away after breakfast, a routine that reminded Gerry of his time with Kate, but Jo always spread a rug on the grass in front of the caravan. It was a totally private area, as the vast barn gave them complete protection from the prying eyes of the punters, relaxing on their different patios, recovering from their journey. It also protected them from any casual visitors who might be imprudent enough to pay a Sunday visit. A large hedge in front of the caravan protected them from the languid, bovine stares of the Charolais cows.

Gerry felt no compunction in having Monday to himself. All the important pleasures and duties had been executed; now was the time for a little roving freedom, which would include a hefty bout of shoplifting. Monday was the optimum day. Calling 'goodbye' to Jo, he shot off down the drive in his battered two-tone Mini. It was about half an hour's drive to Chalon-sur-Saône. Although the route led towards the motorway, it was practically deserted and on that sunny Monday morning Gerry didn't pass more than a dozen cars. The car park at the *Géant Casino* on the edge of the town was equally deserted. Gerry parked his car, donned his bulky jacket with the capacious pockets, pulled out a trolley from the long row of empties and sauntered into the vast *hypermarché* in high hopes of a good morning's loot. He had all morning and the *hypermarché* was completely deserted. Deciding to start with his illegal purchases, he guided his trolley slowly to the far end of the store, housing the wines and spirits. Although now a regular visitor to the *Géant Casino,* Gerry never ceased to marvel at the vast range on display, quite the largest quantity of alcohol he had ever seen in one place. He moved at an imperceptible speed along the serried ranks of different bottles, all carefully arranged; whites, rosés, reds, each in their own sections; the Burgundies and the Bordeaux carefully separated; the non-French wines at the far end of the store. Gerry was feeling expansive. The sex on Sunday had been particularly good and he had slept off his hangover. He was heady, too, with the success of previous shoplifting expeditions. He took a bottle of *Chassagne-Montrachet*, at 189 francs, off the shelf and secreted it in one of the pockets of his capacious overcoat. Pricey, he thought, but it's not as if I'm paying for it. Even if I were, Jo deserves a treat. She's gone through a lot recently. She works hard, not only cleaning up after her punters, but after me as well. He had twinges of guilt when he watched her clean out his caravan and return his clothes, freshly laundered. Gerry patted the pocket of his bulky overcoat containing the bottle of *Chassagne-Montrachet*. Having secreted his first illegal acquisition of the day, he pushed his still empty supermarket trolley slowly along the well-ordered rows of bottles, gleaming on the shelves. What should he go for next? He couldn't go in for quantity, as his pockets only held six bottles with safety, so he may as well go for quality. Should he make it three white and three red? He decided he would, so he selected a bottle of *Sancerre* and one of *Pouilly Fuissé*. He took his time over the reds and decided to go for *Premier Cru*. He carefully pocketed a *Pommard*, a *Volnay* and a *Nuits St Georges* and, happy that his wine selection was settled, decided it was time to turn his attention to some genuine purchases. After all, he would certainly arouse suspicion if he left the supermarket with an empty trolley, wearing a bulky overcoat. On his last visit he had noticed a security guard patrolling the store, but this time he hadn't noticed that a young couple was watching him. Finding himself in the toiletries' aisle, he wondered if the stocks of soap and toothpaste were getting low. He decided they probably were, so he took a large tube of Aquafresh toothpaste off the shelf, followed by a packet of Lux soap. Interesting how so many brands are the same here, he thought, picking four rolls of Andrex lavatory paper off the top shelf. The couple he had noticed following him earlier, were now engrossed in inspecting the vast selection of shampoos at the far end of the aisle.

Gerry made his way slowly past the butter, spreads and yoghurts, to the meat section, planning to buy some tasty morsel, which he and Jo could barbeque. Some chicken pieces, scallops, weren't they called? might be quite succulent. Or perhaps something on a skewer would be more exotic. He selected the meat for the barbeque. After a lot of deliberation he went for turkey kebabs. Then he picked up a large lettuce, still dripping with moisture, a cucumber, some tomatoes, salad onions and two nectarines, glowing red and orange. He strolled past the cheese counter, sorely tempted. But he hadn't really got the hang of the names of French cheeses. There were too many of them, so he thought he would leave the cheese selection to Jo. It was more her domain.

Deciding he had now spent enough money, he pushed his trolley towards the checkout. The store appeared deserted and only two cash desks were operating. Happily there was no sign of any security guard, and the young couple that had been watching him earlier, had now disappeared among the frozen foods. Gerry lifted his genuine purchases carefully out of the trolley, his heart thumping a little louder and faster than usual. It would be too bad if the checkout girl were to suspect anything and enquire as to why he was wearing such a thick coat on a warm day. He probably wouldn't have understood her question, posed as it would have been in rapid staccato French, but he certainly would have understood any sign language indicating that he should remove it. And he would have no option but to comply with her request. The other danger was that if he were to make any sudden gesture, two bottles might accidentally touch each other, making a clinking sound. So he lifted out his purchases slowly and carefully. The consequences if he were caught stealing would be most unpleasant. At the very least he would be taken to the police station; and who knows what information they might have on him there.

Having paid for his rightful and legal items, Gerry pushed his trolley through the exit and walked out into the car park in the bright sunshine. Unaware how ridiculous he looked wearing a heavy coat on such a hot day; he was also unaware that he was being followed by the couple who had spotted him shop-lifting earlier on, as they pushed their heavily laden trolley towards his Mini van.

Chapter Thirteen

Jo waved goodbye to Gerry as he drove down the rutted bumpy drive in his battered old Mini, the two-tone paintwork looking more garish and tawdry than ever in the bright morning sunshine. Although it was only just after nine-thirty, the day promised to be a scorcher. Jo wondered why Gerry had flung a coat into the back of his van. Did he think it was going to rain? Or did he feel the cold in the vast space of the *Géant Casino?* On many occasions she had felt quite chilly herself in the freezer section, thinly clad on a very hot day, as she plunged her arm into a cabinet to extract what she imagined should be the freshest packet of food from the bottom of the pile. Jo was grateful to Gerry for offering to do the shopping. Though goodness knows, if she really thought about it, the debt was surely on his side. She not only took care of Gerry's washing and ironing but she also seemed to be the one who did all the cleaning in the caravan as well. Toiling and sweating, as she tried to remove grease from the cooker deposited over many years by at least one previous owner, she would glance out of the window onto the small private patio she had created in front of the caravan, to see Gerry nonchalantly stretched out in the sun, the inevitable glass of wine in his hand. Then Jo would think back to her life with Alan, about how helpful and caring he had been and how they had always shared the household chores together, particularly since their arrival in Laronne.

Alan. Jo felt a constriction in her throat and a prickling sensation behind her eyes. No. She mustn't cry. She mustn't give way to grief. It was a luxury she couldn't afford. Not only would it be the height of self-indulgence, but she might find that once she had started she wouldn't be able to stop. She went back into the shabby little caravan and put on the kettle hoping a cup of coffee would have a calming effect. How should she spend the day? She had no idea when Gerry would be back. He hadn't even said where he was going. Last week he had gone to Macon on the spur of the moment and hadn't returned until the early evening. But after all, he was free to go exactly where and when he wished. It was no business of hers to enquire where he was going and when he would be back. She must just be grateful that he did some of the shopping when he did go off. He nearly always returned with some tasty little delicacies and several bottles of wine, often of rather good quality. At first she found this rather strange. She had wondered where his money was coming from and was surprised to learn that his father kept him regularly supplied. Somehow Gerry's life-style didn't quite add up: the grubby, tatty little caravan and the battered old Mini contrasted oddly with the seemingly endless amount of cash, much of which he spent on luxury food and fine wine. The oddest thing of all was that Jo never found any letters for Gerry when she went to collect her own from the letter box at the end of the drive. Perhaps he received his mail *poste restante* at the post office in Dracy? But she had never seen him read a letter either, nor had she ever seen a letter addressed to him lying around in the caravan.

As the kettle came to the boil she switched it off quickly so the tiny place wouldn't steam up. The catch on the window behind the cooker was broken, which meant the window could only be opened with great difficulty. Gerry had tried to repair it without success, so they had both decided in the end that it was easier to leave the window closed permanently. Jo put a generous spoonful of Nescafé into a mug, stirred it briskly, added a little milk from the carton in the fridge and put the mug carefully on a placemat on the caravan table. As the tabletop was chipped and badly stained, the placemat was totally unnecessary. Gerry had laughed at her the first time she had used a mat.

'What do you want to use that thing for? The table's in a right mess. Nothing can save it now.'

'True,' Jo had replied. 'I suppose it's just habit,' saving herself just in time from saying that she had been used to protecting better tables in less scruffy surroundings.

Jo took a sip of coffee, almost burning her mouth. As before, she put the mug down carefully on the placemat and stared out of the caravan window at the endless expanse of rolling green fields. It was almost like a Constable painting; the homogeneous line broken only by the odd tree with a small herd of white cows gently grazing, barely moving, as if afraid that any unnecessary movement would spoil the languid tranquillity.

How Alan had loved it! Jo remembered the first winter in London after they had bought the farmhouse in Laronne. They would sit on either side of the living gas fire in their cosy living room in Lavender Garden and discuss their renovation plans. Alan had been so excited.

'Such a well-worth way of spending my godmother's inheritance,' he had said more than once. 'We're going to have marvellous summers there, darling. It's so quiet and peaceful. No distractions. We'll be able to get on with all those things we always promised ourselves we would do.'

'Such as?'

'Oh, you know: writing, painting, gardening. We might try planting some vines. After all, we're right in the middle of one of the greatest wine growing areas in the world. It would be splendid to have our own little vineyard, wouldn't it?'

Jo had laughed at his enthusiasm, little knowing in those very early days how it would all turn out in the end.

Alan had drawn up plans to scale of the main house, the outbuildings, the courtyard and the surrounding land. He wrote copious lists of things to do: essential repairs which shouldn't wait; less urgent renovations which could be done later; materials to be purchased in France, extra furniture they would need, much of which could be bought more cheaply in London. His enthusiasm was infectious. Hours sped by during the cold, wet winter as they discussed plans for their French summer retreat. But no suggestion was ever made during those early eager discussions that they should go and live in Laronne permanently. Jo took another sip of her coffee, cooler now, fragrant and soothing. She wondered how would she have reacted if Alan had suggested right from the beginning that they move to Laronne permanently. She would have been appalled, resisted such an idea with all the force she could muster in the face of Alan's always smooth and logical arguments.

'But we'll be much happier living in France,' he had assured her, more than two years later. 'The weather's warmer, the food's better and the wine's cheaper. There's no hassle in the country; no buses or trains to catch which might arrive late; less cars on the roads; clean air, clear skies and all that glorious, endless space in which to go for walks. The country is so safe: no muggers, no burglars. We'll be able to go out and leave the doors and windows open. Just imagine: we'll sit on the terrace in the evening, sipping our chilled white wine, watching the sun go down over an unrestricted view of the vineyards.'

Alan might have been a very good writer, mused Jo. His descriptions of places transcended reality. He had that extra power of imagination, which made the totally impracticable, seem a possibility. He had built up such a glowing picture of living in France that Jo had started to believe in it herself. It wasn't that Alan had deceived her or lied to her. He hadn't deliberately deceived himself either. He had just got carried away by his own optimism and enthusiasm. Once they were actually living in France he had stopped seeing the drawbacks; he was only able to see the glowing picture he had created.

But now, looking back, Jo wondered if she had ever really believed in Alan's imaginary picture of an idyllic life in Laronne. Had she ever thought hard enough about whether she could give up their London life? She was a city girl, born and bred in North London; brought up in a narrow, early Victorian terraced house, larger and slightly more substantial than the house she and Alan had bought in Clapham. Her father, now retired, had been a GP and shared a surgery in the semi-basement of the house with two other doctors. Jo had spent a lonely childhood. A younger sister had died of meningitis at the age of five. Her mother, utterly distraught, had had a severe nervous breakdown, followed later by a hysterectomy. Her parents were both older than most average parents and although they had lavished every material need on their only daughter, they had remained aloof and rather detached.

Jo had spent an unremarkable adolescence at a conventional boarding school in the Home Counties. School holidays were spent quietly in London visiting the zoo and other suitable places of interest, with occasional visits to the ballet and the theatre. The highlight of the holidays were visits to school friends, who all seemed to live in substantial detached houses, well-protected by elegant rows of cedars, in the stock-broker belt of the Home Counties. These households were teeming with children, cousins, friends, animals and seemingly endless rounds of entertainments and excursions. Jo loved the visits, and although enormously enjoying the company of her school friends, she always felt a little apprehensive about the return visits to her own home. Neither of her parents had any brothers or sisters, so Jo had no cousins. As she grew up she became painfully conscious of the lack of vitality or any real warmth in her elderly parents' rather bleak, well-ordered household.

On leaving school, Jo read English at a northern provincial university. Over-protected by both home and school environments, she was shy and lacking in self-confidence. Until she went up to university she had met few young men of her own age and she felt ill equipped to deal with their advances. At eighteen, slim, petite and pretty with wavy corn-coloured hair and deep violet blue eyes, Jo was surprised to find herself suddenly the centre of male attraction. Young undergraduates buzzed round her like bees round a honey pot. There were invitations to the cinema, theatre, dinners, parties and weekends in the country. At first she was at a loss as to how to cope with her new, hitherto unimagined popularity. But it didn't take long for her to become accustomed to a completely new life.

Oh, those halcyon university days! So full of fun, laughter and no responsibility whatsoever. Jo just managed to attend most of the lectures and hand in her essays, some hastily scribbled late at night, after she had returned, not completely sober, from yet another wild party. And then there was the great joy and excitement of discovering sex. Thinking back over her university days Jo wondered, as she rinsed out her coffee mug in the remains of the water left over in the kettle, whether perhaps sexual awareness and enjoyment didn't create greater problems than they solved. Sex was, of course, hugely enjoyable and totally necessary for procreation - it did literally make the world go round - but so far it seemed to be her experience that the best lovers didn't necessarily make the best companions. One case in point had been her erstwhile fiancé, Simon Lockheed. Tall, dark and extremely good-looking, they had met at university in Jo's second year. Simon was a medical student, from a privileged, wealthy background and had far more money to spend than most of his fellow students. He was enthusiastic, generous and reckless, with the means to indulge in all his whims and passions. They went para gliding, bungee jumping and ballooning. They dined frequently in the best restaurants and flew to London, Paris and Rome for weekends. Simon lavished gifts on Jo: clothes, perfume and jewellery. They visited each other's parents, staying the weekend. Jo was suitably impressed by the grandeur and opulence of Simon's home; he was touched by the simplicity and genuineness of hers. Their engagement was announced in *The Times*, but as they were both considered too young to leap into matrimony so soon, no date was set for the wedding. Simon passed the first part of his medical degree with flying colours, but having developed a strong social conscience while at university, he decided to take a year out and go to Zaire to help with the vast medical and humanitarian problems. Both families applauded Simon's decision. It was considered that the inevitable hardships would be character forming and the enforced absence from Jo would only serve to strengthen their relationship.

Jo was unhappy but resigned to their parting. Simon was everything to her. They had been constantly together for over two years and she couldn't contemplate life without him. Nevertheless, she felt confident that after a year he would return to her, they would marry, settle down and have lots of children. For two months Simon wrote long passionate letters, saying how much he loved her and how much he missed her. Then there was silence for four months. Jo telephoned his parents just to make sure that nothing unfortunate had happened. No, Simon was very well, working hard and enjoying life helping at a refugee camp. Then the bombshell fell. Almost six months to the day after his departure Jo received the following letter:

'*My dear Jo,*

I am sorry not to have written recently. I have been completely swept away by my new life in Zaire. There is so much to do here, so much that is needed that I no longer feel any strong affinity with my life in England, nor have I any desire to return permanently. I hope you will try to understand and not take my decision too personally. You are a most wonderful person, for whom I shall always have the deepest love and affection, but you cannot be part of my new life. I am engaged to a Church of England missionary called Alison and we are to be married next month. Please do not think ill of me. I shall always treasure the memories of our wonderful times together.

Your ever-loving friend, Simon.'

Two years later Jo met Alan at a party. She had spent the intervening time trying to avoid being involved with what she described to herself as 'the wrong sort of men'. At the time she hadn't clearly defined her own phrase. How could Simon have been 'the wrong sort of man?' He was intelligent, wealthy, caring and would certainly make an excellent doctor. Now, almost ten years later, Jo was beginning at last to understand her own definition. 'The wrong sort of man' had nothing to do with wealth, intelligence, good background and sexual excitement. All these things were important, but what Jo was slowly beginning to discover was that the man who was right for her should above all be loyal, dependable and a rock of security. Thinking back to her whirlwind romance with Simon, Jo felt she understood for the first time how a permanent relationship couldn't have worked. Simon had been too impulsive, too stimulating, too impetuous. Like Gerry. His personality had little to do with his background. She had needed someone like Alan, calm and dependable. Sadly, impetuous men appeared to be sexually more stimulating than the dependable ones.

Jo felt it was time to stop musing and brooding over the past. Simon had married Alison the missionary, whom Jo always imagined to be plain, freckled, with thick glasses and buckteeth. Alan was dead. Jo was sharing a caravan with Gerry, who, for all his stories, still remained an unknown quantity. His charm, vivaciousness and recklessness often reminded her of Simon, and he was an equally exciting lover. How long the relationship would continue was anyone's guess. Of one thing Jo was absolutely sure: Gerry may have replaced Alan in her bed, but he would never replace Alan in her heart.

Jo looked at her watch. It was almost midday. The mail would have arrived. A walk down the drive would do her good and help to fill in half an hour before lunch. She closed the caravan door but didn't bother to lock it; there was nothing worth stealing. She whistled for Maxwell who came bounding along from his basket in the barn and started tearing down the drive, hoping for a long walk.

Jo followed slowly, still in a deeply thoughtful mood. An idea was forming in her mind; an idea she wasn't quite sure she would have the courage to put into practice. Should she drive up to the old quarry and see for herself the spot where Alan had met his death? Would it add to her distress if she went, or would it ease her mind? Would it help her to put pressure on the police to come up with some solution, or would it merely make things worse? After all, she had no idea if the police had made any progress or even whether they were making an effort. Since Alan's death Jo felt she had been incapable of making any real decisions. She had just been carried along on the tide of events like a piece of flotsam. She would surely feel stronger and more positive if she were to take some definite action.

She reached the end of the drive where the post box was nailed to a tree by the gate, always left open. She groped for the key in the pocket of her shorts and opened the box. Oh, good! There was a letter for her in vaguely familiar handwriting. She sat down on a tree stump and slit the letter open with the key.

'Dear Jo,

I have been thinking of you a great deal and feel this letter is rather overdue. I am very anxious about your living in France all on your own and I think it's high time I paid you a visit. Life has been extremely hectic in the last two months. I have had to work late most evenings and am now overdue for a holiday. I have decided to take next week off and, hopefully, come and visit you in Burgundy. I am planning to come by train, on the TGV, which I seem to remember stops at Le Creusot, not very far from you. If you are unable to meet me I am sure I will be able to get a taxi from the station.

'The other reason for my visit is that I have an increasingly strong desire to visit the quarry and see the actual place where Dad died. It may sound ghoulish but I think it would help me to come to terms with it all. You have no doubt been up there already and if you don't want to go again I shall quite understand. I'm sure I can find a way of getting there on my own. Perhaps you would be willing to lend me your car?

'I hope you like the idea of my visit? When you've got my letter maybe you could give me a call at work? The number is: 0171 226 0428. I never seem to be at home these days.

'Looking forward to seeing you.
Love from Petra.'

Petra! Petra wanted to come and visit her next week! Alan's daughter was coming to see her, but most of all she wanted to visit the place that had claimed her father's life. Jo felt for the first time since Alan's death that she had been forced to make a decision. Before Petra arrived next week she would go on her own to visit the old quarry and see the exact place where Alan had died. She whistled for Maxwell and started walking briskly back to the farmhouse to make the telephone call to Petra.

Chapter Fourteen

'That's it, Sophie! Higher! Higher! Remember you're a Druid!'

Poor Sophie's arms ached from carrying the heavy wooden banner aloft.

'I can't,' she wailed.

'OK, then. Put it down.'

Sophie let the banner fall to ground with a thud and stood with her arms akimbo waiting for her next line. Chantal, her concentration broken, looked around nervously and spoke the first words that came into her head.

'No, Chantal. You're much too early. You're a page too soon.'

'Prompter! Prompter! Who is the prompter? Henri? I thought Jean-Marc did it yesterday?

'Where's Jean-Marc?'

'He's seeing to the lights, Pierre. He's the only one around here who knows anything about electricity.'

'But we must have the same prompter each time, otherwise there's no continuity.'

'But there won't be any continuity once the villagers join in, will there?'

'The whole point is that we should be word perfect and know all our stage moves inside-out before we ask the villagers to join us.'

'When will that be?'

'End of July at the latest. The pageant is billed for 15 August.'

'The Day of the Assumption?'

'Exactly.'

'Whose idea was that? Yours, Pierre?'

'No,' said Pierre. 'That was the date given to me at *la Mairie*.'

'By the Mayor? Didier Pérnot himself?'

'No, no. Just by the clerk in the office.'

'The little girl?'

'Yes.'

'She knows nothing.'

'Rubbish! She runs the place.'

'You really think so?'

'Certainly. There's never anyone else at *la Mairie*. She runs the show on her own.'

'But surely the Mayor sanctions her instructions?'

'I'd've thought so.'

'Any there any notices up?'

'What about?'

'The date for the pageant, of course.'

'So soon?'

'It's not a bit too soon. It's mid-July. We've got just over two weeks to rehearse all our parts before we ask the villagers to come along and join us.'

'Are all the costumes ready?'

'A lot are. But we're not sure exactly how many we're going to need. That depends on how many villagers will want to act.'

'Oh, everyone will want to join in. They'll all want to be part of it. They always have wherever I've done this sort of thing.'

'Joining in isn't quite the same thing as acting. Lots of people are quite happy to sell programmes or help behind the scenes, rather than actually going on the stage. They prefer it. There's less exposure.'

'Even so, we must be prepared to supply them with enough costumes.'

'I'd go for Druids. Lots of Druids. Can't have too many.'

'Say they don't want to be Druids?'

'Tough. You're not going to give them a choice are you?'

'Well, it is their village, so it's really their pageant.'

'Rubbish. It's our pageant. We're organising it for them.'

'OK. So it's for them, but we're doing the organising. And they've still got to be told what to do. They've never put on a pageant before. That's our job. We're the experts. They've got to listen to us.'

'OK. OK.'

'We're not forcing them, for God's sake. We're just giving them the choice between being Druids or working behind the scenes organising the props.'

'Or doing front-of-house selling programmes and showing people to their seats.'

'Exactly. Let's concentrate on making plenty of Druid costumes. They're much the easiest kind to make. Just a sheet sewn up...'

'... Or even draped round.'

'What about a mask? They'll need a mask.'

'They can supply their own. They'll have to take some initiative themselves.'

'So it's settled, then. We'll run up a load of Druid costumes and let them choose between being Druids or programme sellers.

'Exactly. And find out if there's any publicity about the final date. Any volunteers?'

'Yes,' said Victor. ' I'll do it.'

'Great. Thanks Victor. How many pageants have you done?'

'At least five or six.'

'Do people always argue about it?'

'Oh, yes. I've done pageants where people have argued all the time. I've even known fights break out.'

'How awful!'

Victor and Kate went to check on the date chosen for the pageant with the girl in *la Mairie*.

'It's all arranged for 15 August,' said the girl. 'How are the rehearsals going? All going well?'

'Oh, yes,' said Victor lightly, not wanting to give too much away. 'Everything's under control.'

Victor followed Kate out into the bright sunshine, closing the door of *la Mairie* quietly behind him. They crossed the village square to the other side to where he had parked his car outside the bakery. The door of *La Boulangérie Gautier* stood wide open. Although it appeared dark inside, Victor could just make out the plump, *petite* form of Colette, hands on her hips, holding forth at length to one of her customers. Victor smiled to himself. Kate hadn't yet met Colette Gautier, the baker's wife. He had found it quite an unusual experience, a treat in fact, to meet Colette for the first time. She talked non-stop, very fast and she usually had startling information to disclose. Assuming they were returning to *Les Projets* for lunch, Kate already had her hand on the handle of the passenger car door. For some reason she was feeling a little poorly, queasy might be a better description. She felt tired and had an over-whelming desire to lie down. She thought longingly of her cool, sparsely furnished bedroom back at *Les Projets Créatifs*. When Victor had first shown her the room on the night of her arrival she had gasped with delight.

'Oh, Victor! It's beautiful. It's the loveliest bedroom I've ever seen!'

'Reminds you of home, does it?'

'Oh, no! Oh, yes!' Kate felt a bit confused. She hadn't told Victor, or anyone at *Les Projets*, that her home had been in a caravan on a gipsy encampment under Westway. She thought it would be better to keep quiet about her origins. You never know. People had funny ideas about gipsies. They didn't trust them. It would be a pity to throw away her new temporary lodging through careless unnecessary talk.

'It's nothing fancy,' Victor had said. 'Just the basic essentials. There isn't much cash to spare in this place for anything very luxurious. But it'll do on a temporary basis.'

'Oh, yes.' Kate didn't want to sound too enthusiastic. 'I know it's only temporary. I don't like too much fancy stuff anyway.'

'That's just as well,' was Victor's dry reply.

Kate waited for Victor to unlock the car.

Just a minute,' he said. 'We're going to pop into the bakery to buy some *baguettes* for lunch. Come in and meet Colette. She's quite special. She knows all the local gossip.'

Kate smiled faintly and followed Victor into the shop. Somehow she didn't want to tell him she was feeling unwell. He had been extremely kind. She didn't want to burden him with her problems. It was cool inside the bakery. Kate looked with interest at all the long loaves, in shallow wooden bins, each with a bar across, lining two walls of the shop. The loaves were all graded in size. First there was a bin containing very thin loaves, the thinnest bread Kate had ever seen, called *ficelles*. In the next bin came a slightly thicker variety, which Kate recognised correctly as *baguettes*, the staple diet of many French people. In the bin next to the *baguettes* were the *batards*, a broader, thicker loaf that kept longer. In the next bin were round loaves of different sizes, many covered with a thick coating of flour. These were *pains de campagne*, country loaves, but even when fresh they didn't have quite the same appeal as the *baguette*, with it's crispy crust and light soft centre. There were two large glass cases in front of the counter. In the first one were displayed all kinds of different specialist pastries: large, crab-shaped *croissants*, darkly golden and flaky on top; light, puffy *pains au chocolat*, the chocolate oozing darkly from the centre; *pains aux raisins*, round and flat, dotted with raisins and a rich yellow cream. There were snow white *meringues* copiously filled with whipped cream; chocolate *éclairs*, shiny and gleaming; and *palmiers*, large flat biscuits shaped like two ears joined together, liberally sprinkled with sugar and crispy to the touch.

The second case was devoted entirely to fruit tarts. They came in all sizes: small tarts for one person, medium-sized tarts for four or six people, depending on one's appetite, and extra large tarts for a family or a party. They were filled with a wide variety of fruit: pale golden slices of apple, arranged symmetrically, like a series of sickle moons; plump orange apricots; sliced strawberries, bright red; whole raspberries and cherries, small but succulent. Each tart was in a scalloped pastry case, round, perfectly even and mouth-wateringly appetising.

Victor shook hands with Colette.

'*Bonjour, Colette. J'espère que vous allez bien?*

'*Bonjour, Victoire. Oui, merci. Je vais très bien ; et vous-même ?*'

Victor introduced Kate, who shook hands with Colette. Kate had quickly cottoned-on to the hand-shaking ritual, and the kissing ritual too. She enjoyed both of them. It made meeting people, or even just saying 'good morning' a little bit more special. In fact there were many things she was beginning to enjoy about France, especially the food. All those mouth-watering pastries in the display case. It was a pity she was feeling a little queasy. She really wanted to go outside and get a breath of fresh air but she felt it might be considered rather rude. Colette was chatting nineteen to the dozen.

'And apparently there are two suspects being interviewed by the police at this very moment. No one seems to know who they are yet, but I'm bound to hear about it pretty soon... Such a terrible thing, *n'est-ce-pas, Victoire?*' To lose one's life so suddenly just like that, out walking a dog. Alan Perry was such a charming man too. He spoke perfect French, you know, almost like a Frenchman. You knew him, of course? No? I'm surprised. I would have thought you would have known each other, both being English.'

'Unfortunately not. I'd only been here about three or four weeks when he had that dreadful accident.'

'Only three or four weeks? I see. But I thought perhaps you might have run into each other in England.'

Victor laughed. 'England is quite a large country, Colette.'

'But not as large as France'.

'No. But the population is about the same.'

'Tiens! Vraiment?'

'Eh bien. Il faut s'en aller. Au revoir, Colette.'

'Au revoir.'

Kate and Victor went out into the square, their arms full of crispy loaves of bread. Victor had just opened the boot of the car and put in his load of loaves, when Kate dumped her pile hurriedly and rushed off to the far side of the square, where she threw up in the gutter. Fortunately Victor didn't noticed. On the short drive back to *Les Projets,* Kate sat quite still. She managed to get through lunch, but only just. Luckily she and Victor were sitting at a table by the door. As soon as grace had been said, Kate bolted and threw up again in the loo. Forehead dripping with perspiration, palms sticky, head throbbing, she crept off to her room to lie down. She felt really terrible and fell immediately into a heavy, dreamless sleep.

She woke three hours later feeling greatly refreshed. Funny, she thought, I've never been sick like that before. Must be the change of food. For the next two days Kate felt perfectly all right. The group at *Les Projets* had discovered she could sew, so she was helping to make the costumes for the pageant. Spoken communication between her and the group was virtually impossible, as they spoke no English and Kate spoke no French. But after initial help from Victor to explain exactly what was wanted, Kate took the sewing to a quiet corner of one of the outhouses and got down to work.

Three days later she was sick again after breakfast. She didn't feel nearly as badly as she had done the first time but she began to fear that the change of food was not the cause after all. French food wasn't that different to the food at the gipsy encampment and after all, she had been in France for nearly a month now. There must be another explanation. She was sick four mornings in a row just after breakfast, like clockwork, and then her period failed to arrive. As another week passed, she continued to vomit with monotonous regularity after breakfast and still her period didn't come.

Slowly the truth dawned on her. She was pregnant. There was obviously no other explanation. She and Gerry had taken no precautions. It hadn't occurred to her to do so. Gipsies rarely bothered with such encumbrances and they didn't visit doctors or hospitals unless they were seriously ill. Few gipsy women were on the pill; even less had a coil. Some of the men bought condoms from the local chemist, but most people just trusted to luck or took refuge in abortion if caught out.

Kate hadn't planned her love affair with Gerry. So far she had never planned anything in her life. She didn't lead that kind of life. If she was attracted to a man she went to bed with him. It was as simple as that. The consequences could be worked out later. But somehow her relationship with Gerry had been different. It was more than lust, deeper than mere physical attraction. Kate felt they shared a common bond, something that could even become permanent. If she were carrying Gerry's baby, she would certainly want to keep it. But how could she be sure it was Gerry's child? On the other hand, did it make any difference whether it was Gerry's or somebody else's? Although she definitely felt something approaching love for Gerry, he seemed to have disappeared, vanished abruptly out of her life.

She had absolutely no idea where he could have gone, or whether she was likely ever to see him again. There was also the distinct possibility that he had committed murder. It was even possible that he had been arrested and was, at this moment, languishing in jail awaiting trial.

Then there was Tony, the lorry driver who was responsible for her coming to France in the first place. But that wasn't making love. It was rape, even though she had actually given her initial consent. But how a baby was conceived, whether through loving agreement or by coercion, was beside the point. It was the result that counted, and it was the result she had to face. Here she was, in a foreign country where she spoke hardly a word of the language. She was carrying a baby, whose father she wasn't sure of. Of course she wanted it be Gerry's child growing inside her. As for Tony: well, Tony was nobody in her life. She was grateful to him for giving her the lift. It had certainly relieved the pressure on her blisters. She had expected she would have to agree to sex in return. This is what women did in payment for practical or material favours offered by men. Sex seemed to be the woman's main form of currency. So the woman pays and is left to deal with the consequences. Kate was aware of all this. It was the norm among gipsies. But she didn't think it could ever happen to her. So what should she do next?

The logical, most sensible thing to do would be to go back to England. She could go back to her caravan under Westway and explain to the other gipsies that she had gone off on a holiday. It was none of their business whether she went on holiday or not. She pulled her weight when she was in the encampment, and if she was absent, well then, there were plenty of other gipsies to take her place. She would confide in one of the older women that she had had a little slip-up while staying in France and arrange to get fixed up at one of the local hospitals. After all, the French were renowned for their liberal sexual attitudes. Looked at from that point of view it all seemed quite straight-forward. Then the image of Bert's body, bloody and stiff, lying on the floor amid the chaos in her little caravan, came into her mind. Vicious Bert, whom she hated and was delighted to be rid of. But Bert had been murdered: by whom? Bert's death was the unknown equation. It was the factor, which might prevent her from ever returning to her caravan in Westway. But what could she do instead?

The only person in France she could talk to was Victor. Only Victor spoke her language. But Victor was a man. Would it be possible to discuss such an essentially feminine matter as an unexpected pregnancy with a man?

Kate's narrow, limited upbringing indicated that this was definitely out of the question. Then there was something different about Victor. Kate didn't know quite what it was, but he seemed unlike any other men she had met. He was kind, considerate and courteous. This on its own was unusual. Kate was not used to men showing kindness and consideration towards women. Gipsies were not known for their kindness or good manners towards anyone.

Then there was the question of sex. Kate was used to being propositioned. It had happened ever since she was about twelve. She had become accustomed to fighting off men if she didn't care for their advances. She had only ever given in under protest if she had feared violence. But Victor had made no advances whatsoever, not even the subtlest of overtures. And he had every opportunity. They were constantly together.

At first Kate had felt almost offended. She was used to being noticed by men; she expected physical advances. But when her pregnancy became a reality she was relieved to be left alone. All the same, there was something about Victor, which struck her as being a little bit strange.

Chapter Fifteen

Kate had stopped being sick every morning after breakfast, which was certainly a huge relief. If it hadn't been for the continuing absence of her period she would not have believed she was pregnant. She felt her stomach every morning, stroking it in front of the large mirror in the bathroom after her daily shower; a hitherto unknown luxury, but she could detect no change in its size or shape. It was still as smooth and flat as a pancake. Then a few days later she noticed a small change in her breasts: the area round the nipples had darkened and swollen slightly and the nipples themselves were far more sensitive to the touch than before. Kate knew nothing about pregnancy and had never discussed it with any woman she had known in that condition, but she did know enough to realise that her breasts were certainly preparing themselves to feed the baby. There seemed to be no doubt whatsoever of her condition.

Another week passed and life continued apace at *Les Projets Créatifs*, and as preparations for the pageant became further advanced, Kate found herself so engrossed in all the activity that sometimes she felt she had never done anything else. She had integrated extremely well into the group and was beginning to learn a little French. In fact, if it weren't for the pregnancy hanging over her, she would have been quite content to continue indefinitely in her present way of life. But another life was developing within her. If she didn't make a decision soon it would be too late to return to London and try to arrange a termination.

But did she want a termination? As the baby grew inside her, her breasts continued to swell and her stomach curved a little, Kate felt the last thing she wanted to do was part with the new life developing inside her. It was her baby, growing inside her body. At least the mother's identity was never in question. But how could she be so sure about the father? Mostly she felt it could only be Gerry's child. They had lived and slept together for over a month, making love sometimes as often as three times a day; and making love it had surely been, she thought, thinking back to their wonderful climaxes together, almost always coinciding. At the time she hadn't analysed her feelings for Gerry. He had just arrived, out of the blue, as Bert had done, but with such gloriously different consequences. Thinking back to the brief time with Gerry, her soul yearned and her body ached for him.

It was Victor's week in charge of the shopping. It was all part of the general rota. Everyone put money into the kitty and each week a different member of the group bought all the groceries and necessary household goods. It was the task most favoured by nearly everyone and they all looked forward to their turn for at least two or three weeks beforehand. There was no set shopping pattern. No special shops or supermarkets were patronised for any particular item. The choice of shop or supermarket depended on various factors: the time of year, the merchandise required, and of course, on the person in charge that week. Victor liked to ring the changes. Even though his turn, at the moment, only came round every ten or twelve weeks, he found it more enjoyable to visit different places on these shopping expeditions. As it was the first time since Kate's arrival at *Les Projets* that Victor had been the shopper-in-chief, he thought she would find it both interesting and amusing to visit the *Géant Casino* on the outskirts of Chalon-sur-Saône, the largest supermarket he had ever visited so far anywhere in the world. Mostly, whatever Victor did, Kate did too. It wasn't just a question of their common language. In fact Kate was making very good progress with her French. It was really a question of expediency.

It was Monday. All the rotes at *Les Projets Créatifs* started on Monday. The larder was dismally bare, so Victor and Kate left the house about nine-thirty in the morning, armed with a long shopping list. Victor was most grateful to have a break from the group. Some of the members were beginning to get on his nerves and he really thought his departure for pastures new was overdue. Last week he had been on the gardening rota, which he disliked most of all.

It was a hot still sunny day. The drive to Chalon took about forty minutes, along quiet, peaceful side roads. As she always did, Kate took enormous pleasure in commenting on the passing sights. Nothing was too insignificant for her notice and Victor found her enthusiasm and appreciation both endearing and refreshing. In fact, Victor was developing quite a soft spot for Kate. She was co-operative, tolerant and appreciative of everything around her. She showed remarkable forbearance: she was prepared to take on anything new; nothing was too difficult or too much trouble. Once she had settled down, Victor discovered her sense of humour and fun. He thought she was beautiful, too, although he had no desire whatsoever to take her to bed. Her origins were still a mystery to him. She had arrived in France, apparently in a lorry, although her relationship with the lorry driver was still unclear. What was clear was that this was certainly her first visit to France. No one could feign such innocence and ignorance of all things French. But her appreciation in everything new was most enjoyable and extremely infectious.

Kate remarked on the ugliness of the approach to Chalon.

'Yes, many French towns have hideous suburbs,' agreed Victor.

'Why is that?' enquired wide-eyed Kate.

'Probably because all the hideous buildings, super-markets, factories and conference centres are all built in the suburbs.'

'Why in the suburbs?'

'I suppose because there's nowhere else to put them.'

'Why don't they put some of them in the middle of the towns so as to mix it all up a bit?'

Victor laughed. 'It's probably because there's no room in the centre of the towns. Many French towns are very old; dating from medieval times. Most have very strict preservation orders on them, particularly in the centre. It wouldn't be possible to get permission to build a large supermarket or a modern conference centre in places like, say, Chalon, Beaune or Dijon.'

'Wasn't there any war damage? Weren't there any bombsites? London and Birmingham are full of them.' I probably live on one, thought Kate wryly.

'No. There was very little bomb damage throughout most of France during the war. The French capitulated to the Germans near the beginning of the war so they wouldn't burn down Paris. Another gap in your schooling?' Victor smiled gently.

'No. I seem to remember a bit about that,' said Kate hastily, determined not to show her ignorance, 'but I didn't really specialise in history.'

'Fair enough,' said Victor evenly, wondering, not for the first time, what Kate had specialised in. 'Look! We're here now. Have you ever seen such a vast, empty car park before?'

Victor parked in the large parking space and they strolled over to the trolley park. He let Kate put the ten *centimes* pieces into each of the two trolleys, amused at her childish enjoyment, and they each wheeled a trolley into the store.

'Goodness me!' Kate gasped in wonder. 'What an enormous place!'

'Isn't it just?' agreed Victor. 'Like an aeroplane hangar.'

'Ooh! Have you ever been in an aeroplane hangar?'

'No,' Victor was amused by her literalness. 'But it's how I imagine one to be.'

'Look at those dinky garden chairs!' Kate was off, trying out the chairs, fingering the tables, twisting the knobs on the barbeques and lying on the sun beds. Like a child in a toyshop, thought Victor indulgently, wondering, not for the first time, where Kate had lived before her arrival in France. He let her play around for a while, inspecting the cheaply made furniture, wheeling the bicycles, fingering the tatty clothes. It is a day out, after all, he thought, and decided he would take her out to lunch in the centre of Chalon when they had finished the shopping. 'Come on,' he said, gently but firmly.

'We'd better get cracking. We've a long list to get through. We'll start in the drinks section.'

Like a married couple pushing their babies, they wheeled their trolleys, side by side, along the long wide aisle to the drinks section at the far end of the store. Kate gasped in amazement at the endless rows of bottles arranged along the whole length of the wall.

'Heavens!' she exclaimed. 'I've never seen so many bottles.'

Victor laughed. 'Nor had I.'

'What do we buy?'

'The cheapest, drinkable stuff.'

'How do you know?'

'Experience, I suppose.'

They bent over the bins containing litre bottles of red wine with plastic tops instead of corks. Following Victor's example, Kate picked up two bottles labelled *Vin de Table* and placed them carefully at the bottom of her trolley. As she stood up a movement along the aisle caught her eye. She watched in fascination as a young man with his back to them and quite oblivious of their presence, placed a bottle of wine in an inside pocket of his bulky overcoat. That's shoplifting, thought Kate, but decided to say nothing to Victor. They continued with their wine selection, piling it all into Kate's trolley and moved along to the mineral water.

'Still or sparkling?' asked Kate.

'Get a mixture.' Victor lifted two one-and-a-half litres bottles of Evian water off the shelf and put them in the trolley. Just at that moment he saw a young man take a bottle of wine off the shelf and secrete it inside his overcoat. He gave a little gasp of disbelief and started to say something to Kate but she put a finger on her lips.

Without turning round, the young man sauntered nonchalantly round the corner, into the next aisle.

'But that's shoplifting!' whispered Victor hoarsely.

'I know; but maybe he's poor.'

'What's that got to do with it? You can't have people stealing!'

'But people do.'

'We ought to stop him. Apprehend him.'

'Why? It's not our stuff he's stolen. The supermarket can afford the loss. They're made of money.'

'Even so,' Victor objected, 'it's surely our duty to report a theft to the supermarket manager.'

'I don't think it is. Anyway, I don't want to get involved with the police and things like that.'

Kate's gipsy instinct was coming to the fore as they continued their shopping, arguing from time to time about the shoplifter. But by the time they had reached the checkout there was nobody in sight and they had almost completely forgotten about him. They pushed their cumbersome, heavily laden trolleys out into the bright sunshine towards the parking space. The only other car in the car park was a battered, two-tone Mini van without any side windows. The driver was busy unloading the pockets of his bulky overcoat into the back of the van. He straightened up as they passed. Kate looked straight at him and suddenly felt faint with shock. 'Gerry!'

Gerry stood stock still, too amazed to speak. Kate! Kate, here in France with a young man. His Kate, as beautiful as ever.

'You know him?' Victor sounded incredulous.

'Yes. I - we - he's my husband!'

Neither Victor nor Gerry could think of anything to say.

Chapter Sixteen

Jo was becoming rather anxious. It was Wednesday and she hadn't seen Gerry since Monday morning. She was used to his absence for half a day, sometimes even a whole day. But he was always back by about seven for their first pre-prandial drink before dinner. But now he had been gone for almost three days. He had even missed the weekly wine tasting on Tuesday, one of the highlights of the week. Jo's punters always enjoyed Gerry's company on their weekly outing to the local vineyards. He combined a good nose and experienced palate with a ready wit. And he could taste away to his heart's content; safe in the knowledge that Jo would drive them all home.

As the evening approached, Jo began to think about dinner and wondered whether or not Gerry would turn up. She imagined he would arrive, walking across the courtyard with his long loping gait, throwing sticks for Maxwell, his shirt unbuttoned or slung across his shoulder if the weather were particularly warm. She thought she heard him calling: 'Hi there, Jo!' and then: 'Go for it, Max!' as he threw another stick for the dog.

But seven o'clock passed and still Gerry hadn't appeared. Jo began to think she ought to notify the police; that maybe she should have done so already. Where could Gerry have got to? Had he gone for a longer walk than usual and got lost? Had he gone on a mammoth shopping spree further afield to somewhere like Macon or even Lyon? Could he even have returned to England? But would he leave France without saying anything to her or without planning his departure in advance? After all, if he had gone back to England, it would be without his caravan and all his belongings.

Jo went into the caravan, poured herself a glass of wine and decided she would cook an omelette. This morning's bread was just about edible and there was still plenty of cheese left. There was no point in cooking potatoes just for her. She didn't have Gerry's voracious appetite; like a bottomless pit, that could seemingly only be filled up with large helpings of potatoes. She placed her simple repast on the table outside the caravan. It was a beautiful, calm evening and still broad daylight at just after eight o'clock. She ate her omelette quickly, before it got cold, savouring the chunks of ham and cheese and the succulent, runny centre. She put her plate down on the grass and sipped her wine slowly before starting on her mixed salad. Noise of laughter and the sound of music wafted across the courtyard as the punters settled down for the evening in their apartments, some indoors, some on the patio, listening to Jo's tapes and CDs. She contemplated putting on one of the tapes she had brought across to the caravan. Some Mozart would be rather soothing. She missed hearing classical music, as Gerry only liked pop. But she decided against it. She felt that even Mozart would be too intrusive, and perhaps drown the sounds of approaching footsteps: Gerry's footsteps.

She finished her salad and started on the cheese, eating very slowly so as to fill in the evening and give her time to think: about Gerry. So far she had deliberately tried not to think about Gerry. Gerry's caravan had been on her land now for nearly six weeks. For almost half that time she had been sharing it with him. It had been a big decision to move out of the home she and Alan had created with such care and share a caravan with someone she had only known for three weeks. Jo realised she was beginning to take Gerry for granted. Having made the decision to move in with him, she had made a conscious effort not to analyse all the reasons for doing so. After all, she had met Gerry by accident and she had moved into his caravan almost by accident too. In fact, accidents seem to have played a large part in her life recently. The biggest accident of all, that of Alan's death, had not yet been fully explained. It had happened almost two months ago and Jo was beginning to feel that an explanation was overdue. She had no idea how far advanced the police were in their investigations. Sometimes she felt she should go along to the station and ask them a few questions. But her poor French would make anything more than the most rudimentary enquiries impossible. Then there was the added trauma of reliving the whole ghastly experience. She realised too that she must steel herself to make a visit to the old quarry to see the place where Alan had died, preferably before Petra's visit next week.

Now it looked as if there might have been another accident: this time involving Gerry. But that would be ridiculous. Two accidents in just two months, both involving men she was living with at the time. What on earth would people think? What would the police think? They might even hold her responsible. The whole situation was preposterous. But hang on a minute, she said to herself. Who's talking about another accident when none has been reported and there was every likelihood of Gerry turning up, careless, debonair, having decided at the last moment, to take a little trip to the Midi. Gerry undoubtedly enjoyed and made a habit of doing things without any forethought. His departure for France six weeks ago had been a last minute idea.

I needed a break,' Jo remembered him saying. 'I'd been working too hard and my Dad said to me: "You need a break, Gerry. Here's three hundred quid. Go off and enjoy yourself." So I went off to France. I'd never been before so I thought I'd check it out.'

At the time Jo had thought it was strange that Gerry should just to go off to France without any particular plan in mind. She remembered he didn't even have any guidebooks. His map of France was brand new and priced in francs. He had probably bought it at a service station on the way. No, Gerry was not a long-term planner; he was definitely a spur-of-the-moment man. So, logically she shouldn't worry, but illogically she did. The big question now was: why was she beginning to worry? How important had Gerry become to her? They were poles apart. Of that there was no doubt whatsoever. They looked at everything differently: food, people, education, art, music, and literature. Not that they had had particularly full discussions on the last three subjects. Music had come up in connection with which tape they should play; literature had arisen because of an article she was reading in *The Sunday Times*. But Gerry had shown no knowledge of, or interest in either so Jo had not persevered with the discussions.

Then there were their different life styles. Gerry had talked about his happy childhood in more than comfortable surroundings, and yet he had been prepared to live in a caravan in conditions that Jo could only describe as squalid. She had spent days cleaning up the caravan before moving in, scrubbing, dusting, hoovering, polishing the whole place till it shone. But Gerry had barely seemed to notice the difference. Meal times, too, could be awkward. Jo was accustomed to waiting until everyone at the table had been served, then taking up her knife and fork with some decorum. So she was more than surprised to observe how Gerry seized his knife and fork long before the food had arrived and then tucked in voraciously before his plate had barely landed on the table. Even their washing habits were different. On their first evening of intimacy Gerry had confessed that he was quite prepared to go a whole week without a shower. Jo appeared so shocked that Gerry, to give him his due, soon began to shower daily. Last, but not least, Gerry was five years younger than she was. Jo was used to older men.

Musing on all the differences between them Jo, began to wonder if they really had anything in common. She also began to wonder how Gerry could have turned out as he had, given his undoubtedly well-bred childhood. Or was it? Was Gerry from the background he said he was? Middle-class, well educated, with parents who gave elegant dinner parties in their spacious house with beautiful views of County Wicklow? Jo felt guilty for doubting him.

But the more she thought about it, the more she did doubt him. In short, the Gerry Nolan she knew did not appear to fit into the background of the Gerry Nolan that he described.

Nevertheless, Jo did find Gerry appealing. There were times when his gaiety and infectious enthusiasm reminded him of Simon; now doubtless married to Alison, the buck-toothed missionary, still doing good deeds in Zaire. Simon had been an exciting and inventive lover, as Gerry was too. And Gerry was certainly attractive looking, with his shy smile, warm hazel eyes and lithe muscular body. But often after they had made love and reached their climax together, Jo felt that their physical union lacked either passion or depth. What existed between them was sex between friends, rather than a union of lovers.

Above all it was after making love that Jo missed Alan the most. When Gerry had entered her body and come inside her she felt a terrible sense of despair, as though she had been possessed by the wrong lover. She felt disloyal and deeply guilty for giving herself to another man so soon after Alan's death. As Gerry came to his climax she would close her eyes, as if hoping when she opened them that nothing had changed; that Alan was still with her after all. As her complicated and often anguished train of thought struggled to its conclusion, she wondered that if she and Gerry had nothing in common and were not in love, should she allow the relationship to continue?

It was a question she felt must wait till the morning.

The next day Jo was up early. Rather than take the time to make the ten-minute return car trip to the bakery, she ate some cheese biscuits with a scraping of butter and brewed up her usual mug of coffee in the *cafetière*. She had spent a restless night and had made up her mind, at about four am, to report Gerry's disappearance at the local police station. She had also resolved to screw up enough courage to question them about their progress into Alan's accident. She was beginning to think she ought to start looking round for an English speaking *avocat*, the general French term for lawyer, but the thought of the whole process of searching for the right one drained her energy and sapped her self-confidence. There was also the thought of the legal fees, which would certainly drain her scant financial resources. She had no idea whether the police were investigating a fatal accident or a murder. She had no idea, either, whether France had the equivalent of the English Crown Prosecution Service or Legal Aid.

In fact, poor Jo was at a total loss. Alan's French Dream had turned into Jo's French Nightmare. It seemed that whatever she touched in France had turned into a disaster and the two most important people in her life at the time had disappeared to meet with fatal accidents. Shortly after nine am, feeling very apprehensive and a little tearful, Jo drove slowly down the long, bumpy drive on her way to the police station in Dracy. As she negotiated the right turn into the narrow lane at the bottom of the drive, Marcel Legrand ambled slowly out of his driveway.

'*Bonjour, Jo! Comment-allez vous? Vous-avez entendu la nouvelle?* The police are questioning two people in connection with Alan's death. I wasn't sure whether you would have read about it in the local paper. Come in and have a cup of coffee and Jeanine and I will tell you all about it.'

Chapter Seventeen

'Tu sors?'
 'Oui, Maman.'
 'Ou vas-tu?'
 'Je vais faire une promenade.'
 'On mange à huit heures.
 'Oui, je sais.'
 'Au revoir. Bonne promenade.'

Jean Bertrand had decided to go on one of his increasingly frequent solitary walks. He enjoyed walking. He liked visiting the neighbouring villages and exploring new parts of the countryside. He had another idea too. Since the Englishman's death, for which he felt partly responsible, Jean hadn't revisited the quarry where the fatal accident had happened. He thought it might be worthwhile having a look around. He could even work out how it had happened. Had it been his fault, or the fault of the Englishman with the horrible dog?

Jean felt slightly annoyed with his mother for reminding him that dinner was at eight. Of course dinner was at eight! They had always had dinner at eight ever since he could remember. Most people in France had dinner at eight in the evening. Not all families sat down together, though. That was one of his mother's many little rules: she insisted the whole family ate together every evening and lunchtime at weekends. Jean thought it an imposition at his age to be tied down to set meal hours, especially with the whole family. He didn't see the point. Why couldn't everyone just help themselves from the fridge when they were hungry? But he knew he wouldn't bother. He was hardly ever hungry. He had never eaten very much, even as a child, which was probably the reason why he was so thin. He wasn't very tall either. In fact he wasn't particularly remarkable looking at all. Stick-like arms and legs grew out of his slight, scrawny body in a haphazard sort of way. His neck was too long, like that of some strange bird. His eyes were set too close together in a mean, sallow-skinned face. His nose was long and thin, his lips almost non-existent, only sufficient to form a slit in his face covering his uneven teeth. This strange apparition was topped by a mop of unruly curly jet-black hair. Jean looked young for his age, only about sixteen, but he was, in fact, approaching twenty-three. It was probably just as well he did look so young. It meant people expected less of him than they otherwise might. For Jean was neither bright nor mature. He was bordering on the sub-normal but he wasn't really aware of it himself. He had attended the local school, as twenty years ago there wasn't a great deal of choice. In any case, his parents thought he was just like any other boy. In their opinion all boys, and many girls too, were stupid, disruptive and ill mannered. As they were responsible for feeding and clothing their children, they felt it was the school's responsibility to educate them. They felt no obligation to participate or interfere in any way. Jean was the oldest of seven children: three boys and four girls. His parents hadn't bargained for such a large family and had expressed surprise at the birth of each child. But family planning was quite beyond their comprehension. On the whole the girls were less trouble than the boys.

Jean had not attempted to sit his *Baccalauréat*. No one at his school had suggested it and it was doubtful if his parents had even heard of it. So Jean left school at sixteen, without any qualifications and tried his hand at various apprenticeships, none of which was successful. His last job had been with Georges Lefèvre, the plumber, who after only a few weeks had totally despaired of Jean's incompetence. And when Jean burst into his house one day at lunchtime without knocking and almost found Georges in bed with Chantal Gilot, the postman's wife, Georges sent Jean packing in no uncertain terms.

With each failure Jean became more resentful. He didn't consider himself a failure - he considered himself just as capable as any other young man of his age. He thought the problem lay with his employers, not with him. At first between each apprenticeship Jean lounged around the house, getting under his mother's feet. As he grew older, he lounged around the village and began to steal: just small things from shops to start with, then larger things from peoples' houses. When he was nineteen he was caught breaking and entering, tried, found guilty and received a year's prison sentence. His parents hoped the time in prison would cool their son's heels and make him turn over a new leaf. But it did nothing of the kind: it only whetted his appetite for more mischief.

A year later, when Jean was twenty-one, the family moved to a slightly larger, but equally unsuitable property, on the outskirts of the village of Laronne, barely fifteen kilometres from where they had lived before in Dracy. It was thought advisable not to move too far from Dracy, so not only would Jean-Ives Bertrand, the head of the family, be able to continue in his present job, but also the younger Bertrand children could continue at the same school. Jean was often between employment. His parents, having accustomed themselves for some time to the feckless, idle ways of their eldest son, thought very little about his state of unemployment. From time to time they would make suggestions, but Jean always spurned them, mostly because the work they suggested struck him as being too arduous, but quite often, too, because he knew it would be beyond his capabilities. So Jean Bertrand rose late, lay around the house until lunchtime and then spent the afternoons and early evenings roaming the countryside or snooping around the village shops, his deft light fingers stealing whatever he could. He crossed everyone. Every person in the villages and surrounding countryside knew that Jean Bertrand was up to no good. Most people left him alone, for he was a surly, ill-mannered youth, given to outbursts of violent temper, which seemed to get more violent and more frequent as he grew older. But for their own safety and peace of mind it was impossible always to ignore him. He stole; he vandalised outhouses, sheds and fences; he ripped washing off the clothes' lines just for a joke. He teased small children; even babies in their prams were not safe when Jean Bertrand was about. His vicious streak extended deliberately to hurting, even maiming, animals. He let dogs off the leash, hens out of their runs, rabbits out of their hutches and cows and horses out of the fields. He stoned animals, particularly cows and dogs, for which he seemed to have an ever-deepening aversion.

All the shopkeepers were extremely wary of the arrival of Jean Bertrand on their premises. Whenever possible an extra member of the owner's family would be called in as a precautionary measure. If caught in action, Jean's theft would, of course, be reported immediately to the *gendarmerie*. But this had only happened once, for as he grew older Jean became more and more adept at stealing. Apart from the shopkeepers, who were united to a man, the other inhabitants varied in their approach to Jean's misdemeanours. Usually, as with his shoplifting activities, he was never actually caught in the act, but he was always suspected. His bad reputation preceded him and many people were afraid of him.

His main adversary was Bernard Roger. Bernard, though not tidy in his living habits, was extremely proud of his herd of Charolais - and rightly so. It wasn't a very large herd, consisting of less than seventy head of cattle, which he grazed on several different fields, rented from various neighbours. Bernard had caught Jean Bertrand several times stoning them and letting them out of the field. He had threatened to go to the police if he caught Jean red-handed again. Jean had just laughed in his face. 'Oh, no you won't! I know you won't. You're too lazy - and anyway, who'd believe you? It's only your word against mine.'

On one occasion Bernard had caught him prowling around his filthy courtyard. Jean was planning to steal one of the many chairs that lay around in the chaotic mess, useless and unused. He needed a chair for his bedroom. His dad had refused point blank to buy him the new one he wanted, which he had seen in the *Géant Casino*. It was a splendid chair, roomy and comfortable with a canvas seat in red and white stripes. Jean badly wanted the chair but his dad had said it was too expensive and quite unnecessary. So Jean decided to steal one of Bernard Roger's abandoned chairs and repair it himself. Repairing things, especially made of wood, was about Jean's only skill. So he wandered, quite casually, into Bernard Roger's mucky courtyard and started to examine all the broken furniture. There was a lot of stuff that could be rescued, repaired and used. In fact, if he had a workshop and some proper tools, Jean felt he could go into business and make some money with the contents of Bernard Roger's courtyard alone. It didn't occur to Jean to ask Bernard if he could take some of his abandoned derelict stuff to repair. Jean wasn't that sort of youth. He had learned, quite some time ago, that people didn't want to do him any favours. People didn't like him. So he just helped himself to whatever he wanted without asking.

He selected a chair from Bernard's heap of rubbish. It only had three legs but there was a spare leg a few feet away, which was almost exactly the same as the three existing ones on the chair. He put the three-legged chair over his shoulder, and carrying the spare leg in his other hand, he sauntered towards the ever-open gate of the courtyard, just as Bernard drove in on his tractor. When Bernard saw Jean leaving, carrying one of his chairs, he accelerated into the courtyard. Realising he was trapped, Jean stood irresolutely by the open gate. Bernard swung himself down from the tractor cab and ran towards the gate in a flash.

'You bloody thief!' he shouted. 'Put that stuff down! That's my chair you're stealing!'

Jean looked at him sullenly, still clutching the chair. 'It's broken. You can't sit on it. I was going to mend it.'

'It's not yours to mend. It's mine! You've got to ask my permission to take stuff out of here! Put it down and get out!'

Jean looked around uncertainly. 'Can't I -?'

'No! Put it down! It's not yours.'

Jean put his trophies down on the ground. He knew he was in a no-win situation. Bernard came right up to him and grabbed him by the shoulders.

'Leave my stuff there and clear off! I never want to see you around here again.'

Jean slunk off, frightened. He wondered if Bernard would report his stealing to the police, but after a week nothing had happened so he began to relax a little.

Jean hated Bernard Roger.

Jean's other main adversary was the Englishman, Alan Perry. Alan had caught Jean several times in acts of vandalism or violence. On one occasion he had caught him dismantling a large piece of fencing, thus enabling the cattle to stray out of the field and wander at will, risking injury by passing motorists. On another occasion Alan had discovered Jean demolishing a wooden carport. He had reprimanded him too, for stoning cows and teasing a dog.

Jean Bertrand had also hated Alan Perry.

Jean continued to struggle up the steep path to the top of the hill, memories of Alan Perry and his horrible black dog flooding back. Now he had reached the top and looked down into the vast deep quarry below, remembering with great satisfaction how he had pushed Alan to his death. Fortunately no one suspected him. He had heard that Bernard Roger had discovered Alan Perry's body a few hours later after the fatal accident, but Bernard had no idea that he, Jean Bertrand, had also been on the top of the hill overlooking the quarry.

Chapter Eighteen

'*Vingt-et-un, vingt-deux, vingt-trois, vingt-quatre...*'

'You've won, Jules!'

Jules Gilot, the postman, gathered up his winnings with a contented grin on his lean olive-skinned face.

'Good. And about time too. I haven't won anything for weeks.'

'Nor have I,' said Georges Lefèvre, the plumber, lugubriously stroking his smooth round chin.

'Louis and Pierre seem to do best, especially Louis. Its all that coffin making that brings him luck. He just waits, rubbing his hands, for the next corpse, young or old, whoever it is, it makes no difference. Keeps the lolly rolling in. That right, Louis?'

Georges leant forward, raising his voice and spoke directly into Louis Durant's ear. Although only just touching seventy, Louis had aged more than most of the group. He suffered badly from arthritis and could barely walk unaided. He had also become extremely deaf of late. There was no particular reason why he should have aged sooner than anyone else in the *Commune* of Laronne. Most of the inhabitants aged sixty or more had suffered the same harsh life. Louis saw no connection between poor health and coffin making: rather the reverse. He had started life as a carpenter, but finding he lacked the fine eye and sensitive touch of a cabinet-maker, such as Didier

Pérnot, he had gone into the coffin trade, at first by accident; then realising it's potential, he had quickly established himself in a lucrative, full-time business. There were those who said it was indecent to make one's living from the dead; that there was a curse on all undertakers and coffin makers. But over the years Louis Durant had learned to ignore these remarks, and although he always felt considerable sympathy for the deceased's relatives, he inevitably experienced a deep sense of pride each time he delivered one of his gleaming, hand-finished coffins to the undertakers.

Whenever possible Louis avoided attending the funeral. Of course there were people who criticised him for this, but Louis saw it as a Catch 22 situation. If he came to the funeral people would think he was advertising. If he stayed away he would be accused of indifference. He found it less of a strain to stay away. He made exceptions, of course, in the case of family or close friends. One friend whose funeral he would undoubtedly have attended, if it had been held in Laronne, was that of Alan Perry. Alan had become quite a regular member of their gambling circle. At first the group, known as *les copains,* was suspicious of the foreigner who had only lived in Laronne for a few months. But they all quickly came round to accepting Alan among their select number, seduced by his charming, easy manner and impressed by his fluent, elegant French. Alan's visits soon became almost as frequent as *les copains* themselves and he was even referred to as such.

Louis remembered with morbid horror the request for a coffin for Alan Perry. Lucien Gautier had brought the terrible news, passed on no doubt by his gossiping wife. Louis had no time for Colette Gautier and wouldn't pass the time of day with her if he could possibly avoid it. There had been a knock on the door at about seven o'clock one evening. It was a Thursday. Louis remembered the day quite clearly. He was rushing through an order for a coffin for a little girl of five who had died a few days ago of meningitis and was to be buried on Saturday. Tragic affair. Understandably the parents were distraught. No one knew how distressing it was to make a coffin for a child. Louis went to answer the doorbell.

'*Tiens! Lucien, mon ami, bonjour. Pourquoi es-tu venu chez moi ?*'

Lucien looked grave.

'*Bonjour, Louis.* But it's not a good day. I come with tragic news.'

'Tragic news, *mon ami?*'

'Yes. Tragic. Our good friend, Alan Perry met with a fatal accident yesterday.'

'*Oh, mon Dieu !* Where? How did it happen?'

'It happened up in the old quarry beyond Dracy. It appears that *cher Alain* slipped and fell while walking his dog.'

Louis' eyes widened. 'Walking his dog!'

'Yes. Apparently.'

'And who found his body?'

'Bernard Roger.

'Also walking his dog?'

'That's doubtful. But I have a sad request for you, *mon ami.*'

Louis sighed. 'Yes. I can guess, of course. It is I who will make the coffin for Alain.'

'I'm afraid so.'

As Lucien took his leave, Louis returned to his workshop with a heavy heart. What was worse: to make a coffin for a child of five or one for a dear friend? Of course he would go to the funeral and he would make no charge for the coffin. He sat down for a few moments to get over the shock and let his thoughts go back to the time of Alan's death, the day before, the evening of 4 May. Curious, he thought, that so often they held their gambling sessions on a Wednesday. There was no particular reason. It just seemed to work out that way. With nine *copains,* excluding Jean-Pierre Floret, who, at eighty-five had become too old even to count up on his fingers, never mind see or hear; with nine friends it was easier to have a regular day. But, Louis realised with a sudden flash, that yesterday's session had been cancelled a few days before. He had received a cryptic message from Didier Pérnot, as presumably everyone else had:

Ne venez pas ce soir. La séance n'aura pas lieu.

Why had the session been cancelled and had there been an ulterior motive? And as to poor Alan's untimely death. Had it been an accident? And if not, were there any suspects? With a heavy heart, Louis went into his store where he seasoned all his lengths of oak to select pieces for his friend's coffin.

It was Bernard Roger who had found the body and had, quite rightly, gone to the police. If the police didn't come up with some concrete evidence quite soon, Louis vowed he would do some private investigating. A few days later he was more than relieved to learn he would not have to attend Alan's funeral after all. It would be held in England.

Didier Pérnot was essentially a kindly man but he was also proud. He had been the Mayor of Laronne for over twenty-four years. Next year would be his sliver jubilee.

There would be parties in each village in the *Commune*, which was an unusually large one, comprising Dracy, Laronne and at least half a dozen other small hamlets as well. He was looking forward to being *fêted* and lionised. His only regret was that his silver jubilee didn't coincide with the millennium celebrations for Laronne. It would have been just perfect to walk at the head of the procession, marking not only one thousand years of the founding of Laronne, but his own twenty-fifth anniversary as well. And he had only missed it by a mere nine months. Ironic, really. Perhaps if he had been born nine months earlier...? Who knows? He had contemplated putting back his inauguration by nine months but decided it wouldn't look too good if the Mayor started tampering with the records. And there would be quite a lot of records to tamper with. No. Even before he had formulated his thoughts he realised they were totally inappropriate and rather undignified. But by way of compensation, Didier decided to devise his own smaller pageant, which would be quite independent of the main pageant, but also integrate with it. Didier had given no reason why he had cancelled the gambling session of *les copains* on Wednesday 4 May. He decided he would enjoy a little secret. He loved secrets. He also loved gambling. He could hold his liquor pretty well too, even the rough *marc de Bourgogne,* the viciously strong liqueur made from the residue at the bottom of the wine barrels, sometimes called white brandy or *Eau de Vie.* It was Didier who had inaugurated the gambling and drinking sessions. On one of his rare explorations of remote local places, Didier discovered there was a derelict cottage standing empty in a small coppice not far from the disused tile factory above the old quarry beyond Dracy. He made enquiries as to whom the owner was. No one seemed to know, so he went to see *Monsieur* Bazalet, the local *notaire*. He explained that his enquiries were strictly for mayoral purposes. Any legal fees would of course be waived. That would be quite understood. *Monsieur* Bazalet understood. He had been born and bred in Dracy and was totally familiar with Mayors and unofficial mayoral requests.

It was several weeks before *Monsieur* Bazalet was able to unearth anything about the ownership of the derelict cottage. One day, while he was going through some papers at *la Mairie*, Didier received a phone call. He picked up the phone.

'*Allo, oui. Monsieur le Maire à l'appareil.*'

'*Didier, bonjour. C'est Grégoire Bazalet ici.*'

'*Bonjour, Grégoire.*'

'I have news for you, my friend.'

'Oh, yes. What news?'

'About the cottage.'

'You've found out who owns it?'

'I have indeed.'

'And who is it?'

'Unfortunately, there is more than one. There are several. Seventeen, to be precise.'

'Seventeen people own that little cottage!' Didier was astounded.

'Yes. Seventeen.'

'Can I buy it?'

'It would be difficult at present, particularly considering that five of them live in the United States and three of them can't be traced at all.'

'*Tiens! Extraordinaire!* And what do you suggest, Grégoire?'

'I suggest you rent it. I shall draw up an agreement so the money will go into a trust fund for the owners.'

'Which they will receive when they've all been traced?'

'Exactly.'

'And the rent...?'

'...Will be very low, *mon ami.*'

Well pleased with the way the negotiations had gone, Didier replaced the receiver.

So Didier Pérnot rented the derelict cottage and recorded the expenses as essential to his mayoral duties. He marshalled his friends' support in renovating the place; friends, who of course would become part of the gambling circle once the place was habitable. There was Georges Lefèvre, the plumber, Pierre Bittard, the plasterer and decorator, and Michel Voyou, the electrician. He himself would see to all the woodwork repairs. The four men worked hard in their spare time and made an excellent job of the renovations. Their wives ran up curtains and re-upholstered furniture, which they acquired from junk shops for practically nothing. When it was finished, Didier invited more friends to join them for gambling and drinking sessions at least once a week. He extended his invitation to include Lucien Gautier, Jules Gilot, Marcel Legrand and old Jean-Pierre Floret, who was then far more sprightly, still having his sight and most of his hearing.

All this had happened ten years earlier.

Then two years ago an Englishman, named Alan Perry, came to live in Laronne. Didier had met him when he came with his wife to one of *les soirées à la Salle des*

Fêtes, the village hall, next-door to *la Mairie.* These were always informal, friendly affairs, taking place perhaps six or eight times a year, often for a celebration of some particular event such as Twelfth Night, the village Saint's Day, The Huntsmen's Dinner, or the more important, much celebrated wine festival of *Saint Vincent.* There were various committee members responsible for the different events, who did the catering and organised the drinks. The food and wine were of a high quality and the dancing, to the accompaniment of Lucien Gautier's accordion, usually continued into the small hours. Everyone knew everyone else and any newcomers, a rare event, were introduced all round. Didier Pérnot and Alan Perry took to each other straight away. Alan warmed to the short, rotund Didier's expansive manner and his wicked sense of humour, which lit up his merry, twinkling blue eyes. Didier was impressed by Alan's enthusiasm, his total immersion in all things French and his fluent command of the language. Didier's suggestion that Alan should sometimes join *les copains* up at the deserted cottage met with some resistance at first. Country people are naturally conservative and suspicious. They do not take kindly to change and particularly not to foreigners. But Didier won them all round in the end and Alan became a regular member of the group.

On that fateful day, 4 May, Didier had decided against inviting Alan Perry to join *les copains* at the cottage. It was for no other reason except that he wished to rehearse his own pageant with his friends. Didier wasn't sure whether or not he should include Alan, a foreigner, in his essentially French project. He had been even more doubtful about the reaction of his friends. So in the end Alan had been left out of Didier's pageant altogether and had been none the wiser. Didier had, in fact, cancelled the meeting several days earlier because he had been invited to pay a visit to *Les Projets Créatifs* to see an early rehearsal of their millennium pageant. The group wanted to ask his advice on several matters including historical accuracy and general suitability. Didier was most anxious to accept the invitation, not only because he was Mayor, but also because he was consumed with curiosity about the group and their activities. Didier didn't exactly resent the presence of *Les Projets Créatifs* in Laronne, but he wasn't very keen on their being there either. He couldn't quite see the point in having a group of people, albeit mostly French, interfering in neighbourhood affairs. He felt things such as millennium pageants should be left to him to devise.

Although *Les Projets* and other similar groups received small grants or subsidies, some from the local *Communes* and some from the central government in Paris, they were effectively independent. They were self-elected and almost self-supporting, but because their brief and their purpose was to bring art and drama to the local communities, it was essential that they communicate with the local people, and above all, with the Mayor.

That afternoon Didier spent an interminably tedious four hours watching the slow, tattily dressed dramatic concoction, which the well-meaning, but totally amateur group at *Les Projets* had the nerve to call a pageant. Didier suffered his boredom with as good grace as possible, giving advice where he felt he could. At least it will all be diluted when the villagers join in, he thought, and I suppose they are doing their best. His one consolation was, that by comparison, his own contribution would seem much better.

After an extensive guided tour of the house, the theatre, the workshops and the store rooms, Didier left *Les Projets Créatifs* about seven o'clock in the evening. In fact he was rather impressed by all the renovations and genuinely admired their skill in restoring the house and adapting the factory for their own theatrical purposes.

It was a beautiful evening and still quite early, so Didier decided he would take a short drive and inspect the far side of the old quarry, which he had not visited for a long time. He remembered there was a beautiful view over a lake not far along the road towards La Roche. Having just toured the old tile factory down at *Les Projets*, he thought it might be interesting to see what the old quarry looked like.

He drove slowly along the narrow road, which wound steeply upwards, reaching a sort of plateau. Here the road levelled out briefly before starting its final ascent to the top of the precipice where the cliff fell away sharply to the lake far below. Didier stopped the car and got out to admire the stunning view of Laronne over to the right. Nestling in the hillside beyond the valley, lush with vines, it looked like a fairy tale village. Didier was filled with happiness and pride. This was his village, in his landscape. He was responsible for its care and the well being of all its inhabitants. He hoped he would live forever and always be Mayor of Laronne.

He contemplated parking his car off the road and walking up to the top. This way he would see things better, have more time to admire the view and drink in the beauty of it all. But Didier was a plump man, sometimes short of breath and unaccustomed to walking. So he got into his car again, started up the engine and drove slowly up to the top of the steep hill.

He stopped again briefly at the top and looked down at the lake far below, still and black in the fading light. He thought he heard a crunch of footsteps down below but he saw no one. Looking down at the silent dark lake far below, Didier had a sudden sense of foreboding. It was a remote place, somehow more sinister than beautiful. His pride and happiness suddenly vanished and he decided it was time to leave. He would drive up to La Roche and have a *pastis* at the local *café* with the patron, his friend Jacques Viviers, whom he hadn't seen recently.

Didier drove off just a few moments before Alan Perry arrived at the very spot he, Didier, had just left. He heard a dog barking somewhere but didn't think it was of any particular importance. As he rounded the bend on the road to La Roche, Jean Bertrand came along the cliff path in the opposite direction and saw, just for a second or two, a bright red car driving up the hill.

Didier was totally distraught when he heard of Alan Perry's death the following day. Alan had been a close and fond friend. But he saw no reason why he should mention to anyone that he had, in fact, driven past the exact spot where Alan had met his end. Didier wasn't sure whether he had been there before or after the accident. There had been no reason to look at his watch. If he had been there before the accident there was probably nothing he could have done to prevent it. If he had arrived afterwards, he would certainly have been too late. He had seen no one and, as far as he was aware, no one had seen him. There was no particular reason why anyone should know he had gone for a drive that evening. What he did in his own spare time was his business.

After all, he was the Mayor of Laronne.

Chapter Nineteen

'What made you say that?'

'What?'

'That I was your husband.'

Kate sat up in the bed, cross-legged, pulling the sheet around her slightly swollen abdomen. She looked down at Gerry, lying flat on his back, legs a little apart, his toes extended, twitching idly. He was lean and muscular, without a spare ounce of fat. At the encampment under Westway Kate used to tease him about his tiny bottom.

'It's a wonder you've anything to sit on,' she would say, throwing him a cushion. 'Here have this - so you won't get too sore.' And Gerry would throw the cushion back playfully and they would start a game, which usually ended up by their rolling around on the floor. Then they would begin to undress each other and inevitably make love.

Kate couldn't see Gerry's bottom at the moment, but she smiled with pleasure at the memory of their innocent games. Looking back at their month together on the encampment she thought with regret how carefree and uncomplicated their lives had seemed then. She stroked his rippling chest, feeling gently for the nipples underneath his soft tangle of hair. Her hand moved down, caressing his stomach, hard and concave, unlike her own, now slightly extended, full of child, Gerry's child. She twirled her finger in his belly button, tickling him slightly. Gerry laughed with a mixture of pleasure and pain as Kate pulled sharply at a few hairs and then began to stroke his penis.

Gerry turned on his side and looked up at the beautiful woman sitting cross-legged on the bed beside him, her thighs slim and supple, her skin silky to the touch. Her shapely calves tapered to tiny ankles and the most exquisite feet he had ever seen on a woman. He noticed the sheet pulled loosely round her stomach and wondered why. She had never done that before on the encampment under Westway. He thought her breasts seemed larger than he had remembered too, not pendulous or over-ripe, but full, sensuous and even more desirable. The area around the nipples glistened darkly; the nipples themselves were pointed and hard.

Gerry stroked her leg, as Kate remained sitting cross-legged, quite still, stiffening a little as Gerry's hand moved upwards, savouring the silky feel of the skin at the top of her thigh. He continued to stroke for a few moments, then searched for her vagina, feeling it swell and grow moist. Kate started to moan softly as Gerry withdrew his finger and pulled her gently down beside him. He reached for her mouth with his, but before he kissed her he whispered: 'Kate! My dearest Kate! I love you! I love you!'

'Do you really love me, Gerry?'

'I said I did a few minutes ago.'

'Did you mean it?'

There was a long pause. 'I think so.'

'You think so?'

'Kate, my darling Kate. I don't know anything about love. I've never loved anyone, not even my mother, and I don't think anyone has ever loved me.'

'If you don't know anything about it, how do you recognise it?'

'How do you recognise anything you're experiencing for the first time?'

'You compare it with something similar.'

'And if there's nothing similar?'

'Then you can't really compare it.'

Gerry laughed. 'You sound like some psychologist.'

'What do they do?'

'Try and explain to people why they think as they do.'

'And can they?'

'I don't know. I've never met any.'

Kate giggled. 'Gerry! You are a card!'

Gerry stroked her cheek. 'You still haven't answered my first question.'

Kate took his hand and held it against her cheek.

'What question? It must have slipped my mind. We've been very busy these last fifteen minutes.'

Gerry kissed her, lightly and tenderly. 'We have.'

'What was the question?'

'Why did you say in front of your friend that I was your husband?'

'To be quite honest, Gerry, I don't really know. I think it was a shock just seeing you there in the car park, unloading your loot into the back of your old Mini from your thick overcoat, which looked ludicrous on such hot day. So I said the first thing that came into my head.'

'It made me very proud and happy.'

'Really?'

'It made me feel... Kate...'

'Yes?'

'Do you remember at the camp I once asked you if you were married?

'You did?'

'I did.'

'And what did I say?'

'You said gipsies hardly ever got married because they didn't live within the law, so they didn't see the point in being locked in a marriage.'

'I said that?'

'Yes.'

'And then what did you say?'

'I said had you ever thought of having kids.'

'Yes?' Kate stiffened a little. 'And what did I say to that?'

'You said a gipsy camp was no place for kids.'

'Quite right. Nor it is,' said Kate firmly.

'Then you said: "why don't we go away and get a place of our own." '

Kate frowned. 'Yes. I remember.'

'I said I'd get a proper job. Remember?'

Kate laughed. 'Like a waiter in a restaurant. I remember.'

Gerry joined in her laughter. 'A waiter in a restaurant! It'd be great gas, wouldn't it? I could be in charge of wines. I know a lot about wine now, well, French wines anyway. Kate! Kate! Shall we do that? Shall we go off together and get married? I'll get a good job; any good job and we'll raise a family. Would you like that, Kate? Kate, will you marry me, my darling and have my children?'

There was a pause. Kate leant up on her side and looked at Gerry very hard.

'Yes, Gerry. I'll marry you. I don't know a lot about love either but I think I love you too. And Gerry, the family's already been started. I'm pregnant. I'm carrying your baby.'

Gerry sat bolt upright and stared at Kate in amazement for the second time in two days.

'That's great,' was all he said. 'Kate, there's something I have to tell you.'

'And what's that?'

Kate's heart missed a beat. He was going to tell her about Bert. How he had knifed him and left him for dead. But it had been an accident. Of course it had. He had done it to protect her. Bert had probably had a go at him as well, so he had done it in self-defence. But the undisputable fact was that Bert was dead. And he had been murdered. That was no suicide. So someone was guilty of murder. And that someone would eventually be tracked down by the police and imprisoned to await trial. But Kate didn't want the 'someone' to be Gerry. God, please don't let it be Gerry, she prayed, several times a day.

They were sitting in Kate's room. It was the only private place at *Les Projets,* the only place where they could talk without being overheard. Even though no one except Victor understood English, they still felt constrained in having any sort of personal discussion if anyone else was around. And they certainly had plenty of things to discuss.

Kate felt guilty about Victor. Since Gerry had arrived she had hardly spoken to him. She was certainly extremely grateful to him. If it hadn't been for Victor, God knows where she would have ended up: in the cab of another rapist's lorry. She gave an involuntary shudder. Gerry took her hand and stroked it. He was sitting on the side of the bed; she sat opposite him on the only chair.

'OK?'

Kate nodded.

'Not feeling sick?'

'No, thank God.'

'It's dreadful for you to have to go through all this sickness and swelling up just to have my baby.'

'It's OK. I'm getting used to it now. It'll all be worth it in the end. What do you have to tell me, Gerry?'

She had better steel herself for the worst. She would have to face up to it some time.

'When I left the campsite under Westway that time...'

'Yes...?'

'I didn't mean to run out on you like that...'

'No. But you did.'

'Yes.'

'So where did you go?'

'First of all I found a scrap-yard not far from the campsite.'

'Oh, yes. I know the one.'

'Most of the stuff was in a pretty bad state and only fit for the dump. But there were a couple of cars that still went, including my old Mini van, so I offered the bloke fifty quid for it. He said for that price I could take the caravan as well.'

'So you were all set. To go where?'

'Anywhere.'

'Why did you have to go at all?'

'I had to think things out.'

'What things?'

'You and a few other things.'

'Why did you come to France?'

'I just seemed to be driving in that direction. Of course, when I got to Dover it was either cross over or drive back.'

'So you decided to cross over.'

'Yes.'

'Curiosity?'

'Line of least resistance.'

Kate laughed. 'You're a scream. You certainly don't go in for long term planning. But what did you do about a passport? Had you thought that one out?'

'No, I hadn't.'

'So what did you do? Steal one at a filling station?'

Gerry laughed. 'It had crossed my mind. But I did better than that. I had a bit of luck.'

'What sort of luck?'

'I was just leaving the gents at one of those large motor way-service stations when I saw something lying on the floor. I picked it up and discovered it was a little mauve book with a coat of arms on it and a photo of a man inside who looked very like me. I'd never seen a passport before but I realised what it was. What a bit of luck! I thought. I'm all set now. When I arrived at the passport place the bloke didn't even look at my passport. He just waved me through. It was all dead easy.'

'And when you arrived in France, what made you come all the way down here to remote and empty Burgundy?'

'It was probably because of the person I met on the boat.'

Exactly, thought Kate. If I hadn't met Tony on the road I wouldn't have come to France either.

'So who was the person you met on the boat?' she said out loud.

'I'm coming to that. She's the person I want to tell you about.'

'Aah! What's her name?'

'Jo. Jo Perry.'

'And how did you run into her on the boat?'

'We had breakfast together.'

'Together?'

'Well, we sat at the same table in the canteen.'

'That's quite different.'

'Yes. I suppose it is.'

'So you told this Jo Perry that you had planned a trip to France and you either asked her the way to Burgundy or you asked her to suggest somewhere nice for you to go.'

'Not exactly.'

'What happened then?'

'We didn't talk at breakfast - well, hardly at all. I just happened to see her on the road in front of me later on. I recognised her car, you see. I'd seen her get it into it on the boat. It was a French car and as she was English, I thought maybe she'd be able to show me the ropes.'

'If you were both in your cars how did you speak to each other? I shouldn't have thought your Mini has a car phone.'

Gerry smiled. 'No, it doesn't. I saw her turn off at a stopping place and I just followed her.'

'To a service station?'

'Somewhere like that. Only there weren't any services. Just a picnic bench.'

'And so you ate your picnic together?' Kate realised she sounded a bit proprietorial. 'After all, that's no harm. You'd already had breakfast together.'

Gerry was beginning to realise that explaining about Jo was going to be more difficult than he'd thought.

'No. We didn't have a picnic.'

'You asked her the way?'

'In a sense, yes. I asked her if she knew anywhere where I could park a caravan. And she said: "How about my place?"'

'And you said: "how lovely, I'll follow you down" and you did and a great time was had by all.'

Gerry could detect the tinge of jealousy in her voice. 'Kate, I had to go somewhere.'

'No, you didn't. You didn't have run out on me like that and go off and park your caravan at another woman's place.'

It was on the tip of her tongue to tell him about Bert, lying dead on her caravan floor in a pool of dried blood, stinking of death. But she was afraid. She didn't want to know the worst yet. She had to think of the baby: Gerry's baby.

'It was only temporary. I had to have a bit of space: time to think. And we weren't married.'

'No. We weren't married. We're still not married.'

'No. Not yet.'

'Tell me more about Jo. Is she pretty?'

Gerry smiled and stroked her cheek. 'Not nearly as pretty as you are.'

'Is she married?'

'She's widowed.'

'So she's old?'

'Not too old. About ten years older than you.'

'What's she look like?'

'Fair hair, blue eyes, nice figure.'

'Fair hair, nice figure. Well, I'm dark and very soon I'll have no figure at all.'

'I prefer brunettes. And your figure'll come back when you've had the baby - our baby.'

'Does Jo have children?'

'She never mentioned any.'

'And her husband… When did he die?'

'Quite recently. Just a few weeks back, in fact.'

'How did he die?'

'He had an accident. He fell down a cliff face when he was out for a walk.'

'With his dog?'

'How did you guess?'

'I heard something about it. I heard Victor talking about it recently. It seems it mightn't have been an accident after all. Gerry…?'

'Yes?'

'No. It's nothing.'

'What's nothing?'

'Did - did you and Jo make love?'

'We went to bed together but I couldn't call it love. I don't love Jo. I love you.'

'It just happened because you were both there?'

'Yes.'

'Often?'

'Quite often.'

Kate sighed. 'I suppose it's unavoidable really. I've got something to tell you, too.'

'Victor?

'No. Not Victor. Tony.'

'What makes you so sure this Tony geyser isn't the father of the baby?'

'I know he isn't.' Kate was determined to blot out any idea of Tony's paternity from her mind.

'How do you know?' Gerry was persistent.

'Women know these things.'

'How?'

'Cos I'd missed my period before I went with him.'

'Which would make me the father?'

'In this case, yes.'

'What do you mean: in this case?'

'Cos there was only you and Tony.'

'In this case.'

'Yes.'

'What about...?'

Kate was terrified Gerry was going to say Bert.

'I said there was no one else, Gerry. Just you and Tony. And I didn't choose Tony. He raped me.'

'I know. That was evil.'

'That's why it couldn't be his baby. Surely babies only come out of love? Or caring anyway.'

Gerry felt happier. 'I'm sure you're right. I'm sure women know these things better than men.'

Kate seized on the chance. 'I'm sure they do.'

'I can't help wondering...'

Please God, not Bert.

'...Wondering about Victor.'

'Victor!'

'Yes. Victor.'

'Gerry! Haven't you noticed anything about Victor?'

'I've hardly seen that much of him. Well, no. I'm always with you.'

'Fair enough.'

'What about Victor?'

'I think he's gay.'

'Gay!'

'Yes.'

'What makes you think that?'

'Well he didn't make a pass at me.'

'Did you expect it?'

'I suppose I did. Men usually do.

Gerry laughed. 'Does that make Victor gay just because he didn't make a pass at you?'

'Not necessarily. But have you seen the way he looks at Pierre?'

'Can't say I've noticed.'

'I think Victor fancies Pierre.'

'Well, I'm pleased you didn't go with him. That might've given you a choice of three dads.'

'Gerry! I told you it can't be Tony. And it certainly can't be Victor. That only leaves you. Are you jealous of other men?'

'Maybe just a tiny bit.'

'But I'm not allowed to be jealous of Jo?'

'She's not having my baby.'

'As far as you know.'

'As far as I know. Kate. But I'm going to have to go and see Jo and explain the situation.'

Chapter Twenty

Jo drove back along the narrow rutted driveway to the farmhouse, deep in thought. There was no point in going to the police now. It appeared they had the case well in hand. They were questioning two people in connection with Alan's death. Though, heavens above, it had taken them long enough. Jo couldn't decide whether the slow progress was due more to the ineptness and stupidity of a country police force or the canniness and caginess of the local inhabitants.

Marcel and Jeanine had been so kind. They had also seemed concerned. Concerned not only that the riddle of Alan's death should be solved as speedily as possible; but immensely concerned about Jo's own welfare: how she was coping without Alan at her side, with the enormous amount of practical problems which they knew must constantly arise in running a guest house in a foreign country, where she hardly spoke the language.

The conversation with Marcel and Jeanine had been a great struggle. Jo knew she had understood very little of what they had said. Often the elderly couple had been forced to resort to sign language. Jo knew her French wasn't improving. In fact, she thought it had become worse since Gerry's arrival in Laronne. While Alan was still alive he would at least correct her terrible grammar and atrocious accent. He would translate for her when necessary, which seemed to be most of the time, and put her right when she had completely misunderstood something simple and basic. Now there was no one to help her at all. Gerry spoke no French and wasn't attempting to learn any except for the names of vineyards, bottlers and shippers. Most of the punters spoke no French either and relied on her to help them.

Gerry. In the relief of hearing that some positive progress had been made into the police investigations of Alan's death, she had temporarily forgotten about Gerry. He had gone off again. Only this time he had been away for two days and nights. Of course. That had been her other reason for going to the police station. She had forgotten for the moment. But she was already half way up the driveway now. She would have to continue up to the house, turn round in the courtyard and come back again. Better go to the loo first, though, just as a precaution. So she might just as well park the car in the proper place, as she tried to persuade everyone else to do. She drove carefully into the enormous barn, part of which was used as a car park and got of the car. Maxwell came bounding towards her, black and gauche, seemingly larger than ever. I really ought to put him on a diet, thought Jo vaguely, but I bet the punters feed him scraps; all that chewy tough steak that looks so appetising in the supermarket, but which, in fact, turns out to be almost inedible. Maxwell sniffed at her crutch, trod on her feet, almost bare in thin strappy sandals, put his wet nose and slobbering mouth into her hand and then jumped up, his paws reaching as high as her neck. He wagged his long, heavy tail against her legs, barking incessantly.

'Down, Max, down.' Dear God, what a bloody nuisance he is. I'd have him put down if Alan hadn't loved him so much. The dog kept barking and started to pull at her trouser leg with his teeth. Jo tried to push him away. 'Get off Maxwell! You're a bloody nuisance!'

Maxwell let go and stood quietly for a second. Jo heard shouts coming from the house and then the sound of running footsteps crunching across the gravel. Gerry, she thought. It must be Gerry. He's back!

As Jo got out of her car, the footsteps approaching the barn grew louder. Let's hope its Gerry, she thought fervently. The footsteps stopped suddenly just outside the barn door and Maxwell began to bark again, more frantically than ever. Jo shut the car door and went swiftly across to the dog.

'Shut up, Max! It's probably only Gerry.'

The dog stopped barking for a few seconds and Jo heard a man's voice outside the barn door.

'Is that you, Mrs Perry?'

Holding Maxwell by the collar in case he should frighten her visitor, Jo went to the barn door.

'Yes. Oh, good morning, Mr Penrose.'

'I'm so relieved you're back, Mrs Perry. I've been looking for you everywhere. You didn't say you were going out.'

'No.' It's a free country, thought Jo rather bitterly. I don't have to tell the punters each time I go out. She hadn't taken to the tall, thin Mr Penrose, with his drooping moustache, steel rimmed spectacles and watery pale blue eyes.

'No, I don't necessarily inform my guests each time I go out,' she replied tartly.

'Oh, I didn't realise. I thought the place was constantly supervised.'

'So far I've never found that necessary. Why? Is there a problem?'

'In a matter of speaking, Mrs Perry. There's been an accident...'

'An accident? What kind of an accident?' Dear God, not another accident. 'A bad accident? Is anyone hurt?' Jo felt her heart thumping louder. The palms of her hands grew sweaty.

'No one's hurt, Mrs Perry. It's not that kind of an accident. More of an environmental accident...'

'For God's sake stop talking in riddles and tell me what's happened,' snapped Jo. She was loosing patience with her punters. Each lot seemed worse than the last.

'There's a fault in the plumbing, Mrs Perry. Claire can't turn off the shower. The waste outlet seems to be blocked as well. The water's pouring down the staircase and beginning to drip through the ceiling into the apartment below.'

'Jesus Christ!' shouted Jo rushing into the house followed by Maxwell, barking hysterically.

All the paying guests had all tried to turn off the water without success. Jo tried to phone Georges Lefèvre, the plumber, but met with no success there either. Unbeknown to Jo, at the very moment the strident sound of the telephone echoed round the Lefèvre household, Josette Lefèvre was happily gossiping to her neighbour about how trying it was to have a husband who demanded even occasional sexual favours, while the said husband was relieving his sexual urges in a most powerful orgasm, his face tucked in between the soft, capacious breasts of his miraculous Chantal.

It wasn't until lunchtime that Jo made contact with *Monsieur* Lefèvre, by which time one of the more enterprising punters had finally managed to locate the water main and turn off the stopcock. The devastation was terrible. Jo could never have imagined that mere water from a shower could do so much damage. Luckily the staircase, hewn from robust Burgundian oak by the skilled craftsmanship of Didier Pérnot, only needed wiping up with a dry cloth. The walls had been splashed, but they would soon dry out. The floor of the shower room itself was awash, but with the aid of buckets, mops and willing hands, it was soon cleared up. It was the apartment underneath the shower room that had received the worst damage. It appeared that a pipe had burst in the shower itself and the water had gone through the ceiling, damaging furniture, rugs, a curtain and a whole case of Alan's books. Jo was appalled, shocked and constantly on the verge of tears as she cleared up the mess with the help of her visitors. She was extremely grateful to them. After all, it was hardly an appropriate holiday occupation to have to clear up the mess in one's guesthouse. Jo felt that when they had all finished, a few bottles of wine all round wouldn't go amiss.

Georges Lefèvre called round in the afternoon, inspected the plumbing and declared that nothing could to be done until the following morning at the earliest, provided he could lay his hands on all the necessary piping for executing the repairs. He was a very busy man. He had a lot on his plate at the moment but he would, of course, do his best. Until his best materialised they would just have to manage without water.

'Isn't there a water tank in the attic?' enquired one of the guests.

'No,' replied Jo, by now totally fraught and exhausted. 'The French don't have tanks in the attic.

They don't see the necessity for them. They think they might burst and cause a flood.'

By five o'clock poor Jo was utterly worn out, while the punters went off to the swimming pool.

'At least there's one way of keeping clean,' remarked one.

Jo went round to the far side of the barn to the caravan, half expecting to see Gerry stretched out on a sunbed with a glass of wine beside him. But there was no one. The caravan was shut up and completely deserted. Jo's heart sank a little lower. I'd meant to go to the police station this morning to make enquiries about him, she thought, but of course it wasn't possible. I'll have to wait till tomorrow now. She unlocked the caravan, went in and sat down on the bench seat. Petra was arriving next week, probably Tuesday, she had said on the phone.

'I'll phone you on Saturday to confirm it.'

'That's fine,' Jo had replied.

'And Jo...'

'Yes?'

'Do you remember what I said in my letter about going up to the quarry to the place where - where Dad died?'

'Yes, of course.'

'Have you been up there yet?'

'N-no. Not yet?'

'Shall we go together?'

'We could do. Why don't we discuss it when you arrive?'

'Yes. Why not. Good idea. Phone you Saturday. Bye.'

'Bye, Petra.'

There was less than a week to go before Petra's arrival. She seemed quite set on seeing the place where her father had met his death. Jo now felt more strongly than ever that she should go up there on her own before Petra's arrival. She would at least know what was in store and might be better able to help Petra cope with her distress; help to heal her grief. As Petra was younger by twelve years, Jo felt it was up to her to take the lead and be the stronger person. It was an idea, which had been forming for some time now and should no longer be postponed. Today was Wednesday, 29 June. She calculated it was exactly eight weeks since Alan's death. This might be a very good moment to revisit the scene of his accident. She would go this evening. But first she would have a half-hour kip to give her a bit more strength.

Chapter Twenty-One

'*Maman!*'

'*Oui, chéri*'.

'The 4 May was a Wednesday'.

'Was it, dear?'

'Yes. I've checked in the calendar. You said it was a Thursday.'

'Did I, dear?' *Madame* Paillard sounded vague. 'Is it important? It's quite a long time ago now.'

'Nearly eight weeks ago,' replied Roland Paillard. 'But yes, it is important.'

'Why is that, dear?'

In the last two months *Madame* Paillard had become increasingly vague. Her piano pupils turned up as previously arranged and *Madame* assiduously passed on her knowledge and her skills. Meals were served regularly and punctually by Vivienne, the servant, who had been with *Madame* Paillard for over thirty years. *Madame* Paillard no longer had to plan or arrange anything. She had planned and arranged it all years ago. Now all she had to do was sit and wait for it all to happen, and it did; like clockwork.

'What was that you were saying, Roland?' *Madame* Paillard put down a photograph of her husband, now dead for over twelve years.

'I was saying, *Maman*, that I was under a misapprehension about 4 May.'

'The 4 May?'

'Yes.'

'And why is that?'

Mon Dieu, thought Roland. *Maman* does seem to be losing her marbles a bit.

'Well, I had thought, or been led to believe, that 4 May was a Thursday. I now have confirmation that it was a Wednesday.'

Madame Paillard picked up another photograph of her husband and studied it closely.

'So handsome,' she murmured. 'Does it matter, Roland?'

'Yes, *Maman*, it matters a great deal. Alan Perry met with his fatal accident on Wednesday 4 May around seven-thirty pm. I spoke to him at ten-minutes-past seven. I may have been the last person to see Alan alive. I think I should go to the police.'

Jules Gilot had two things on his mind. One was his wife, Chantal. They had been married for eleven years now and although childless, Jules felt that they were as happy as most couples could reasonably expect to be. He had married Chantal on the rebound. His family and friends had expressed a little initial surprise at his choice but they quickly took to the large, bouncy woman with her warm smile, big laugh and huge breasts. It was her breasts that Jules had first noticed. In fact, no one could avoid noticing Chantal's breasts. They sailed before her wherever she went, swinging and swaying like gargantuan fleshy pendulums. Jules had fantasised about those breasts after only one meeting. What would they look like naked? How would it feel to put his face between them? He hadn't been disappointed. He had had the full benefit of those remarkable breasts for eleven years. But now he suspected that someone else was enjoying them too. It wouldn't take him long to find out. There weren't that many people in Laronne who would be attracted to such enormous breasts in such an intimate way. It was really only a question of matching up the shaving lotion. The perfume was quite an unusual one.

Jules' second problem concerned Alan Perry. He remembered the evening of 4 May very clearly. He was on his way to deliver an urgent letter to Roland Paillard, the architect who lived with his rather dotty mother in the big house above the old quarry beyond Dracy. He didn't know either *Monsieur* Paillard or his mother particularly well. Nobody did. They kept themselves to themselves and gave the impression, *Madame* Paillard in particular, of being a little bit superior to the ordinary people in Dracy and Laronne. But duty is duty, and Jules took his very seriously. As the only postman serving an increasingly wide area it was essential that he made all the deliveries promptly, especially the urgent ones, however inconvenient the time of day might be.

He remembered Alan Perry's cheery call: '*Bonjour, Jules!*' as he struggled valiantly up the hill on his battered old bicycle. He remembered dismounting with relief and his pleasure in greeting such a good friend. He remembered, too, much of the conversation. It was all about walking dogs. Bizarre, how the English seem to enjoy walking their dogs. He couldn't see the reason for it himself. Dogs were for guarding property, and as for walking - well! Jules, detesting any sort of exercise, would have swapped his battered old bicycle for a car any day.

But now Alan Perry was dead, struck down by a freak accident, leaving behind him a charming, pretty but confused and defenceless widow. Had it been an accident? The talk in Laronne was that such an accident would have been almost impossible. An experienced walker, an Englishman (all English people were experienced walkers) strolling along the cliff top with his dog? How could he have had an accident? He knew the dangers. He knew what to look out for. Surely he had been pushed? Or had a rumour to this effect been deliberately circulated in Dracy and Laronne? And who would circulate such a rumour? Colette Gautier of course! Who else! Nosy parker with her wagging tongue. Over two hundred years ago people had been guillotined solely through rumours set in motion by people like Colette Gautier.

And what about Lucien, the master baker so beloved by all? Jules certainly loved his *baguettes* and *batards*, but perhaps Lucien also loved to put his head between large, fleshy breasts? Jules felt he ought to check out Lucien's shaving lotion.

Meanwhile, the image of Alan Perry's handsome, open, sun-tanned face was beginning to haunt Jules Gilot. He had spoken to him about seven o'clock on that fateful evening. According to the pathologist, forty minutes later he was dead. Jules might have been the last person to see him alive. He couldn't have it on his conscience for the rest of his life. It was time he went to the police.

Lucien Gautier scratched his thick mop of curly dark hair and wiped his hands on his heavy baker's apron.

He was in a thoughtful mood as he shoved the large tray containing the long *ficelles, baguettes* and *batards* into the vast oven where the red-hot wood burnt merrily down below. Lucien loved his baker's job. He was proud of his skill, both as master baker and *patissier.* He loved to see the differently shaped loaves coming out of the oven, light, crispy and golden. He enjoyed kneading the dough and cutting the pastry to make his famous *tartes aux fruits.* He enjoyed chatting to the customers, both in the bakery and outside their houses during his daily morning delivery round. But most of all he enjoyed the calm and solitude of his early morning labours, baking the bread in the vast hot ovens. He rose at three am, slipping quietly out of bed so as not to disturb his wife, Colette, still sleeping soundly, her arm above her head, caressing the hair curlers, which she put in every night to achieve her attractive fluffy hair-style. She looked as pretty as a baby doll in her pink nightie, tied at the neck with a pink satin bow. There were many people over the years who had offered Lucien sympathy for his unsocial working hours but he brushed these unnecessary sentiments aside.

'*Je les aime bien,*' he would reply. 'I enjoy working alone in the early hours of the morning while the rest of the world sleeps. It's peaceful. I can think.'

And now Lucien was thinking.

It was almost two months since Alan Perry's tragic death. Lucien remembered the day well. It was Wednesday 4 May. He remembered it for several reasons. One was the cancellation of the by now fairly regular Wednesday meeting of *les copains* up in the cottage in the woods on the way to Dracy. Lucien enjoyed these sessions. He thought they all did. It made a nice change, just men together, gambling and drinking in the cosy little cottage in the woods. At first he had been suspicious, as all the others had too, of the inclusion in the group of the Englishman, Alan Perry. Lucien had never met a foreigner before. He had seen them, of course, gawping at the medieval church in Laronne; staring at the decorative *Mairie* in Dracy. He had sold them bread and pastries at the bakery, inwardly scornful of their inability to speak any French, resorting to sign language to point out the items they required. He had been amazed by Alan Perry's fluent, almost perfect French. Alan's command of the language and his absorption in all things French set him apart from all other foreigners. It was so easy to include him in everything. He had integrated so well that he was completely accepted in their group. Lucien thought of him as a really good friend. He had been totally devastated by Alan's death.

As the days turned into weeks and the police investigation into Alan's death remained static, Lucien began to wonder if there was any connection between the cancellation of the meeting of *les copains* and Alan's fatal accident. But why should he think such a thing? It was, after all, Didier Pérnot who had cancelled the meeting. That was Didier's privilege. It was he who had found the cottage and inaugurated the sessions. He was the Mayor of Laronne and had probably had a more pressing engagement to attend to. Even so, it did appear to be a strange coincidence.

Lucien clearly remembered his meeting with Alan on that fateful evening. He was out on a special delivery, bringing a large *tarte aux fraises* to Jean-Pierre Floret for his eighty-fifth birthday. He had met Alan on the way up to *Monsieur* Floret's house. Alan was on one of his walks, a renowned English habit apparently, usually accompanied by his dog. His meeting with Alan on that evening had been extremely brief. Lucien was in a hurry. He had to leave the *tarte aux fraises* with *Monsieur* Floret in time for his birthday celebration and get home for dinner with Colette by eight o'clock. He remembered Alan's surprise at his late delivery round in such a remote area. He hadn't told Alan that he had one more call to make after *Monsieur* Floret.

It was a private call. Quite private. He had recently started a nice little affair with Anne-Marie Marceau, the wife of the schoolmaster, Emile. Annie, as Lucien called her, was bored and lonely. Living in Lille, in northern France near the Belgian border, had been bad enough after a lifetime enjoying the wonders and excitement of Paris. But when her husband took up his new teaching post in Laronne, Annie was in the depths of despair. She had never lived in the country before and she was finding the experience oppressive in the extreme. She couldn't bear the silence, the greenness and the emptiness of it all.

'Nothing ever happens,' she complained. 'Nothing moves - not even the cows - and the silence is quite deafening.'

Annie and Emile had no children and Annie couldn't find a job. Another rural problem, she complained to Lucien. So when Emile went off to the classroom each morning, Annie stayed in the teacher's house and somehow tried to fill in her day. Gradually Lucien began to make the Marceau's house his last port of call and helped Annie fill in her day too. They both knew their affair couldn't last forever and they both tried not to become too emotionally involved but just enjoy the physical side to the full. Annie, married to a very silent, rather taciturn husband, was delighted with Lucien's friendly patter and chatter. And Lucien, with a wife who never stopped talking for even one second, was delighted to have found a mistress who enjoyed his stories and his jokes.

One morning, during school break, Emile returned to the house to collect a clean handkerchief. He strode into the bedroom so quickly, that he caught Lucien and Annie totally unawares in bed together. They were taken so completely off their guard that Lucien had no time to leap into the wardrobe or even roll under the bed. They both just shot under the duvet, clutched each other and stopped breathing. Their luck held. Emile, in a great hurry, as he had momentarily left his class unattended, grabbed his clean handkerchief and rushed out of the bedroom, without even bothering to close either the drawer or the bedroom door. But it had been a very close shave indeed. It was known, through Colette Gautier of course, that many of the inhabitants of Laronne were engaged in extra-marital affairs. After all, the country being the country, and very remote country at that, there was very little else to do. It was difficult for couples who had been married, or even just together, for some considerable time, to think up new variations on a well-worn theme. A re-coupling brought new ideas and fresh excitement into a very old pastime. If their affair were to continue it was imperative to find different, safer premises. So Lucien, with the advantage of his widespread deliveries to give him a cast-iron alibi, finally found another derelict cottage, past the one where *les copains* held their sessions up by the old quarry towards the lake. Structurally, it was in a much better condition than the cottage discovered by Didier Pérnot. There was nothing inside in the way of floor covering, carpets or furniture. But Annie and Lucien didn't need much: just a bed and maybe a table and a couple of chairs. Between them they furnished it simply from junk shops and parents' fund-raising donations at the school.

They met often. Annie was free all day and Lucien had no problem in extending his delivery times without arousing the least suspicion. They had no problem in communicating to arrange the next *rendezvous*. Lucien just made an extra call at the teacher's house and no one except Annie was aware of it.

On Wednesday 4 May they had a wonderful afternoon. So wonderful that they had decided to seal it with a final orgy of love-making that evening after Lucien's call to *Monsieur* Floret. When Lucien left in the late afternoon to prepare his *tarte aux fraises* for *Monsieur* Floret at the bakery, Annie stayed on at the cottage to clean and tidy up a little and continue running up curtains, which they had both decided would make the place more homely.

Having left Alan Perry at about ten minutes to seven and delivered his tart to *Monsieur* Floret, Lucien drove back along the narrow road which wound its way up past the old quarry and along by the dangerous precipice down to the lake, where, unknown to Lucien, Alan Perry was about to meet his death in a few minutes time. Lucien's heart was singing at the thought of making love to his beloved Annie so soon again. So deep was he in thought and fond feelings for Annie, that he was quite unprepared for what happened next.

A red car came round the corner, quite close behind him. In his rear mirror Lucien could see the face of Emile Marceau, brows knitted in concentration as he tried to remember the exact spot where he had taken his class for a picnic that afternoon, so he could retrieve the anorak belonging to the little girl. It gave Lucien quite a start to see the face of his lover's husband so close behind him in his rear mirror. He wondered, with alarm, what Emile was doing in this remote spot. Did he know about the cottage? Had he already been there and found his wife inside, patiently and contentedly waiting for her lover, for him, Lucien? Had his cover been blown? Was his wonderful affair soon to end? Was he, the master baker of Laronne, renowned not just for his produce but for his loyalty and kindness as well, soon to be exposed and, inevitably disgraced?

Thoughts rushed through his mind, different thoughts now, no longer those of peace and love, but of confusion and torment. He decided to drive on. If Emile followed him, he would be forced to drive past the overgrown path to the cottage and forgo spending another precious few minutes with Annie that evening. Annie would wait a little. She wouldn't worry. She was always calm and composed. He would explain everything when he delivered the bread to the Marceau household in the morning. Lucien had no idea, of course, that Emile was out only to search for a little girl's anorak, which had been lost on a picnic.

The red car slowed down and stopped. Lucien could no longer see Emile's eyes in his rear mirror. He wondered if Emile had recognised him. Thank God he wasn't in his baker's van, which had gone into the garage for an emergency repair. Lucien was grateful for that now; relieved he was in his own private car, rarely used and quite unidentifiable. Still glancing constantly in his rear mirror, Lucien saw Emile Marceau park his car in a lay-by, get out and walk across the cliff top, near to the spot where Alan Perry was shortly to met his death.

Lucien drove on a short distance and rounded a steep corner. There, not far off, on a promontory overlooking the lake far below, stood the unmistakably slight figure of Jean Bertrand. As Lucien drove past, presuming that Jean was up to no good and hoping against hope that he would not turn round and recognise him, the youth bent down and picked up a stone, which he hurled down the cliff side. Lucien carried on towards the haven of his secret cottage, hoping he would not encounter anyone else on the way before he found himself in the soothing embrace of his beloved.

Chapter Twenty-Two

There were just two things in his life that gave Bernard Roger immense pride and satisfaction. One was his herd of Charolais cattle; the other was his son Luc.

It was hard work being a cattle farmer, especially if one worked single handed, as Bernard did. His two brothers were also farmers in the *Commune* of Laronne, but they were busy on their own land and had their own problems. They offered to help at harvest time, as did everyone in the area, but otherwise it was each man to his own, particularly where the livestock was concerned. So mostly Bernard struggled on alone.

He was equally busy in winter and summer. In winter he had to clean out the mucky stables where he had driven the cattle for the season. He also tried to get round to all the hedging and ditching in the numerous fields he rented from other landowners in the area. In the summer the cattle were out in an assortment of fields, so he had to check they weren't wandering too far. He also had the vegetable and cereal crops to attend to.

In France, unlike England, there is no law of primogeniture. In England this law forbids estates from being broken up and divided equally between all the sons. In France, almost all property is divided up with each succeeding generation, so in the end there is hardly any land left at all. Bernard's grandfather had had a considerable holding, but as his wife bore him nine sons, all of whom survived into adulthood to inherit a ninth share, there wasn't a great deal left for Bernard's father. By the time it was again divided into three, the land was hardly a viable commercial proposition. So the three brothers were forced to rent land from families who had sold their livestock and gone to live in the cities in search of adventure and prosperity. But Bernard was determined he would do everything possible to help his son, Luc, to avoid the loneliness, poverty and the back-breaking hard work of a farmer's life.

He was less interested in the future of his daughter, Claire. At twelve, she was a pretty girl with long blond hair, blue eyes and a cheeky upturned freckled nose. Already heads turned when she walked down the street, on the few occasions he had taken her on a day's outing to Chalon or Macon. Bernard felt that education for girls was unimportant, especially pretty girls. All Claire needed was a rich, attractive husband, preferably one who lived in a town. Bernard hadn't the faintest notion how he would set about finding such a husband. His daughter was only twelve. There was plenty of time.

Bernard had never discussed his plans with his wife, Denise. He had long given up on her. After fifteen years of marriage and observing her sluttish ways, he now put what hope he had left in life in his cattle and his son, Luc.

Bernard was delighted that Luc had a new teacher for his last year at primary school. Emile Marceau had given Luc such tremendous encouragement and extra help after school that Bernard was finally planning to go to a parents' evening in order to meet Emile. He knew his wife, Denise wouldn't stir herself sufficiently to come along with him. Sadly, Denise had no interests in life beyond staying in bed as long as possible and reading glossy women's magazines.

Even without going to the official parents' evening Bernard knew his son was doing well. Long after the boy had gone to bed, he poured over Luc's exercise books, noting the ticks, the stars, the high percentage marks and the lack of red corrections. After he had studied Luc's books, Bernard felt proud and confident: proud he had such an able son; confident he would have a successful future ahead. As the weeks passed into the final phase of Luc's last term at Laronne primary school, Bernard waited with pleasurable anticipation for his first official meeting with his son's new teacher, to whom he felt he owed a great debt of gratitude for all his help and encouragement.

Bernard was perfectly aware, as indeed were most of the other inhabitants of Laronne, that somebody was hiding something from the police regarding Alan Perry's tragic death. It had not fully been established as being an accident; nor had there been any proof of foul play. No one had come forward with any information as to where they had been on that fateful evening of Wednesday 4 May. The only certainty was the assurance of Alan's widow, Jo Perry that her husband had left home with the dog shortly after five-thirty on that sunny May evening, planning to be back by seven-thirty for dinner. Even Colette Gautier, variously known as useful informant or irresponsible gossip, depending on one's point of view, was unable to throw any more light on the subject. Anyone who knew anything was keeping quiet. No one in the entire *Commune* of Laronne wished to get involved with the police.

Luc Roger had come top of his class and would go on to his secondary school with a special commendation for industry, good behaviour and outstanding achievement. Bernard's fatherly pride knew no bounds, as he waited for the parent's meeting the following week with mounting interest and impatience.

Then the most unfortunate thing happened.

Throughout Emile Marceau's first year at Laronne Primary School, various items of school property had gone missing. Textbooks, exercise books, jotters, pens, pencils, rubbers and rulers were slowly disappearing. At first Emile was totally at a loss as to what to do about it. He regarded stealing and violence as a purely urban phenomenon. Having never lived in the country before his present post, he was under the misapprehension that all country dwellers, adults as well as children, were happy, fulfilled and materially well off. It hadn't occurred to him that rural deprivation was far more harsh and deep-rooted than any suffered in the towns. But as more and more school property began to disappear, Emile Marceau was forced to take a stand. One morning during the Easter Term he addressed the whole school: twenty-eight young country hopefuls, looking as if butter wouldn't melt in their mouths.

'...And so, children,' he concluded in his address, 'I very much regret to say that if the thief is caught, he or she will be severely punished, stripped of any awards they may have gained during the year and given a poor end of year report.'

The next morning Emile walked into the classroom and found Luc Roger standing in front of the stationary cupboard, filling his pockets with pens, pencils, rubbers and rulers.

In the end, Luc confessed to all the thefts. He admitted stealing the items to give to his friends. He was socially embarrassed by his own lack of material possessions and held himself in such low esteem that he was over-anxious to improve his standing among his peers.

Emile had no alternative but to carry out his threat. For a week Luc was kept in every day after school and given tedious tasks to do such as sweeping floors, scouring hand basins and generally tidying up. Emile knew extra academic work would be no punishment for his star pupil. Luc's stars and his special commendation for excellence were taken away and a footnote for unseemly behaviour was added to his end of term report. The only honour remaining to him was that he was still top of his class. It was impossible to remove the simple fact: there was no one to touch Luc Roger academically.

Bernard was distraught. He thought his son's life's prospects were ruined. Being just a simple peasant, his only thought was revenge. He would go to the police and tell them he had seen Emile Marceau at seven-thirty pm on Wednesday 4 May, driving a red car on the cliff top, a few yards from where Alan Perry had met his death.

He had no fear whatsoever of the consequences.

Chapter Twenty-Three

'Pierre wants me to go with the whole group to this remote cliff top for a rehearsal of their new pageant. But I don't want to go at all. What'll I do, Gerry?' Kate looked at him pleadingly.

'Don't go, that's all.'

'How can I get out of it?'

'Don't be around when they leave.'

'Say they come looking for me?'

'Hide.'

'Where?'

'We'll find somewhere. It's a big enough place. Anyway, why don't you want to go? It could be a bit of a laugh wandering about on a deserted hill top all dressed up in medieval gear.'

Kate shuddered. 'It's anything but a laugh. You don't know anything about their new pageant.'

'No. Tell me.'

'It's all about this poor woman who was branded a witch about four hundred years ago. The locals chased her up to a deserted cliff top above a lake. They slit her throat, disembowelled her while she was still alive and then threw her body into the lake. They want me to play the part of the murdered woman.'

Gerry put his arm around her. 'We'll find somewhere to hide this evening, don't worry. Or we could always go out somewhere?'

'I don't like it here any more, Gerry. There's something odd about these people. There's something – well, sinister and sadistic about them. Let's leave. Let's go back to England tomorrow.'

'As soon as we can. But I can't leave without explaining things to Jo.'

'No. I can see that. When are you going to do it?'

'Tomorrow.'

'Tomorrow?'

'Yes.'

'Promise?'

'Promise. Tonight we'll hide here. It'll be less obvious than going off somewhere. I know a good place.'

Lucien Gautier sang as he drove up the steep narrow road towards the old quarry above Dracy. In a couple of minutes he would pull off the road, hide the car behind some bushes and walk the last few hundred yards to the cottage, secluded in the woods, where his beloved Annie would be waiting for him. It was unfortunate his car was bright red, he thought, as he parked it behind some large bushes, hopefully hidden from the road. If he had known at the time he was buying it, that he would be having assignations in the woods with a mistress, he would, of course, have bought a green, or perhaps a black one. Curious that Emile's car, which Annie borrowed whenever possible, was also red. So was Didier Pérnot's, come to that. Odd, because most people in the area had white cars, which showed up better against the green of the countryside. Lucien walked up the now well-worn path to the front door of the cottage, his heart singing. In a few moments he and his beloved Annie would be naked in each other's arms.

Georges Lefèvre couldn't wait to take his beloved Chantal to the deserted cottage he had found up in the woods. *Mon Dieu!* It had been a difficult day. Josette had yapped and nagged more than usual and the phone had never stopped ringing during lunch. You'd think people would leave you alone at lunchtime. How can a man function on any level without a decent lunch? It was difficult enough to persuade lazy, frigid Josette to produce an appetising, satisfying meal, but on the odd occasion when she did, he wasn't even allowed to eat it in peace. Of course the English didn't understand food. He had heard that in England people took only half an hour for lunch, which might explain their lack of sexual appetite. To have good sex, a man needed good food. So it followed that the English had little understanding of the Frenchman's need for a peaceful two-hour lunch break. *Madame* Perry had no idea he was tucking into the first *poulet roti* that Josette had produced in nearly a year, when she had telephoned about her burst pipe. *Et mon Dieu!* What a mess! What a state the poor lady had been in! And all her mad English guests rushing around with buckets and mops tying to stem the flood, which was coming out of the bathroom like a waterfall. It seemed that no one had thought to turn off the main water tap. Even *Madame* Perry, the owner of the house, hadn't known where it was. Poor lady. Georges was sorry for her: widowed so young, struggling to make ends meet in a foreign country where she barely spoke the language. *Cher Alain*. It had been a dreadful tragedy.

Georges pulled off the road well before the path to the cottage came in sight. He parked his discreet black car behind some bushes on the right, got out, locked it and made his way up the narrow over-grown track to the cottage where he planned to meet Chantal in just a few minutes time. It was after seven-thirty and although still fully daylight out in the open, it was dusky in the woods. Something made Georges move quietly and cautiously as he walked round to the back of the cottage, even though he was not expecting it to be occupied. It had looked very silent and deserted earlier in the afternoon, but there was something sinister about the whole place that signalled caution. There was an aura of sombre expectancy.

Suddenly he heard a woman laugh. A bright, tinkling laugh, in stark contrast to the gloomy surroundings. For a moment he couldn't make out where the laugh had come from. Absurdly it seemed to come from the bushes behind him. He stood stock still, not daring to breathe, his heart beating a little faster. Then he heard a man's voice, laughing too. There seemed to be something distinctly familiar about the male voice. Could it have come from the cottage? Georges crept forward as silently as possible towards the slightly open window. In spite of himself he wondered why he was being quite so cautious. After all, in the afternoon the cottage had seemed deserted and as far as he knew, the wood was public property. But at the moment it did seem possible there was someone inside the cottage. He picked his way carefully over what had once been a flower-bed and reached the window. He almost gasped out loud in surprise at the sight, which met his eyes. There was a soft light on in the far corner beyond a double bed. The bed covers had been thrown back and both the floor and the bed were strewn with clothes. Clothes belonging to a man and a woman who were stark naked, hard at it on the bed. The woman was kneeling on the bed on all fours. The man, with an enormous erection was fondling her from behind. The woman was slight with long fair hair falling forwards, cascading over her face. The man was well built, with thick dark hair, a darkish complexion and a very hairy chest. At the moment his face was in shadow.

Georges watched, fascinated. In all his long and varied sexual experiences he had never before seen another couple at it. The woman was moaning with pleasure, punctuated with light little laughs. The man was laughing too and murmuring endearments. Georges caught a glimpse of his face for a split second, before he gently turned the woman over and came into her. Georges stared in utter amazement. The man was Lucien Gautier.

He thought he recognised the woman as the wife of Emile Marceau, the new, rather dull schoolmaster. Obviously he was also rather dull in bed. Feeling sexually aroused by what he had witnessed, Georges looked around for his own beloved Chantal. On no account must the lovers in the cottage be disturbed. He and Chantal would have to make do with the car.

As Jules Gilot let himself into the house, he met his wife, Chantal, in the hall, dressed for going out.

'You're going out? Now? So late?'

Chantal knew she was trapped. She knew she couldn't leave now and meet Georges in the woods tonight. He said he had a surprise. Something really special to show her in the wood near the old quarry. 'Something for both of us you will really like,' he had said.

Chantal looked straight at her husband who was regarding her in slight puzzlement. Whatever surprise Georges had in store would have to wait. Jules was, after all, her husband. Her first loyalty should be to him. It was just that Georges was - well - different. Chantal wasn't fully aware that she had a low boredom threshold.

'I've just come in,' she said lamely.

'And where did you go?' enquired Jules, thinking how really attractive Chantal looked in a billowing navy dress with white polka dots. She wore high-heeled shoes, which was extremely rare, as, with her large bulk, she didn't always find it easy to balance. She was lightly made up, carried a smart navy handbag and smelt quite delicious.

'I - I just went to visit *Maman*,' said Chantal, feebly.

Huh! Dressed to kill just to visit your mother! thought Jules. More lightly going on an assignation with that Lucien Gautier. But he didn't say anything of the kind.

'Is *Maman* quite well?' he enquired. 'No problems?'

'Oh, yes! *Maman* is very well. No problems at all.'

'You look very lovely, *chérie*.'

'Merci, *chéri!*'

'I - I thought it would cheer up *Maman* if I made a little effort to look nice.'

'And, I am, of course, also a beneficiary.'

Jules took a step towards his wife. She suddenly seemed very desirable. He put out a hand and touched one of her massive, exploding breasts. Chantal gave a little frisson of pleasure. He continued to stroke the breast, then he brought up his other hand to give the second breast equal attention. Chantal let her smart handbag fall to the ground with a thud. Jules had never been so subtle before. This was marvellous! As Jules continued to stroke, she felt a rush of dampness between her legs. Then he took hold of both breasts, squeezing large quantities of flesh in each hand.

'How does the dress undo?' he enquired. 'I wouldn't want to spoil it.'

'It unzips down the back. Then it just lifts off over my head.'

Jules let go of the magnificent breasts, turned his wife round, unzipped the dress and lifted it carefully over her head. Without looking at her, he laid the dress over the back of the hall chair. Then he turned back to look at her, gasping in amazement and delight. She was a *tour de force* of womanhood. Her pure white unblemished flesh hung in great folds around a frame in which not a bone was to be seen. Her breasts hung down, bigger and fleshier than he had ever imagined, rolling onto her huge stomach, the nipples enormous, dark and erect. Her vast bottom seemed to spread out across the hall, soft, fleshy, glistening white. He came towards her, frantic to have her. He grabbed the enormous buttocks and held them for a second. Then he put his face between the two great breasts and went: 'Brrrrah.'

It was the first time in eleven years of marriage that Jules Gilot had seen his wife naked.

Georges Lefèvre sat in his car in the wood for almost two hours waiting for his beloved Chantal. The owls hooted, the bats flew around and a full moon came up, casting a pale, eerie light around the wood. No sound came from the cottage but he could hear raised voices on the cliff top above the lake. He wasn't sure whether to worry about Chantal or not. More than likely she had mistimed her departure to coincide with Jules' arrival at home. No matter. They would have other times together. There would be many more occasions on which he would be able to grasp those succulent, fleshy breasts.

In the meantime he might just as well go home to the frigid Josette and see if she had anything to offer him; either nutritionally or sexually.

Didier Pérnot parked his red car beside some bushes on the cliff top overlooking the quarry and waited for the others to arrive. It was eight o'clock on a beautiful still summer night. The sun was setting, golden in a pink sky over Laronne on the opposite side of the narrow road. Down below, the lake looked dark and sinister in the shadows. The perfect setting for a cruel medieval tale of witchcraft and murder, thought Didier, well satisfied with his choice of subject and venue. He was fully attired in his pageant garments: long black robe with a hood, a white mask with blood red lips and two holes for the eyes; the surrounds painted a luminous green. Didier was playing the executioner and he totally looked the part. He hoped the others would arrive just as dusk was falling over the cliff top, so they would fully appreciate the sinister spirit around the place: the very spot where poor Alan Perry had lost his life eight weeks ago. No one yet knew for certain how or why he had died. Had he seen a ghost, a spirit from the past; had such a bad fright that he had lost his balance and slipped on the sheer, treacherous surface? Or perhaps, while he was gazing down below at the view of the lake, someone had come up behind and pushed him over? But who?

Didier looked at his watch. Eight-thirty. Everyone should be here by now. Unfortunately the woman who had volunteered to play the part of the victim had been unable to attend at the last moment. She said she had forgotten about an important committee meeting. As she was to play such a major part, her absence was most regrettable. Louis Durant had been excused. With his bad arthritis he could hardly be expected to leap about on a cliff top with any safety. Michel Voyou had also been excused because his wife had suddenly been taken to hospital. But that still left Pierre Bittard, Jules Gilot, Lucien Gautier and Georges Lefèvre. Where were they all? What were they up to on this beautiful summer evening? Why were they not on the cliff top, where they had been bidden by Didier Pérnot, who was, after all the Mayor of Laronne.

Chapter Twenty-Four

Jo woke up with a start, aching all over. For a moment she couldn't remember why she had fallen asleep on the bench seat without making up the bed properly as she usually did. She couldn't remember either why she ached so much. Then it all came back in a flash: the flood in the shower; the tiresome Mr and Mrs Penrose; the massive clearing up operation; the helpfulness of the other guests and the belated arrival of the plumber, Georges Lefèvre, stating baldly that he didn't have the correct equipment to do any repairs today, so they would just have to manage without any water for the time being. She remembered, too, the ironic question of the water tank. Why were there no water tanks in the loft in French houses? Because of the risk of flooding, of course! But she had had the flood without the water tank and the inconvenience of being left without any water into the bargain. Jo felt she had had enough problems with French houses, French plumbing and unreliable English paying guests. It was high time to put her rambling, inconvenient French property on the market and return to live in England.

But for the moment she was still living in Laronne and stuck with all her problems. Petra was coming to stay next week and wanted to visit the spot where her father had died. Jo had already decided to see the place first: to be prepared and forewarned, so she would be better able to comfort and support Petra. She had decided to go up to the old quarry this evening. Should she go alone? Or should she take Maxwell with her for protection and companionship? If Gerry had been around would he have offered to come with her, just to keep her company? She had hardly spoken to Gerry about Alan. There hadn't seemed much point somehow. The two men were totally different. Alan, the academic, the dreamer, the scholar, the long-term planner, sensitive and responsible. Sexy too, in his own refined way. Gerry, in complete contrast, seemed to have little or no education despite his avowal of private schooling. He totally lacked any sense of responsibility, and as for long-term planning! Jo felt Gerry couldn't plan further than the next ten minutes. But he was fun: a warm and lively companion and very good in bed. Jo had realised right from the beginning that their relationship couldn't last. They came from different planets and only seemed to be fully united in the sexual act, and then strictly only in the physical sense. Even so, Jo felt great affection for Gerry. She was grateful to him for having filled a terrible void at a most crucial time in her life. She sat up and looked at the clock on the table. Ten minutes to eight. Good Lord! She'd slept for over two hours! She dabbed her face with a flannel in a bowl of water, which luckily she had the foresight to save, and brushed her teeth. She looked down at her bare legs. Shorts? No. You never know what kind of bushes and brambles might be encountered on a cliff top. Better put on stout shoes too, with soles that would grip as much as possible. It would be too ironic if she were to slip on the cliff top and end up in the lake only eight weeks after her husband's fatal accident in the same place.

Jo put a light cotton sweater over her tee shirt and went out of the caravan, locking it behind her. She went round the corner to the front of the barn and called for Maxwell, expecting him to come bounding along, tail wagging furiously, body wriggling ecstatically, in joyous anticipation of a walk. But there was silence.

'Maxwell! Maxwell!' she called. 'Max-y!' But the dog didn't appear. Jo wondered whether she should tell the punters she was going out for a walk, especially in view of Mr Penrose's comment this morning: 'I didn't know you'd gone out. I thought this place was always fully supervised.' But it wasn't. And it never had been fully supervised. And why, for God's sake, should she pander to the punters?

Jo got into her car and drove off alone down the bumpy, rutted drive.

Jo wasn't sure of the exact place of Alan's tragic accident, so she followed the route she knew. It was the way she and Alan had always driven when they went to have dinner with *Madame* Paillard and her son, Roland. It was sad that since Alan's death she had not been invited to dine with the Paillards. Was it because she was a widow: a woman alone? Or was it because her French was so poor that the Paillards felt she couldn't cope with an evening in French on her own? Goodness, how her life had changed since Alan's death. The unwanted widow. Sometimes she felt only half a person.

She passed the entrance to the Paillards' house: a steep curving drive up to the big house well hidden in the trees: a very private house. The Paillards were not the sort of people one called on without a formal invitation. The road became narrower and more winding. Jo couldn't remember ever having been along this section before. There was a path through the woods off to the left. Jo thought she saw some lights twinkling in the distance. Just a little cottage, she thought, belonging to some Burgundian peasants. She could imagine them. The husband, rotund and red-faced; his wife, wearing a stained floral pinafore over a very old dress, lined and strained-looking, with wisps of untidy grey hair, preparing dinner for her husband and two surely-looking children. Not a contented family, too impoverished to be happy: but at least the four of them were together, leading integrated, companionable lives. She drove on and a huge complex of barns and outbuildings appeared through the woods, on the right this time, lights gleaming from various windows. She realised what it was: an artists' centre called *Les Projets Créatifs*. She had heard they were mounting a big pageant on 15 August to celebrate the millennium of Laronne. Posters to advertise it were already going up. She had heard too that they were in constant need of new recruits and welcomed visitors at any time. Feeling curious, she drove into a vast deserted courtyard through massive iron gates, standing wide open, with a large notice on one side saying: ENTRÉE LIBRE.

Jo had really no idea what she would say if she met anyone. She had arrived by accident (another accident!) with absolutely no purpose in mind. The notice on the gate saying 'entrance free,' was quite welcoming. But there was nothing else welcoming at all. Jo parked her car and walked up the driveway, the surface rough and full of weeds, to a large impressive house at the end. The handsome front door, the shutters and the window frames all needed painting. The downstairs windows were uncurtained and the curtains upstairs looked torn and tatty. The whole place was very run down and needed a vast sum of money spent on it. It was quiet, as if all the occupants were out or away. Jo had no wish to go inside, so she didn't ring the doorbell, but curiosity persuaded her to have a quick look round the outhouses. She was hardly likely to make another visit to such a God forsaken spot. She peeped through half open doors into the vast sheds and barns, housing scaffolding, paints and other building materials. She inspected smaller buildings containing theatrical costumes, lighting and sound equipment. In one of the smaller buildings at the very far end, there was a light on. Her rubber-soled trainers making no noise, Jo padded along a narrow outside path between two rows of outbuildings. Darkness was beginning to fall and a pale half-moon had already appeared in the sky. She heard the scuffling noises of little animals out in the woods beyond and began to feel a bit frightened. At the moment she seemed to be the only occupant of this enormous building complex deep in the wood. But curiosity continued to overcome her fear and she felt more determined than ever to investigate the outhouse with the dimly lit window at the farthest end. Reaching the window, she stood at the side in case the room was occupied. Everything was enveloped in total silence. She peered cautiously into the window and almost gasped out loud in amazement. A man and a woman stood in the middle of the room, both completely naked, locked in embrace. The woman had long, lustrous dark hair, falling in a thick sheet round her shoulders. She was petite, olive-skinned and slim, with a small bulge protruding in front. She was clearly pregnant. The man released the woman's mouth and took a step back to look at her, gently caressing her full breasts.

'You're so beautiful, Kate,' he said. And he picked her up and carried her over to the bed.

The man was Gerry Nolan.

Jo raced along the long narrow path between the two rows of out-houses, tears pouring down her face. Gerry! Gerry in this ghastly place about to make love to another woman! A pregnant woman, whom he had probably made pregnant himself. He had walked out on her, to meet up with this woman in the woods who looked like a gipsy and who was carrying his child. Jo ran across the courtyard, running faster in the open space. Now sobbing wildly, she reached her car, fumbled for the lock with difficulty and tumbled in. Tears were blinding her. She could barely see to drive but she had to get out of this silent sinister place, where Gerry was by now deep inside this other woman. She started up the engine, turned on the headlights and drove out of the open gates, turning right to continue in the same direction as before. She drove on a few yards. The road wound steeply upwards, each bend becoming narrower. Jo realised she was too upset to drive with safety. She might have an accident. She really must stop somewhere and give herself a chance to calm down. But at the moment there was nowhere safe to stop, so she was forced to drive on, ever upwards, round more bends, each steeper than the last. The difficulty of the drive and the potential dangers absorbed all her concentration and helped her to stop crying. Finally, when she had rounded the last bend and found herself near the top of the cliff, she had calmed down considerably, albeit feeling drained and exhausted.

She had now reached the highest point, very near the spot, which had claimed Alan's life. Now she had the final emotional hurdle to surmount. Should she or should she not get out of the car, walk along the cliff top and see for herself the very place where her husband had died? She had made all the effort to come and now she had finally arrived. She felt she should go through with it. It wasn't dark yet, by any means. It was a great deal lighter out here on the cliff top than it had been in the woods. Over to her right the light was soft and pink, where the sun was sinking fast over Laronne. The half-moon was brighter than it had been in the woods, even twenty minutes ago, shining over the lake where Alan had drowned. Jo decided she would sit in the car for a moment and collect her thoughts, which now turned to Gerry. Her first reaction of shock and dismay at seeing her lover in the arms of another woman was quite natural. Gerry had been hers for over a month. But was he really hers? Had she really ever been his? They had found each other quite by accident. He had turned up out of the blue, just when she needed someone. The 'someone' need not have been Gerry. It had just happened to be. Their relationship could never have been permanent. She had always known that. Gerry had probably realised it too, if he had ever given the matter any thought. No. It was for the best that the relationship had ended, although it wasn't the way she ideally would have wished.

Darkness was falling. The half-moon had become much brighter even in the last few minutes, casting it's pale, eerie light over the cliff top. She felt she ought to take a quick look before darkness fell completely. She was about to get out of the car when a strange procession of masked people, wearing the kind of cloaks that Druids wear, approached from the opposite direction. They were intoning chants and gesticulating. Jo was puzzled and a little frightened. Perhaps the cliff top was haunted? Perhaps these weird people had appeared while Alan had been out walking and he had been so badly frightened that he had lost his balance and slid down the steep slope to the lake? Or perhaps one of them had pushed him over the edge? Jo felt fairly safe in her car. Or at least safer than she would feel out on the cliff top. Should she drive off and leave them to it? These bizarre, Druid-like people, prancing about and chanting even louder. But curiosity got the better of her again. She would stay. No one could see her car in this light. The Druids continued their dancing and prancing, when suddenly a lone figure appeared from the opposite direction. When he saw the Druids walking slowly towards him, he stopped stock still in his tracks. Just as the first Druid reached him he seemed to take fright and tried to run away in the opposite direction. But he turned too quickly, lost his footing and fell, sliding down the cliff face out of sight.

Huddled in a little bunch, the Druids crowded together at the top of the cliff. Shaking like a leaf, Jo started the engine and began to reverse the car, ready to return home the way she had come. She was convinced she had witnessed a repeat of her husband's murder. But before she could straighten up the vehicle, a Druid in a hideous white mask, with green eyes and blood red mouth, came up to the car. He leaned in through the window and said: '*Madame* Perry! Are you all right?'

Jo fainted.

Chapter Twenty-Five

Drat! Where is that girl? 'Kate! Kate! We're leaving *now!* Victoire! Can't you find that girl?'

Pierre was becoming impatient. He had really pinned his hopes on having Kate as the murder victim. She looked quite perfect with her stunning, dark good looks and her heavy thick mane of dark hair. She had an almost gipsy-like appearance. Beautiful figure, too. Was there a suspicion of a bump beginning to show in front? But it wouldn't matter for the pageant, as it wouldn't show in the voluminous cloaks they were all going to wear. They were the same as the cloaks the Druids would have worn in the original pageant, but that wouldn't matter either. No one except that silly little mayor, Didier Pérnot, had seen their first tedious effort so they wouldn't be any the wiser.

Kate seemed to have a new companion at *Les Projets*. A tall, thin young man called Gerry. He also had just appeared from nowhere. Another non-French speaking Englishman, who wasn't very useful either. Ah, well! Pierre felt it was really none of his business who came and went at *Les Projets*. He was only their self-appointed leader. But his pride made him determined to make the best of the available material, stage a pageant that would do them credit and hopefully bring in other commissions.

Curious that Kate appeared to look pregnant. Or was he just imagining it? Probably. He was afraid Victor might be the father. Afraid Victor might have been making love to a woman when he wanted Victor for himself. It was difficult. Pierre didn't know how to broach the subject with Victor. He didn't want to make a mistake about Victor's sexual orientation, especially as they were living in such a small community. Perhaps tonight? Out on the cliff top? If it was dark enough maybe he could just brush Victor's hand and see if there was any response. Meanwhile, there seemed to be no response from the girl, Kate. Maybe she had gone out with this new Gerry chap? Maybe they were lovers? Could he live in hope? They would have to leave without Kate. If they didn't leave now it would be too dark to see and that would be dangerous. Pierre didn't want the risk of anyone else falling over the cliff top into the lake far down below.

Victor was coming along the corridor. 'Sorry. Can't find her anywhere, Pierre.'

'Too bad. We'll have to go without her or it'll be too late.'

He caught Victor's gaze. Their eyes held for a second. Could it be…? thought Pierre. Maybe later.

'*Allons-y tout le monde!* Let's go!'

They all filed out of the courtyard onto the woodland path dressed in medieval costumes with cloaks and masks, looking very threatening, rather like the Ku-Klux-Klan. Kate crawled across to the window and peered out without standing up. She watched the small motley band of people disappear along the woodland path, all dressed up in very strange outfits.

'They've gone. Thank God for that.'

'Thank God indeed,' said Gerry.

'You've picked a great hiding place.'

'I did, didn't I?' Gerry tried to sound modest, despite feeling proud of himself. 'It's even got a bed in it.'

'Yes. That's nice, isn't it?' Kate sat cross-legged on the floor beside the window. She was trembling.

'Come and sit over here.' Gerry patted a space on the bed beside him.

'I will in a minute.'

Gerry got up and came to sit beside her on the floor. She was still shaking.

'You're frightened.'

'Yes.'

'It's bad for the baby.'

'Is it? How do you know?'

'Must be. Babies like peace and quiet. A nice relaxed atmosphere.'

'Then let's get out of here, Gerry. I hate these people. They're evil. Let's go. Anywhere.'

'Let me love you first.'

'Oh, Gerry!'

He helped her to her feet, hugged and kissed her tenderly, then slowly started to undress her.

Jean Bertrand walked slowly and aimlessly along the narrow country road kicking a stone. He was always aimless now. He no longer saw the point of anything. He had also started biting his nails. He raised his left hand and inspected it. Nothing much left to gnaw on. All the nails were bitten down to the quick. His index finger was bleeding. He knew, without looking, that his right hand was even worse. Jean was worried. He was worried that Bernard Roger might have seen him push Alan Perry over the cliff. Though it couldn't be proved that he had done it deliberately. Bernard would have had to be much nearer to see that. Besides, it hadn't been deliberate, had it? It was just an accident. Jean, having a poor memory and no conscience, was easily able to convince himself that it had definitely been an accident. But the police mightn't think so. He had heard the police had been interviewing people; at least two people. No one knew for certain, although the rumours abounded. Even that gossiping bitch, Colette Gautier, wasn't sure who had been interviewed. No one had been arrested yet, so there were no real suspects.

Jean was pretty sure that Bernard had been one of the people the police had interviewed. Only two days ago Bernard had caught Jean looking idly into his filthy courtyard. Jean was merely gazing at the mess, wondering how anyone could leave his premises in such a shocking state. Bernard obviously thought Jean had his eye on another piece of his abandoned broken furniture. He came right up to Jean and grabbed him by the shoulders.

'I thought I told you to stay away from here! You lousy, good-for-nothing little thief! And that includes hanging about near the gate. And what's more - you're not only a thief - you're also a murderer! I saw you on the cliff top pushing that poor *Monsieur* Perry around. They're saying it was an accident...'

It was a calculated gamble. Bernard hadn't seen the struggle at all, but he had heard the noise of Alan's fall and he had found the body. He saw the fear in Jean's eyes. That'll teach him, thought Bernard.

'Clear off! I never want to see you here again.'

Jean had slunk off, thoroughly frightened. He wondered, in rising panic, how much Bernard had seen of his struggle with Alan Perry on the cliff top. He remembered seeing Bernard walking down by the lake below. He wondered how much of it could be seen from the lake. It would do no harm to go back to scene of the accident and try to work out whether or not Bernard could have seen anything. He would go up to the old quarry first, try and work out the exact place where the accident had happened, and then find a way down to the lake below to find out how much he could see of the scene above. Jean didn't realise that it was exactly eight weeks since Alan Perry's death. He had long since lost touch with the date, or even the day of the week.

Jean struggled up the steep path to the top of the hill, memories of Alan Perry and his horrible black dog flooding back. Now he had reached the top, and looking down into the vast deep quarry below, he remembered with great satisfaction how he had pushed Alan over the edge of the cliff. He thought he heard a dog barking. No. Surely not. He took a step forward, leaning over to survey the scene more easily. Then he heard quite a different sound coming towards him up the steep slope from the direction of Dracy. It sounded like people trying to sing. Having had no religious upbringing, Jean was completely unaware of the existence of chanting monks. Looking in the direction of the strange moaning noise he saw a group of people in fancy dress costume coming towards him. Not having had much education, he had no idea that the group was dressed up as Druids. And of course, being a recluse, he had no idea they were rehearsing for a pageant soon to take place on 15 August. He stared in fascination as the people came slowly towards him.

Jean was frightened. Who were they? Why were they here? Did they know who he was? Did they know that he was the person who had pushed Alan Perry over the cliff? He had to get away from this ugly, threatening crowd. Without thinking he moved closer towards the edge of the cliff. As the Druids came closer, he was right on the edge. Suddenly he lost his footing. He tried grabbing onto a stone; but the stone was loose and pulled him down further. He slid down on his back, the stone rolling on top of him. He tried holding onto a bush, but it had no roots. He began to roll over, faster and faster to his death, to drown in the lake beside the quarry.

Just as Jean's inert body landed in the lake, the group of mock Druids reached the top of the precipice. Their chanting ceased as they stood in horrified silence, gazing down at the ugly scene below.

Chapter Twenty-Six

Kate and Gerry woke early, feeling rested and refreshed, despite having spent the whole night together on a narrow, single bed. They had slept in each other's arms, entwined as one being, as if they had never been parted. They made love, as they usually did in the morning, now quietly and gently. Their lovemaking had calmed down. It was no longer the frantic, physical orgy of the early days. They were both conscious of the well being of the baby. And they were very much in love.

Gerry swung his legs over the bed. 'Come on. Let's go.'

'Where?'

'To a town.'

'What town?'

'Any town.'

'What about Beaune?'

'Beaune'll do as well as any other place. I can't wait to get out of the country and I need to get out of this goddam place.'

'Don't blame you there. This place is evil.'

'It's like a prison. Everyone doing everything at the same time.'

'What do you know about prisons?' Kate seemed mildly amused.

'Well, nothing. But I can imagine it. And they don't even speak English.'

'Gerry! We are in France. It's up to us to learn French.'

'I can't. I'm too old.'

'Too old at twenty-seven! That's rubbish.'

'Anyway, it's hardly worth making the effort. I shan't be here much longer. It's time I went back to England and got a job.'

'Suits me. Maybe I could cadge a lift; hitch-hike in your cab?'

They both laughed.

'When do we leave?' Kate asked, thinking of the baby.

'As soon as we can. I have to explain things to Jo first. I can't just walk out on her without a word.'

'Seems you just walked in on her without a word. On me too, if it comes to that,' Kate added dryly. 'And you never even told me where you'd come from.'

'Did I not?' Gerry was beginning to realise his life was becoming more complicated than he had bargained for. But he couldn't keep running away. He would have to make a decision sooner or later: either to return to England, probably to face a murder charge, or go off somewhere else, with Kate, where he could find work.

'Would you like to go to Spain?' he asked innocently.

'Spain! Why Spain?'

'I thought maybe I could find a job as a waiter in a Spanish restaurant.'

'In Spain?'

'That's what I just thought.'

'Why Spain? A minute ago you were planning to return to England.'

'I had an idea we could check out Spain first. As it's so near.'

'Near? I should think England's nearer than Spain.'

'We're half-way to Spain from here.'

Kate was becoming more convinced than ever why Gerry was postponing his return to England. In her mind's eye she saw the chaos and destruction in her caravan. Bert lying dead on the floor in a pool of congealing blood. The bloodstained knife beside his body, probably covered in Gerry's fingerprints. But could she be absolutely sure that Gerry had murdered Bert? It could have been one of the other gipsies. Suppose Gerry and Bert had had a fight and Gerry had run off, fearing for his life. Suppose Bert had run after him, brandishing the knife. Suppose Gerry had shouted out in fear: 'help! Help me! He's got a knife. He'll kill me!' Then suppose one of the gipsies had come to his rescue, had managed to overpower Bert, grab the knife and twisted it in his stomach. Then, with Gerry's help, the two of them might have carried Bert, dying, perhaps already dead, back to her caravan and left him there. Then Gerry would have been an accomplice, an accessory after the fact. He would have been arrested too, along with the murderer if he had stayed there. But he hadn't. He had left the encampment without any warning, without making any plans at all. He must have fled from justice, otherwise why would he have left so suddenly? He must be guilty of something. Perhaps she could help him to talk about it. Lead up to it somehow. She could say: 'I wonder what happened to Bert after I left? Did he run off? Or did you have a fight? Did Bert hurt you with the knife? Or did you hurt Bert? Did you hurt him a little or quite a bit, or did you, Gerry, did you kill Bert?' But she knew she couldn't ask him that. What would happen if Gerry were to say, quite simply and truthfully: 'Yes, I killed Bert. But I didn't mean to.

It was an accident. The knife slipped.' Then what would happen? Would she have the strength and the courage to say: 'Gerry, you should confess. Give yourself up.'

But what if he just said: 'No. I didn't kill Bert. One of the other gipsies did.' Or if he said: 'I had no idea Bert was dead. I just thumped him and ran off.'

But if Gerry hadn't killed Bert, why had he run off? Why had he bought a motorcar and a caravan and come all the way to France? He must have been running away from something or he would never left her in the encampment under Westway. But maybe he was running away from something that had happened before he had arrived at Westway. Maybe he had heard some news, seen something in the paper. The paper. That was it. They would go into Beaune and buy an English newspaper. They must sell English newspapers in Beaune. Kate had heard it was a pretty little town, packed with English tourists in the summer. They would all want to read English newspapers. But there mightn't be anything in an English newspaper about Bert's death. Anything could have happened since she had left England. His body might still be lying undiscovered on the floor of her caravan, festering, stinking, covered in flies. The very thought made her stomach heave. Beads of perspiration broke out on her forehead. She was afraid she was going to throw up. She must have gone white. Gerry was concerned and put his arm around her.

'You OK? You look a little poorly.'

'No. I'm fine. I'll just sit here a minute.'

Kate felt she was being cowardly. She wasn't facing up to the facts: the fact that the father of her baby was possibly a murderer. If this were true, what would happen to her and their baby if Gerry were to confess to the murder? If he just confessed to her first of all, would she have the courage to say: 'Gerry, if this is really true, you must go to the police.' He would be taken away in handcuffs and put in a cell at the police station. He would be cautioned: 'Anything you say, Gerry Nolan, may be used in evidence against you.' He would be allowed to make one phone call to his solicitor. If he didn't have a solicitor - and somehow that seemed the more likely option - then the duty solicitor would be appointed by the state; some spotty youth with buckteeth, or an earnest, skinny young woman in horn-rimmed spectacles, just recently qualified. He would have no chance of fair representation under such circumstances. He would be interviewed at length and sent before the magistrate. The magistrate would remand him in custody. No bail would be given. He would be sent to prison to await trial for murder.

And what would happen to her?

The baby would be born, probably before the trial even came to court. A child born out of wedlock to a father who stood accused of murder. Her child. Was she becoming hysterical? How much of it was true? Was any of it true? One little question would provide the answer: 'Gerry, did you or did you not kill Bert?'

But Kate was too frightened the answer would be the wrong one. Instead she asked:

'What do you want to do in Beaune?'

They found an empty table in a *café* in *La Place Carnot* and sat down on metal chairs. The sun was hot, but a breeze rustled the huge plane trees surrounding the square. Small fluffy white clouds floated gently, high up across the azure blue sky. A waiter in a white shirt with sleeves rolled up to the elbows and baggy black trousers covered in a long white apron, appeared at the table to take their order. He had a white napkin over right his arm and a circular brass tray squeezed under his armpit. He clutched a notepad in his left hand, pencil poised in his right.

'*Bonjour, monsieur-dame. Je vous écoute.*'

Gerry looked blank. 'Yes?'

'You ready?' enquired the waiter, in strongly accented English.

'Ready?'

'*Oui, monsieur.*' *Mon Dieu,* some of these foreigners were slow.

'I think he wants to take our order,' hissed Kate.

'Oh? Yes…Two *cafés*?' asked Gerry hesitantly.

'*Oui, monsieur. Tout de suite.*' And the waiter sped off.

Kate looked round the pretty square. 'Shame about the cars,' she said.

'What do you mean? What's wrong with the cars?'

'They spoil the view.'

'Oh!' Gerry looked round the square. It was impossible to see the doorways or any of the picturesque French shutters on the houses opposite.

'Yes. I see what you mean. I suppose you're right. Cars can be a bit intrusive. How sensitive you are!'

'You're going to become a bit more sensitive in a minute. There's a man in a uniform who looks like a traffic warden or a policeman inspecting your van, which happens to be blocking a gate.'

'Should I move it?'

'Better not till he's gone.'

'D'you think you need a ticket to park over there?'

'Probably.'

'It doesn't matter anyway. He won't be able to trace my car.'

The waiter arrived with two coffees on the circular tray and placed a cup in front of each of them with great ceremony. '*Voilà, monsieur-dame!*'

Kate flashed him a winning smile. '*Merci.*'

Gerry looked at her in surprised admiration. The two small cups contained steaming, dark, inky-looking liquid. Gerry picked his up cautiously. 'Hot.'

'Yes,' agreed Kate. 'Strong too. Look, there's a newsagent over there. While the coffee's cooling I'll go over and see if I can get an English newspaper.'

'An English newspaper?' Gerry's voice was raised a little in alarm. 'What do you want an English newspaper for?'

'To read it, silly. What else do you do with a newspaper?'

Kate stood up and put her hand on Gerry's shoulder for a moment. 'It might be a bit of gas to find out what's going on at home, don't you think?'

Gerry hesitated for a moment. He thought of trying to restrain her; to stop her from buying a newspaper, saying it was a waste of money. But he couldn't do that. Kate was free to buy whatever she wished, whenever she liked.

'Good idea,' he said. 'Get a couple while you're at it.'

After all, it was over a month since he had left the encampment. Bert was probably up and about now after a spell in hospital. He had nothing to worry about: nothing at all. Gerry watched Kate walk across the square to the newsagent. Slight, slim and elegant, Kate was beautiful. He loved her. She was going to have his baby. Nothing could go wrong now. He sat and admired the view in the pretty little square, as the uniformed official placed some paper on his van. No matter he thought, they can't get me here. No one can get me here for anything.

Kate came out of the newsagent, the newspapers tucked under her arm. She was smiling confidently as she walked across the square, tossing her head, shaking her long dark hair in the sunlight. She wore freshly laundered jeans and a white shirt hanging loosely over the waistband. The bump was beginning to show now, just a little. She had complained this morning that her waistbands were becoming a bit too tight. She would need some new clothes, a loose dress or some maternity trousers so she would be more comfortable carrying the baby. But new clothes cost money. The baby would cost money, too. Maybe not to feed at first, as Gerry presumed Kate would want to feed it herself to start with. But it would need clothes, a cot and a pram. Having a baby involved more than he had realised. That's why people plan babies, thought Gerry ruefully. Middle-class people with good jobs who lived in nice houses. People with money and education. Not people like Kate and me: a gipsy girl who has never lived in a house, an ex-prisoner who has done time for murdering his mother. Was it too late? thought Gerry. Was it too late now to start finding a proper job and a permanent home for the woman he loved, who was shortly to bear his child? Or was it all just a pipe dream. There must be a way, thought Gerry desperately. There must be a way to a successful and comfortable life without resorting to stealing and violence. If only he could return to England with a clear conscience, get a job and somewhere decent to live.

The sound of a metal chair scraping the flagstones brought Gerry back to the immediate present with a start. Kate sat down beside him and unfolded the newspapers.

'What did you get?' he asked, his heart beating a little faster.

'*The Daily Mail* and *The Daily Express*. Which one do you want to start with?'

'I don't mind. It's up to you.'

Gerry looked at both newspapers guardedly, slightly fearful, as if they were about to reveal some dark and dire secret.

'I'll start with *The Express*.'

Kate passed it over, leaving *The Mail* folded on her knee while she sipped her coffee. Gerry apprehensively took *The Express* and opened it. On the front was a photograph of a caravan. An old, rather scruffy caravan. It could have belonged to a gipsy or a new age traveller. Underneath the headline ran: more clues found to murder at gipsy encampment under Westway. Then in smaller print: for more details turn to page 2 column 4. With trembling hands and sinking heart Gerry opened the paper. There, in the middle of page 2, was a photograph of Kate. The photographer had caught her pose to perfection: her head tilted back, her long dark hair streaming down like a thick, lustrous curtain, laughing at some joke or pleasantry. Underneath he read: 'over a month ago the body of Bert Mercer, aged 30, of no fixed address, was found in a caravan at the gipsy encampment under Westway. His death is now believed to have been the victim of a jealous gipsy feud. It is thought he was stabbed to death by a previous girl friend, Kate O'Leary, aged 22. It is rumoured she may have left the country and

Interpol have been alerted. A police warrant has been issued for her arrest.'

Gerry put the open newspaper down on his knee and looked up to find a *gendarme* standing beside him with a paper in his hand.

'*Monsieur, la voiture...*'

The policeman looked down at the newspaper photograph and then across at Kate sitting opposite, cool and calm, still totally unaware that anything was amiss.

Chapter Twenty-Seven

Le gendarme sat across the table from the two young people in the Dracy police station feeling confused. He couldn't understand what was going on. He had decided on the spur of the moment to drive his arrestees to his own base in Dracy rather than struggle with unknown surroundings in the Beaune *gendarmerie*. For the past two months the police in Dracy had been trying to discover why an Englishman, Alan Perry, had lost his life up on the cliff by the old quarry. What had he been doing in such a remote place? The man's very presence in such an out of the way place struck the policeman as very odd. Walking a dog? Were all the English quite mad?

Of course, the locals were no help at all. A canny breed, these country people. The policeman himself (whose name was Michel) was from Paris and since his arrival in Dracy a few months ago, he had regretted joining a force, which patrolled such an empty region of France. How he longed for the hustle and bustle of his beautiful native city! So they had one unsolved murder on their hands and now it appeared that Interpol wanted their help in finding a suspect responsible for a murder in England, shortly after Alan Perry's mysterious death. Curious how the English kept turning up in France, both as murder victims and suspects. He looked directly across at the young couple sitting on the opposite side of the table, holding hands.

They had been absolutely no trouble. Michel had gone across to the young man sitting in the *café* by the side of the square in Beaune to enquire if he were the owner of the battered old van, which was blocking a doorway. Then he had seen the photograph of the girl in the English newspaper. A girl they had been told to watch out for. A violent vicious girl, they were told, who had brutally attacked her boyfriend in a caravan on a gipsy encampment, leaving him for dead and then escaping at night, hitch-hiking her way across to France. Her picture was up in the station. There could be no mistake about it.

What puzzled Michel was that the girl didn't seem in the least bit vicious or violent. In fact, she seemed gentle and very vulnerable, with her magnificent mane of heavy dark hair, olive skin and big black eyes, like two dark pools of water. As soon as he had shown her the photograph in the paper, explaining he must ask her to accompany him to the station, she had stood up, ready to go with him. No need to bring out the handcuffs. No restraint of any kind had been needed. She had come like a lamb.

Her companion, too, her boyfriend or *fiancé?* He had been charm and co-operation personified. He had insisted on calling the waiter and paying the bill. Michel could hardly have stopped him settling his bill before asking him, also, to come along to the station.

Now they were deep in conversation. The young man was earnestly insisting on something. The girl was rather upset and on the verge of tears. The trouble was that Michel couldn't understand a word they were saying.

And they couldn't understand anything he said either. No one at the station spoke any English; so he realised he would have to engage an interpreter.

Various police officers came in and out of the interview room during the morning as Michel bustled about getting cups of coffee for the two young people he had arrested. Everyone had shaken hands with the suspects, trying their little bit of English, which didn't amount to very much. A slightly festive air began to pervade the interview room. Then as the clock crept closer to midday, Michel realised he would have to make arrangements for their lunch. Even a murder suspect had to be fed, *et mon Dieu,* he couldn't really believe that this beautiful girl was guilty of murder. Michel could hardly take his eyes off her when he was in the room with her.

It was mid-afternoon when Victor Fleming arrived. One of the officers knew of the existence of the rather eccentric group of artists who called themselves *Les Projets Créatifs*. They lived in the vast complex of run-down buildings at the edge of the wood near the old quarry, very near the scene of the two fatal accidents that had happened recently. He had seen Victor a few times in the *café* in Dracy, and he knew enough English to realise that Victor was reading an English newspaper. When Victor came into the interview room at the police station, Kate threw her arms around him and burst into tears, leading to even more confusion.

'*Monsieur* Fleming, would you please be kind enough to explain to us what is going on?'

A sergeant was in charge now, a neat, dapper little man with a small ginger moustache, very smart in his pale blue shirt with two stripes on the epaulettes.

Victor looked blank. '*Monsieur,* I have absolutely no idea at all. I don't know why these people are here.'

'Do you know them, *Monsieur?*'

'Yes.'

'Do you know their names?'

'Yes, I do.'

The sergeant sighed with relief. 'Thank goodness for that. At least that makes identification easier. By what name do you know the gentleman, *Monsieur* Fleming?'

'I know him as Gerry Nolan, sergeant.'

'Very well. And would you spell that for me, please, *Monsieur* Fleming?'

Victor spelt out each letter slowly as the sergeant laboriously wrote down the name in his notebook in his flowery French handwriting.

'And the young lady's name, *Monsieur?*'

'Kate O'Leary.'

The same procedure was repeated, the name O'Leary presenting some difficulty.

'And how long have you known these young people, *Monsieur* Fleming?'

'I'd say I've known *Mademoiselle* O'Leary about six weeks and *Monsieur* Nolan about two.'

'Weeks, *Monsieur?*'

'Yes. Two weeks.'

'And you have no idea at all why they are at the police station?'

'None at all.'

'They have been arrested, *Monsieur* Fleming.'

'Arrested! Whatever for? What have they done? Have they committed a crime?'

'It appears that *Mademoiselle* O...O...,' he looked down at his notebook, struggling to pronounce the name

O'Leary. 'It seems she has been charged with murder in England.'

Victor gasped with horror. 'That's not possible! Kate couldn't kill a fly! She's the most gentle and one of the loveliest women I know!' He turned and looked at Kate. 'Kate, did you understand what the policeman has just said?'

Kate shook her head. She could guess of course, but she didn't actually understand any of the conversation at all.

'This policeman says you've been accused of a murder in England. This can't be true! There must be some mistake. There is a mistake, isn't there?'

'There certainly is,' Gerry cut in. 'Kate has done nothing. I am the one who should be accused of murder.'

Victor turned to the sergeant. '*Monsieur,* would it be possible to have a word with my friends in private for a few minutes?'

The two policemen looked at each other, a little surprised. After all, as the conversation would be in English it would, in effect, be private anyway. But as all the young people had been so co-operative and well mannered the sergeant didn't see it would do any harm. He relented and said with a shrug: 'well, why not? See that the door and the window are well guarded from the outside, Michel.'

It would be a quicker and surer way of getting the information he needed.

Kate stared straight ahead as Victor drove her in his car back to *Les Projets.*

'It was very difficult saying goodbye,' she said at last.

'Yes. It must have been.' Victor steered the car carefully around another steep bend.

'He couldn't have done it, you know. It must have been an accident.'

'I'm sure it was.'

'Gerry's just not that sort of person. He wouldn't kill a fly; never mind a person.'

Victor smiled inwardly to himself. It was exactly the same phrase that he had used to the police about Kate.

'Bert Mercer was a fucking evil bastard.'

Victor winced. He had never heard Kate use foul language before.

'He was going to kill me. No doubt about it. Gerry went to my defence; then Bert went for Gerry. I was so scared I - I ran off. That was when it must have happened. But it would have been self-defence. You do think he'll get off, don't you, Victor?'

Poor Kate! How desperately she needs reassuring, thought Victor. 'There'll be mitigating circumstances, certainly.'

Kate, not quite sure what that meant, said simply: 'I'm going to have Gerry's baby.'

'I thought as much.' Victor wasn't quite sure what to say. Congratulations were hardly in order.

'I love him, Victor and I'm pretty sure he loves me. We come from the same sort of world. A world where people never had much luck or any opportunity to get things right. A sort of underclass, if you like. But Gerry was absolutely determined to pull himself out of it. He had great plans to go back to England and get a job. A waiter in a restaurant, he said once. We were planning to go to the council and ask for a place to live, especially for the baby. But it was too much to hope for. It was an unrealistic dream.'

Victor found it very difficult to know what to say. He felt extremely sorry for her.

'Have you - do you have anything in mind as to what you might do - for the moment, I mean?'

'I just want to go back to England so I can visit Gerry in prison. He'll be on remand, won't he? I might even be able to see him every day. It'll be important to him to know that I'm OK and the baby is growing inside me.'

'That sounds like a good idea. Where will you stay? Are you planning to return to your caravan?'

Kate's heart sank. She hadn't decided whether to return to the gipsy encampment or not. On the one hand she wanted to return home to her caravan, filled with her few possessions. It was the only home she had ever known and she couldn't really imagine any other. On the other hand the gipsies might take a pretty dim view of her return. They must have known that Bert's death had been the reason for her fleeing the campsite. Although they had originally accused her of murder, they must have realised by now that all along she had been shielding Gerry. They would certainly be in no doubt once they saw her pregnant condition.

Kate sighed. 'I think it might be better if I stayed in a hostel until after the baby is born. Gipsies aren't always friendly, even towards their own. A hostel near the prison would be ideal, wouldn't it?'

'It would be a good start.' Victor wondered whether she would ask him to help her find a hostel. He rather hoped she wouldn't.

'Have you seen a doctor since you knew you were pregnant?' He wasn't sure he should ask her such a direct question about a very personal matter.

'No. Should I?'

'Yes. I'd say so. Most women do.'

'Do they?' Kate sounded a little surprised. 'Most gipsy women don't, as far as I know. But a lot of their babies die.'

'Exactly. You wouldn't want that to happen.'

'No.'

'I'm planning to return to England very soon, Kate. Maybe in a couple of days. I could give you a lift in my car.'

'Oh, would you? That'd be wonderful. Thank you, Victor!'

'That's OK.' Victor felt embarrassed. He felt it was the least he could do.

'Do you think Gerry's on his way already?

'He could be.'

They passed the spot on the cliff top where Alan Perry had lost his life. It was cordoned off with tape and several police officers were searching in the grass for something.

'What happened here?' asked Kate.

'A youth fell to his death over the cliff last night.'

Kate shuddered. 'How dreadful. It seems near the spot where Alan Perry also lost his life.'

'The same one, I believe.'

'How weird!'

'Who told you about Alan Perry?'

'Gerry, of course.'

'Of course?'

'Yes. But that's the part of the story you probably haven't heard yet. When Gerry left the gipsy encampment after the fight with Bert, he bought an old van and a caravan and fled to France.'

'Yes. I'd gathered that much.'

'And on the motorway he met up with this woman, Jo Perry, who invited him to park his caravan on her land.'

'Good Lord! Just like that!'

'Apparently. And after a while she moved into the caravan with Gerry.'

'Really?' Victor felt Gerry's story was becoming more and more unbelievable.

'Yes. Gerry said it was because she needed the space in her house to let to her paying guests. Punters, she called them.'

Victor felt Jo Perry must be quite an original person, too.

'And why did he leave?'

'Because he met me again with you in the car park of the *Géant Casino*. Don't you remember?'

'Yes. Of course I remember. But I had no idea he had been sharing a caravan with Alan Perry's widow.'

'Victor, could I ask you something?'

'You can certainly ask.'

'Jo Perry will be worried about where Gerry's got to. Do you think you could explain it all to her?'

Dear God, thought Victor. I've got a tricky assignment here.

'OK,' he said. 'I'll try.'

'Oh, thanks Victor! You're an angel!'

Kate leaned across and gave him a peck on the cheek.

Chapter Twenty-Eight

'*Allo, oui.*'

'Mrs Perry?'

'Yes.'

'My name's Victor Fleming. I don't think you know me...'

'I don't know most of the people who call me, Mr Fleming. I assume you're phoning from England and I can save you money by explaining at the outset that we are totally and completely booked up until the end of September...'

'I'm not calling to make a booking, Mrs Perry and I'm not calling from England either. I'm phoning from just up the road, near Dracy. I've got some information about Gerry Nolan.'

'Gerry Nolan! Oh, thank goodness! Is he safe and well?'

Victor felt a pang of dismay at the relief in her voice.

'He's quite safe and extremely well, Mrs Perry.'

'You've seen him, have you?'

'Yes. Just this morning, in fact.'

'Oh, good. And where is he now?'

'I think it would be better if I came and explained to you in person.'

'Oh, very well. Do you know where I live?'

'Yes. In the big farmhouse just outside Laronne.'

This came as no surprise to Jo. Most people in the area knew where she lived. 'When would you like to come over?'

'Would about twenty minutes suit?'

Better get it over as soon as possible.

'Yes, of course. Any time.'

Didier Pérnot thought he would never live down the shame and embarrassment of having frightened poor *Madame* Perry so much that she had fainted. The evening on the cliff top, which had promised so well, had turned into a nightmare. Originally he had had such high hopes of inspiring the cast of his pageant to greater heights by letting them experience the sombre atmosphere of the old quarry at twilight where, four hundred years ago, an unfortunate witch had been disembowelled alive and then flung into the lake. Today the event would just be a mock-up, hopefully well enough stage-managed to look realistic. Didier sat in his bright red Renault on top of the cliff, waiting for his friends to arrive. After he had been there for nearly an hour-and-a-half, a large group of people had come along the path dressed in medieval costume. They had leaped about and acted scenes, which bore an extraordinary resemblance to his own pageant. Gradually the truth began to dawn. He guessed, quite correctly, that the group were all members of *Les Projets Créatifs* who appeared to be rehearsing his pageant.

Then the most ghoulish thing had happened. Just as the murder victim was horribly, realistically being disembowelled, a figure appeared along the cliff top as if from nowhere. He walked towards the actors as if he hadn't seen them. Then suddenly, appearing to have noticed them, he had taken fright, and turning round too quickly, he had lost his balance. In seconds he had fallen over the edge of the cliff and slithered into the lake far below.

Didier had got out of his car and started to walk towards the scene of the tragedy. On the way he had passed *Madame* Perry sitting in her car, in a state of total shock at what she had just witnessed. Completely forgetting he was dressed up as a Druid and wearing the most frightening mask, he had put his head into the car to reassure the poor lady. *Madame* Perry, unable to cope with another shock, had fainted.

From then on the evening had dissolved into total chaos. The girls from *Les Projets* were sobbing with fright and shock. The men wandered about, totally distraught. Even that efficient, though sadly effeminate Pierre, seemed at a loss as to what to do next. Didier realised, that as Mayor of Laronne, it was up to him to take charge. He must phone for the police and an ambulance right away. Not having a car phone, Didier decided to drive to the nearest cottage and ask the occupants if he might use their phone in such a grave emergency. He drove back along the road and saw a light coming from a house in the woods. As the track appeared to be unsuitable for vehicles, he parked his car at the side of the road, walked up the narrow overgrown path and knocked at the front door. Getting no response, he walked around to the back and looked in through a lighted window. The curtains were half open and he could see two figures in bed. He knocked at the window. The couple in the bed stirred. He knocked again. He was becoming impatient. There was no reason why anyone should sleep in peace when he had an emergency of vast proportions on his hands. He knocked a third time.

'Who's there? I need to telephone for an ambulance and the police right away. It's extremely urgent. There's been a fatal accident on the cliff top by the old quarry. I am Didier Pérnot, the Mayor of Laronne.'

Two figures sat up in bed. Then the man got out of the bed and came to the window. It was Lucien Gautier. And the woman sitting up in bed, her shoulders covered with a sheet of golden hair, was certainly not his wife.

Arriving back with Kate at *Les Projets Créatifs* in the late afternoon, Victor was most relieved to learn the pageant had been cancelled. Through some dreadful stroke of fate a young man had fallen to his death out on the cliff top last night, just at the moment that the disembowelling of the unfortunate fourteenth century witch was about to take place. Nobody knew how it had happened. A young man, apparently taking a late evening stroll along the cliff, had presumably taken fright on seeing an eerie group of Druids about to dispose of a young female. It was thought he had turned so suddenly to run away, that he had lost his footing and slipped over the edge. The body, when recovered later by the police, was identified as that of Jean Bertrand, eldest son of Jean-Yves Bertrand of Laronne. It was a shocking event but sadly, everyone knew the youth would not be missed.

Instead of a pageant, the good inhabitants of Laronne would celebrate their millennium with a sequence of music and dancing to be devised by *Les Projets Créatifs*. Not being in any way a dancer or a musician, Victor felt he could now leave *Les Projets* at any time and return to

England. He took the letter from Vincent out of his pocket and re-read it for the umpteenth time.

'Dearest Vic,

'It may come as a surprise - and I hope not too much of a shock - to hear from me after such a long time. It's been utter hell living without you. I didn't realise how much I needed you until you had left. And I didn't realise either, how very much I love you. I don't know whether you still feel the same about me, or whether you have found another, better partner. I don't know anything about your life in France; whether you are happy and fulfilled with your amateur theatrical group, bringing culture and beauty to the French peasantry. You always did have a strong philanthropic streak. On the other hand, you might be missing England, the real world and the professional theatre. If you are considering a move back across the water and would consider taking up with your old lover, I'm sure we could make it work better this time.

'And by the way, there is a job going as assistant director here at Reading Repertory Theatre which might be just up your street and give you more impetus to return. Although I shall quite understand if I don't hear from you, I do, of course, hope with every fibre of my being that I shall.

'Your devoted friend and lover, Vince.'

Victor folded up the letter carefully and put it back in his pocket. He hadn't decided yet whether or not he would reply. He had not expected to hear from Vince again and the letter had come as a bit of a shock. He thought about Pierre. Last night he had realised that

Pierre was desperate to have him, whether fleetingly or permanently he couldn't yet make out. He had made his intentions quite clear out on the cliff top just before the terrible accident. They had all been in such shock that no one could be said to have been fully responsible for their actions. After the police and the ambulance had arrived and the whole hoo-ha had died down they had all trailed back to *Les Projets* in disconsolate little groups. Emotionally exhausted by the whole day, Victor had gone straight to bed. He was aroused about an hour later by a knock on the door. It was Pierre. Without saying a word, he had got into Victor's bed and they had made love. But it was love born of desperation, rather than real affection. Pierre had been very possessive and very dominating. Victor had been rather unnerved by the experience. No, he had decided, Pierre would never be for him. It would be simpler and kinder to leave before things got too complicated.

Now it was time to return to London, to real life and the real theatre. Life at *Les Projets* was no longer for him. He would ask Kate first thing in the morning how soon she would like to leave for England. On his return he would put himself forward as a candidate for the post of assistant director at Reading Rep.

Chapter Twenty-Nine

'*Allo, oui!*'

'Jo?'

'Yes.'

'It's Sebastian.'

'Oh, hello, Sebastian.'

Jo's heart sank. Sebastian was usually bad news.

'I've got bad news. Gran's dead. She died last night.'

'Oh, dear. I'm sorry to hear that.'

Jo had to think quickly. Was Gran Alan's mother or Melissa's mother? 'What did she die of?'

'A heart attack following a severe stroke. She had a stroke soon after you left after Dad's... After you were here last.'

'Why didn't you tell me?'

'We thought you had enough on your plate.'

'Yes, I did. Thank you. So now you're phoning me about the funeral.'

'Yes. It's next Wednesday.'

'Oh, yes.' Wednesday again. 'Where?'

'South Norwood Crematorium.'

'Oh. The same place where...'

'Yes. I'm afraid so. But we'll quite understand if you don't want to come.'

'Thank you. Would you and Petra like me to come?'

'If you feel up to it, Jo. It's always nice to see you.'

'Even at a funeral?'

'Yes. Even at a funeral. By the way, I got a first.'

'A first! Congratulations, Sebastian! Your father would have been very proud.'

A first. How like Sebastian.

'It's a beautiful property, *Madame* Perry. We'll get some really nice photos done and put it on the market right away.'

'How much do you think I'll get for it?' Jo asked hesitantly.

'It's extremely hard to say, *Madame* Perry. At this stage, I really don't know. It's a beautiful property but of course it is fairly isolated and a long way from shops and schools. Even a fairly large town such as Chalon must be a good half hour's drive.'

'Yes, it is. But don't you think people prefer to be isolated? On holiday, I mean.'

'On holiday? So you would think of it purely as a holiday place?'

'Well that's what it's been up till now. I've been letting it by the week to English visitors. There are four apartments.'

'Then it might be more suitable to advertise it in England.'

'And here as well. Why not? As long as it's sold quickly. I no longer wish to stay here. I want to return to England as soon as possible.'

'Of course. I quite understand. We'll do our best, *Madame* Perry.'

'I'm sure you will. *Au revoir.*'

'*Au revoir, Madame* Perry.'

Despite the warm September sunshine outside, it was chilly in the crematorium chapel. Jo shivered in her thin navy dress. She sat in the front row between Sebastian and Petra. They had been very kind, very welcoming, as far as anyone could be at a funeral. The chapel looked exactly the same as it had done for Alan's funeral barely four months ago, stark and chilly, with white lilies everywhere. The effort to be ecumenical had only succeeded in making it look impersonal. The service was coming to a close. Soon the coffin would glide gently through the curtains into the flames below. The contents were the remains of Mrs Perry, eighty-years-old last week. Not that old any more for this present day and age, but the rapid onset of Alzheimer's Disease had prematurely aged Alan's mother.

Alan's mother. It was hard to think of her as being part of Alan. Shrivelled, wizened and sharp-tongued, she had never been one of Jo's favourite people. But she had loved Alan and would never have recovered from his death. Jo wondered if Melissa was in the chapel. She had half expected her to be there in a scarlet sari, the red oriental mark on her forehead, as Alan had described her appearance on their wedding day. How Jo had laughed at the time. She had met Melissa only once before, at Alan's funeral four months ago, right here, in the very same chapel. Understandably the two women had not taken to each other. Melissa had felt usurped. Jo had felt threatened. Melissa was so clever. She had produced two children, which Jo had failed to do. Two children who were as clever as Melissa herself. They were thoughtful, too. They had taken Jo under their wing as soon as she had arrived in London and they were looking after her now, at their grandmother's funeral, which was reminding them all so much of Alan's funeral.

As the coffin began to slide slowly forward, Jo felt weak at the knees. Only four months ago Alan's body was starting out on exactly the same journey. Beads of sweat appeared on her forehead and her hands felt clammy. Instead of praying for the soul of old Mrs Perry, Jo began to pray that she would be able to get through the service without vomiting. The curtains opened and a red glow appeared behind the coffin.

'Ashes to ashes; dust to dust,' intoned the clergyman, sounding as if he were thinking of his lunch.

Nearly over, thought Jo, clenching her hands. Sebastian, dead white, was staring straight ahead. Petra was sobbing noiselessly. Just as the coffin withdrew into the curtains, a figure clad in a scarlet sari with a red mark on her forehead appeared from the shadows. She danced in front of the coffin, and a chanting a mantra; she threw down rose petals and ran out of the chapel.

Jo stayed on in London for a couple of weeks, partly to delay her return to Laronne, so full of memories and problems, but also to arrange the sale of the farmhouse from the London end. Although she stayed again with her parents, Jo found Sebastian and Petra offered her even more support. Petra had offered to drive back with her to Burgundy and see her 'settled back in,' as she put it. But Jo didn't want to be 'settled back in.' She didn't want to return at all. She wanted the property to be sold as quickly as possible so she could return to London and start a new life. A calm, peaceful life without punters, pageants or living in a caravan with a murder suspect.

It had been a great shock to discover that Gerry might be a murderer. Although she hadn't believed most of the things he had told her about himself, she had always suspected he had invented his past. He didn't fit in with his own story. She couldn't really imagine his living in a large Georgian house called Laragh Lodge with beautiful views of lush County Wicklow. She couldn't quite visualise his wealthy parents; his riding to hounds, going off to boarding school in Dublin in a pukkah uniform. But she had never imagined that he might be a murder suspect. He had always seemed such a gentle man; so kind and considerate.

It had been a bad enough shock when she had seen him making love to the gipsy girl through the uncurtained window in one of the outhouses at *Les Projets Créatifs* on that fateful evening. Now, of course, Gerry's disappearance made sense. He had accidentally met up again with the gipsy girl who was pregnant with his child. After murdering the girl's boyfriend in a jealous rage, he had left the gipsy encampment and come to France. He had met her, Jo, accidentally on the ferry and taken advantage of her knowledge of France. Jo now realised, with frightening clarity, that Gerry Nolan was a skilful manipulator. He exploited people to his own advantage. He also seemed to be rather accident-prone. But was she not rather accident-prone herself? What with losing her husband in a fatal accident and then sharing a caravan with a suspected murderer, she could also be in the hands of fate. But hopefully something better would turn up. She hadn't yet recovered from witnessing the dreadful accident on the cliff. Perhaps the place was haunted? It had been bad enough watching the rehearsal of the grisly pageant. Who on earth could think up such a horrible idea as disembowelling a woman for being a witch and then throwing her body into the lake? Despite having been based on a fourteenth century story, only a twisted mind could think of selecting such a morbid theme and actually turning it into a performance for people to watch. Jo had come to the conclusion that all the people at *Les Projets Créatifs* had very strange minds indeed. No wonder Victor Fleming had left *Les Projets* after less than a year. She didn't blame him at all. She had quite taken to Victor when he had called round to the farmhouse to explain in person what had happened to Gerry. He had been kind and gentle, the perfect gentleman. She owed him an enormous debt of gratitude. He had returned the following day with two policemen: Michel, *le gendarme* who had arrested Gerry and the gipsy girl, and the sergeant who had asked Victor to come to the station as interpreter. He came to Jo's house in that role to translate the results of the police investigation into Alan's death. *Les gendarmes* were most apologetic. They assured Jo they had spent a great deal of time in search of their quarry but they hadn't come up with a great deal of evidence. Several well-known local people had been questioned and the police had been convinced of the truthfulness of their statements. There seemed no reason to doubt them. The one person constantly under suspicion had been Jean Bertrand. He had been spotted on the cliff top by several of those interviewed, but as they had no proof of foul play, the police were unable to bring any charges. It was certainly odd that Jean should have been walking on exactly the same part of the cliff during the evening of the pageant rehearsals. The police would, of course, have questioned him about his walk had he survived. Had it been an accident or had Jean taken his own life? If the latter were true then the boy certainly had a sense of the theatrical. They would never know.

When Victor came to say goodbye a few days later before returning to live permanently in England, Jo felt a strange sense of loss. She hardly knew him, but he was English and a contact with home. She couldn't imagine any romantic attachment, perhaps because he was a little bit too young? But she had envied his departure. Lucky Victor Fleming was a free agent. He wasn't mortgaged to a rambling French farmhouse in Laronne.

Selling the farmhouse was now her chief preoccupation. It was a serious worry too. If she couldn't sell it, she couldn't return to England. It was as simple as that. All her money was tied up in the farmhouse. Oh, how foolhardy she and Alan had been to sell the cosy little house in Lavender Garden! How she longed for it now! A charming Victorian house in a tranquil street within five minutes of a pleasant stroll on Clapham Common. She would do anything to live there again, in spite of the burglary.

Chapter Thirty

This time the ferry was almost empty. Jo took her heavily laden lunch tray to a table over by the window, deliberately avoiding the far side of the canteen where she had shared a table with Gerry those short four months ago. Over half the tables were unoccupied, so she was rather surprised when a well-modulated male voice asked:

'Do you mind if I join you?'

'No, of course not.'

Jo looked up, non-plussed, as a well-dressed man, possibly in his early forties, put his fully laden tray on the other side of the table. She watched him as he methodically placed the main course centrally, the knife and fork on either side. He put his glass towards the middle of the table, slightly to the right of his plate, the bottle of mineral water just level and to the right of the glass. He put his apple tart dessert above the plate, holding the main course a little to the left. He looked for the correct place to deposit his empty tray, laid it tidily on top of the pile of other trays, returned to the table and sat down. He picked up the paper table napkin, put it on his lap and smiled across at Jo.

'How pleasant to be able to join a young lady for lunch.'

Jo couldn't think of a reply.

'Would you mind passing the salt and pepper, please?'

'Yes, of course.' Jo passed over the cruet set, studying her companion as she did so. He was tall, well built, though not fat. He had a mop of thick dark slightly wavy hair and brown eyes. He wore a navy jacket over an open-necked blue and orange check shirt and he had a light suntan. He ate his food slowly and deliberately, in complete contrast to Gerry. Inevitably, Jo thought back to her first meeting with Gerry on this very ferry almost exactly four months ago, when he had wolfed down his food as though he hadn't eaten for days.

'Cross over often, do you?'

The man's question broke into Jo's thoughts.

'Yes. No. Well, I mean it depends what you mean by often.'

Jo wasn't sure how much she wanted to get involved in another casual meeting with a complete stranger.

'You look very experienced.'

Jo laughed in spite of herself. 'How does one appear to have experience of a ferry?'

'Oh, you know. Knowing which exit to take from the car deck. How to find the restaurant without studying the plan. What food to select without looking at the menu.'

So he had been watching her!

Jo felt a slight constriction in her chest. Was he another stranger looking for somewhere to stay, somewhere to park a caravan? Or would he just be casually chatty, making small talk to fill in the one-and-a-quarter hour crossing. She had chatted to strangers on trains, aeroplanes and ferries often enough and until she had met Gerry, they had all seemed quite harmless.

'You're quite right. I have done this crossing several times before.'

'Know France well? I see you drive a French car.'

There he goes again! It was the French car that Gerry had noticed and which had encouraged him to follow her down the motorway.

'Yes, I suppose I do know France quite well...'

'And speak the language perfectly,' he said lightly.

'No, I speak French very badly,' said Jo ruefully. 'Though my husband was fluent.'

'Was?'

'Yes. He had a fatal accident a few months ago.'

'Oh, I'm so sorry.' The man seemed embarrassed. 'My wife died too, last year.'

'Oh.' Jo couldn't think of anything else to say. It seemed they were becoming too intimate too soon.

'So you're hardly going on holiday.'

'What makes you think that?'

'Well, you wouldn't drive through France in your French car all on your own ...'

'I could be going to stay with friends,' replied Jo, 'but I'm not, as it happens.' In spite of herself, and feeling the need for caution she was warming to her companion.

'You're - let me guess: you're going back to your holiday home in Provence to collect some things and decide what you're going to do next.'

'No. Wrong.' Jo couldn't help laughing. 'I'm going back to the house where we lived for two years, hoping to sell it as quickly as possible.'

'Well, I wasn't all that wrong. You're about to make a major decision in your life.'

'I think I've already made it. It's now a matter of putting it into execution. Why are you going to France?' She felt it was her turn to ask the questions.

'I'm looking for suitable properties to sell on the English housing market.'

'Oh! Come and see mine,' said Jo, without thinking.

'I'd love to. Perhaps we could do each other a mutual favour.'

'Yes. Who knows?'

Jo was thinking of past mutual favours: living in a caravan with Gerry, who turned out to be a suspected murderer.

'Where is your house?

'In remotest Burgundy. Near places you would never have heard of.'

'Try me,' he laughed. 'I know Burgundy extremely well. That's where my company does most of it's business.'

'It's in a small village called Laronne. About thirty kilometres from Chalon-sur-Saône.'

'Really? Anywhere near Dracy, and what's that other place called - La Roche?'

'No! Surely not! What an amazing co-incidence.' Jo couldn't believe it.

'I'm spending the week in Dracy. More picturesque than Chalon. I'm making it my base for exploring the region. Look,' he put his hand in his breast pocket and drew out a business card. 'Here's my card. I run my own property company.' He handed her the card. She read: LEWIS PROPERTY SERVICES.

'My name's Edward Lewis.'

'I'm Jo Perry.'

They shook hands solemnly across the table.

'Why don't you give me a call tomorrow and I could come and inspect your house. I hope you won't be all alone in your remote place. I mean to return to an empty house after a long journey...'

'No,' Jo replied, 'I have a house full of eight paying guests.'

'Oh, good.' Edward Lewis sounded genuinely relieved.

Jo stood for some time with her hand on the telephone handset. Should she, or should she not, call Edward Lewis? Of course, it was for business purposes only, but one never knew... She picked up the phone and quickly got through to the hotel in Dracy.

'*Bonjour, Monsieur,* please would it be possible to speak to *Monsieur* Lewis? I believe he is staying at the hotel.'

Un moment, s'il vous plâit, Madame.' Jo heard the sound of high heels clacking on a stone floor. There was a moment's silence, then the heels returned.

'*Madame, Monsieur* Lewis – he is now out. He go to visit large house near Dracy. I ask him to call you on his return. Would you your name and number to me give, please.

www.ingramcontent.com/pod-product-compliance
Lightning Source LLC
Chambersburg PA
CBHW021504240626
47154CB00002B/500